BY NIGHT UNDER
THE STONE BRIDGE

In gratitude
to my good comrade

G.P.

BY NIGHT UNDER THE STONE BRIDGE

Leo Perutz

*Translated from the German
by Eric Mosbacher*

ARCADE PUBLISHING • NEW YORK

CONTENTS

PESTILENCE IN THE GHETTO

In the autumn of 1589, when the great pestilence was raging in the Prague ghetto and children were dying off like flies, two wretched, greying professional entertainers, who made their living by amusing guests at weddings, walked down the Belelesgasse that led from the Nicolasplatz to the Jewish cemetery.

It was getting dark. Both of them were weak with hunger, because for two days they had had practically nothing to eat but a few crusts of bread. These were hard times for entertainers, for the wrath of God had descended on innocent children, and there were no weddings and no occasions for celebration in the ghetto.

A week before, one of the two men, Koppel-the-bear, had handed over to Markus Koprivy, the money-lender, the worn skin in which he performed his comic leaps, dressed up as a wild beast. His companion, Jäckele-the-fool, had pawned his silver bells. All they had left were their shoes and the clothes they stood up in, though Jäckele-the-fool still had his fiddle, for which the pawnbroker would give nothing.

They walked slowly, for it wasn't quite dark yet, and they didn't want to be seen entering the cemetery. For years they had earned their daily bread, and a little extra for the sabbath, by honest toil, and now they were reduced to looking for copper coins that pious visitors to the cemetery left behind on gravestones for the poor.

When they reached the end of the Belelesgasse and could see the cemetery wall on their left, Jäckele-the-fool stopped and pointed to the door of Gerson Chalel, the cobbler. "The cobbler's Blümchen is sure to be up still," he said. "I'll play her

I

'I'm still only six and my heart is still happy', and she'll come out and dance in the street.''

Koppel-the-bear started out of his dream of hot radish soup with pieces of meat floating in it.

"You're a fool, and if the Messiah comes and heals the sick you'll still be a fool," he snapped. "What do I care about the cobbler's Blümchen? What do I care about her dancing? I'm aching with hunger in every limb."

"If you're aching with hunger, take a knife and sharpen it and go and hang yourself," said Jäckele-the-fool. He slipped the fiddle from his back and began to play.

But, however much he played, the cobbler's little daughter failed to appear. Jäckele-the-fool dropped the fiddle and thought for a few moments. Then he crossed the road and looked through the open window into the cobbler's shop.

It was dark and empty, but there was a gleam of light from the living room, and Jäckele-the-fool saw the cobbler and his wife sitting on low stools facing each other and singing the prayer for the dead for their daughter Blümchen, whom they had buried the day before.

"She's dead," said Jäckele-the-fool. "So the cobbler's another who has fallen from the heavens and landed on the hard earth. I have nothing, and yet I'd give everything if only she were still alive. She was so small, and yet when I saw her it was as if the whole world were in her eyes. She was only five, and now she has to chew the cold earth."

"When death goes to market he buys up everything," Koppel-the-bear murmured. "Nothing's too small, nothing's too petty for him."

And they walked on, quietly muttering the words of the psalm of King David:

"Because thou hast made the Lord, which is my refuge, even the most High, thy habitation:
    there shall no evil befall thee, neither shall any plague come nigh thy dwelling.
For He shall give His angels charge over thee to keep thee in all thy ways.

They shall bear thee up in their hands, lest thou dash thy foot against a stone."

By now night had fallen. A pale moon hung in the sky between dark rain clouds. So quiet was it in the streets that you could hear the murmur of the river. Nervously and fearfully, as if what they were going to do was contrary to God's law, they passed through the narrow gate into the garden of the dead.

It lay in the moonlight, as quiet as the dark, mysterious river of Sam-Bathyon, whose waves stand still on the Lord's day. The grey and white gravestones leant against one another, propping each other up as if unable by themselves to support the burden of their years. The trees stretched up their bare branches as if in anxious complaint to the clouds in the sky.

Jäckele-the-fool led the way and Koppel-the-bear followed him like a shadow. They walked down the narrow path between the jasmine shrubs and the elder trees until they came to the weather-worn gravestone of the great Rabbi Abigdor. Here, on the grave of the holy man whose name was a shining light in the darkness of exile, Jäckele-the-fool found a flat Mainz pfennig and a copper three-pfennig piece and two foreign coins. Then he went on towards where the gravestone of the famous physician Rabbi Gedalya stood under a maple tree.

But suddenly he stopped and clutched his companion's arm.

"Listen," he murmured softly. "We're not alone. Can't you hear a whisper? Can't you hear something moving?"

"Fool!" said Koppel-the-bear, who had just picked up and pocketed a bent Bohemian groschen. "Fool! It's the wind blowing dead leaves along."

"Koppel-the-bear," whispered Jäckele-the-fool, "can't you see something shimmering and shining over there by the wall?"

"If you're a fool, drink vinegar, ride broomsticks and milk billy goats, but leave me in peace. What you see is white stones gleaming in the moonlight."

But at that moment the moon vanished behind dark clouds, and Koppel-the-bear realised that it wasn't white stones that he

3

could see over there just by the cemetery wall, but gleaming forms floating in the air, children in long white shifts, holding hands and dancing over the new graves. And above them, invisible to the human eye, was the Guardian Angel appointed by God to watch over them.

"May the Lord have mercy on me," Koppel-the-bear groaned. "Can you see what I see, Jäckele-the-fool?"

"Praised be the Creator, for He alone works wonders," Jäckele-the-fool whispered. "I can see Blümchen, the darling little innocent, and I can see my neighbour's two children, who died a week ago."

And, when it dawned on them that it was the next world that was being revealed before their eyes, they were seized with panic. They turned and fled, jumping over graves, crashing into branches, falling and picking themselves up again. They ran for their lives, and did not stop until they were outside in the street.

Then for the first time Jäckele-the-fool looked round for his companion.

"Koppel-the-bear," he said with his teeth chattering, "are you still alive and are you there?"

Koppel's voice came out of the darkness.

"I'm still alive and I praise my Creator," he said. "Truly the hand of death passed over me."

And, as they had both survived, they realised that it was the will of God that they should bear witness to what they had seen.

For a time they stood whispering in the dark, and then they went and sought out the hidden king in his own house, the Great Rabbi who understood the speech of the dead, listened to the voices of the deep, and could interpret and explain God's fearful signs.

He was sitting in his room, bent over the Book of Secrets that is called Indraraba or the Great Collection. Lost as he was in the infinitude of numbers, signs and effective powers, he did not hear their footsteps as they entered, and not till they greeted him with the words: "Peace be with the holy light" did his soul return to the terrestrial world from the remoteness of the spirits.

And when the Great Rabbi directed his gaze at them the two

began to speak, calling on God and exalting His power; and Jäckele-the-fool breathlessly described in a torrent of words how terrified he had been in the cemetery by the rustling and the whispering and the gleams of light between the elder trees, and he told him what he had said to Koppel-the-bear and what Koppel-the-bear had said to him, and how, when clouds suddenly hid the moon, they had seen the spirits of dead children dancing in a ring over the graves.

The Great Rabbi, who in dark nights had paced the Thirty-two Hidden Paths of Wisdom and in magic disguise had passed through the Seven Gates of Knowledge – the Great Rabbi understood God's sign. He now knew that a sinner was living in the streets of the ghetto, a secret sinner who was sinning again and again, day after day: and that it was because of this sinner that the great pestilence was ravaging the ghetto and the dead children's souls found no peace in the grave.

The Great Rabbi gazed for a time in silent contemplation. Then he rose and left the room, and when he came back he held in his right hand a bowl of groats and two pieces of unleavened bread and in his left a small embossed silver bowl containing spiced apple sauce, the sweet Passover dish.

"Set to and eat," he said, pointing to the groats and the bread, "and, when you have eaten your fill, take this bowl of sweet nourishment and go back to the children's graves."

The two men were terrified at being told to go back to the cemetery again. But the Great Rabbi went on:

"Have no fear. He through Whose word the world came into being has power over the living and the dead, and His will alone prevails. You will sit by the graves and wait until one of the children approaches and wants to taste the apple dish, for the dead have not yet forgotten the food they ate on earth. But you will seize the hem of the child's garment with both hands and ask in the name of the One Who is the Beginning and the End what sin it is that has caused the great pestilence to descend upon this town."

And the Great Rabbi spoke over them the words of the priestly blessing, and their fear vanished, and they rose and went, determined to do as he bade them.

5

They sat between the graves, leaning against the cemetery wall with the bowl of spiced apple sauce on the damp earth in front of them. As they sat there in pitch darkness not a sound was to be heard, not a blade of grass moved, and there was not a glimmer of light in the cloud-covered sky. And, while they waited thus, fear overcame them again, and Koppel-the-bear started talking to himself, because he could stand the quiet no longer.

"I don't like sitting here in the dark, I wish I had a penny candle," he said. "There's supposed to be a full moon tonight, but I can't see it, a cock must have crowed and the moon fled. It would be better to be sitting at home beside the stove. Frost is rising from the earth and creeping into my clothes, frost is my enemy. Jäckele-the-fool, I can see you're freezing too, you're shivering. There are hundreds of rooms here in this graveyard, well built all of them, with no windows and no doors, and frost can't get in and nor can hunger. Both of them, having to stay outside, can keep each other occupied. The grave is the same, and that's the truth, for prince or beggar, age or youth . . ."

He fell silent, the last words stuck in his throat for, standing in front of him, bathed in white light, was Blümchen, the cobbler's daughter, holding the silver bowl in her hands.

"Blümchen!" said Jäckele-the-fool in a hoarse whisper. "Alas that you had to go. Don't you recognise me? I'm Jäckele-the-fool, and Koppel-the-bear's here sitting beside me. Don't you remember how you used to jump about and dance when I played my fiddle in the street? And how you used to laugh when Koppel-the-bear dashed about on all fours and made everyone split their sides with his antics?"

"All that's over and was only in time," the girl said in a strange voice. "But now I'm in truth and eternity that has neither limit nor end." The silver bowl slipped to the ground and the girl turned to rejoin her companions. But Jäckele-the-fool remembered what he had been sent to do. He held the child by the hem of her garment and would not let her go, and he said:

"In the name of the One Who is the Beginning and the End I call on you to tell and reveal the sin that caused the great pestilence to afflict this town."

There was silence for a while. The girl stood motionless, looking into the darkness to where, invisible to the eyes of the living, the angel of God, the guardian of souls, was hovering over the graves. Then she said:

"The angel of God has spoken, the servant of the Lord has said: 'It happened because of the sin of Moab committed by one of you. And He, the Eternal, saw it, and He, the Eternal, will destroy you, as he destroyed Moab.' "

At that Jäckele-the-fool dropped the hem of the garment, and the child was gone as if carried away by the wind, and the glory and the light that surrounded her vanished behind the dark shadow of the elder trees.

And the two men, Jäckele-the-fool and Koppel-the-bear, left the cemetery and went to the house of the Great Rabbi and told him what they had heard.

At first light the Great Rabbi sent his messengers from house to house, summoning the community to the house of God, and they came, all of them, men and women alike, and no-one stayed away. And when they were all assembled, he mounted the three stone steps, and under his coat he wore a white winding sheet and over his head there was a banner on which was written:

"The Lord of hosts fills the world with his glory."

And when all was quiet he began to speak. Among them, he said, there was a woman who was living in the sin of adultery, like the children of the accursed race whom God had destroyed. And he called on the sinner to come forward and confess and accept the punishment that the Lord God would inflict on her.

A whispering and a murmuring arose among the women, and they looked at one another in terror, but none of them came forward, none of them would confess to the sin of Moab.

Then the Great Rabbi raised his voice a second time. It was because of this secret sin, he announced, that the great pestilence had afflicted the town, carrying off their children. And he called on the sinner in the name of the Holy Letters and the Ten Terrible Names of God to come forward and confess, so that the calamity might be brought to an end.

7

But once more the Great Rabbi had spoken in vain. She who was guilty of the sin kept silent and would not be diverted from the path she had chosen.

Then a dark cloud of anger came over the Great Rabbi. He took the sacred rolls from the tabernacle and spoke the words of the great curse over the sinner, that she might dry up like the cliffs of Gilboa accursed by David, so that the earth might do to her what it had done to Datam and Abirom and that her name might be extinguished and her race be accursed in the name of the Sparkling One and in the name of the Flaming One and in the name of the Shining Lights and in the name of Zadekiel, who is the Ear and the Eye, and so that her soul might descend into terror and remain there until the end of time.

Then he left the house of God. And in the streets of the ghetto there was fear and dismay and bewilderment and despair.

When the Great Rabbi had returned to his house and was sitting in his room again, he remembered something that had happened many years before. Two butchers had come to him and complained that they had lost everything during the night. A thief had broken into their stall and wrought havoc with their meat. He had taken away as much as he could carry and befouled the rest.

Then too the Great Rabbi had summoned the community and called on the thief to confess and make good to the best of his ability the damage he had done. But, as the evil-doer kept silent and refused to abandon his evil ways, the Great Rabbi had pronounced a curse on him, expelling him and his family from the community of the children of God.

During the night that followed a dog had appeared outside the Great Rabbi's house and had howled and howled so long and so dreadfully that he had eventually realised that it was this dog that was the thief, and he had lifted the curse he had pronounced on the creature.

Now, the Great Rabbi reflected, if the curse is so effective that it is intolerable even to an animal into whose dark soul no gleam of the knowledge of God enters, how can it be possible for this adulteress to go on living under the burden of it without

8

appearing before me and confessing her sin before the day is over?

But the hours passed, night came and went, and the Great Rabbi waited in vain. So he called his silent servant, the work of his hands, who carried the name of God on his lips, and sent him to look for Koppel-the-bear and Jäckele-the-fool in the streets of the ghetto, for he needed them. And when they came he said to them:

"When daylight has faded and the shadows have fled, you will go once more to the cemetery, and you, Jäckele-the-fool, will play on your fiddle one of the songs that children sing on the feast of Tabernacles. And the spirits of the dead will hear you, because for seven days they remain bound to this world by terrestrial tunes. Then you will both come back, and you, Jäckele-the-fool, will go on playing without stopping until you enter this room. Then you will leave it immediately, and you must be careful not to look back, for what I want to do is the prerogative of the Flaming Ones, who are also called the Thrones, the Wheels, the Powers and the Hosts, and your eyes must not see them."

The two men did as he bade them. Jäckele-the-fool played on his fiddle the cheerful tunes of the feast of Tabernacles and Koppel-the-bear performed his leaps, and so they made their way between the graves in the cemetery and back again through the lonely streets, and behind them there was a bright light that followed them up the steps and into the Great Rabbi's room.

And, as soon as they left, the Great Rabbi spoke the forbidden word that is written in the Book of Darkness, the word that shakes the earth, uproots rocks, and calls the dead back to life.

And the child was standing before him in human form and was of flesh and blood and its light was extinguished. And it flung itself to the ground and wept and complained that it wanted to go back to the garden of the dead.

But the Great Rabbi said: "I shall not let you go back to Truth and Eternity, and you will have to begin life on earth all over again unless you answer my question. In the name of the One and Only One, in the name of Him who was and will be, I call on you to speak and reveal who is guilty of the sin because of

9

which the great pestilence has afflicted the town and carried off its children."

The child dropped its eyes and shook its head.

"I don't know who the sinner was because of whom God summoned us to Himself, and the servant of the Lord who is set over us does not know either. Apart from God, there is only one who knows, and that is you."

A groan came from the Great Rabbi's breast, and he spoke the word that undid the spell, and the child fled back to the home of souls.

And the Great Rabbi left his house and made his way alone through the dark streets of the ghetto and along the river bank past the fishermen's huts until he came to the stone bridge.

Below it was a rose bush with a single red rose, and next to it a rosemary was growing, and they were so closely intertwined that the rose leaves touched the white rosemary flowers.

The Great Rabbi bent down and pulled the rosemary out of the ground. Then he lifted the spell from the adulteress's head.

Black clouds chased each other across the sky, and the pale light of the moon clung to the piers and arches of the stone bridge. The Great Rabbi walked to the water's edge and dropped the rosemary into the river, and it was carried away in the waves and sank into the murmuring depths.

That night the pestilence in the ghetto streets came to an end.

That night the beautiful Esther, wife of the Jew Meisl, died in their house on the Dreibrunnenplatz.

That night Rudolf II, the Holy Roman Emperor, in his Castle in Prague, awoke from a dream with a shriek.

THE EMPEROR'S TABLE

On an early summer day in 1598 two young Bohemian noblemen were walking arm in arm through the streets of the Old Town of Prague. One of them was Peter Zaruba of Zdar, a student of law in Prague University, a young man of restless and enterprising spirit who busied himself with plans to help the Utraquist Church to establish its rights, to diminish the Emperor's powers in Bohemia, to increase those of the Estates, and perhaps even to put a Protestant king on the Bohemian throne. Peter Zaruba was deeply interested in such ideas. His slightly older companion was George Kaplíř of Sulavice, who lived on his estate in the Berau district. He did not take much interest in political or religious matters, his chief preoccupation being the lard, poultry, butter and eggs he delivered to the Master of the Imperial Household for the imperial kitchen, and the Jews, whom he regarded as responsible for the evils of the age. He had come to Prague to see about the money due to him, for the Master of the Imperial Household was many months in arrears with the settlement of his accounts. He and Peter Zaruba had become kinsmen a year previously, when a member of the Kaplíř family had taken a Zaruba bride.

The two young men had been to the Church of the Holy Spirit, and George Kaplíř had been surprised at the large number of Jews they passed on the way. Peter Zaruba explained that this was a Jewish neighbourhood, for the church was surrounded on all sides by Jewish houses and Jewish streets. Kaplíř said it was disgraceful not to be able to go to church without coming up against all those big Jewish beards, but Peter Zaruba replied that, so far as he was concerned, the Jews could wear beards as big and long as they liked, it was all the same to him,

For a man like George Kapliř, who spent his time in the Berau district, there was plenty to see in the Old Town of Prague. The Spanish Minister went by in his state coach with an escort of bowmen and halbardiers on his way to the Archbishop's Palace. In the Wacholdergässlein a comic beggar assured potential clients of his willingness to accept anything – ducats, doubloons, portugalosers or rosenobles – there was nothing he would turn up his nose at. The Tein church was filled to overflowing for the baptism of a Moor who had entered the service of Count Kinsky – the Bohemian aristocracy flocked to see the spectacle. The printers and the tent-makers were both holding their festival that day, and their beflagged processions clashed in the Plattnergasse. They nearly came to blows because neither was willing to give way to the other. In the Johannesplatz a Capuchin friar was addressing the Moldau fishermen, telling them that he too was a fisherman, the *Miserere* was his rod, the *Our Father* was suspended from it like a golden line, and the *De profundis*, the favourite nourishment of the dead, was the bait with which he pulled poor souls from the fires of purgatory like carp or white fish. And outside an inn on the Kreuzherrnplatz two master butchers were quarrelling, because one of them was selling pork at a heller a pound less than the other.

But George Kapliř of Sulavice had no eyes or ears for any of this. All he saw was the Jews he met on his way. On the Altstädter Ring one of them was in the pillory with an iron ring round his neck because, as a notice on his chest explained, he had "repeatedly and blatantly infringed market regulations". George Kapliř could not resist telling this Jew to his face what he thought of him. He called him Moses or Eisig, for those were the names of the two Berau Jews he knew.

"Hey, you, Moses or Eisig," he called out, "is it your Day of Atonement today? If your Messiah came and saw you like this, he wouldn't be at all pleased."

As he got no answer and expected none, he walked on and caught up with Peter Zaruba on the Small Ring.

Beyond the Moldau bridge, where the island was, they came across a whole party of Jews who were being taken, under strong guard to prevent any of them from escaping, to the church of Our Lady by the Lake to listen to a special sermon to the Jews to be delivered in Hebrew by a Jesuit in the hope of persuading them to accept baptism. They walked like drunks for, to avoid having to listen to the sermon, they had resorted to an ancient and well-tried expedient: they had not slept for two days and two nights, and were so exhausted that they were bound to fall asleep as soon as they sat down in church.

"Jews here, Jews there, Jews everywhere," Kapliř exclaimed indignantly. "They're multiplying so fast that soon they'll outnumber the Christians in the country."

"That's in the hands of Almighty God," said Zaruba, who was beginning to be bored by his new relative's inability to talk about anything but his lard, his eggs, and the Jews.

"I regard their numbers and their wealth as nothing but a bad sign that God has become angry with us Christians," said Kapliř.

Zaruba picked up and developed this idea.

"Perhaps," he said, "as they're still unconverted, God has sent them to us as an example to follow for our enlightenment."

"Get away with you and your enlightenment, don't make me laugh," exclaimed Kapliř, half amused and half indignant. "They come to noblemen's farms, not with enlightenment, but to buy up our lard, butter, cheese, eggs, linen, wool, skins, cattle, and poultry. True, they pay cash, for a stone of wool your Jew lays four gulden on the table, and if they don't pay cash they give good security and guarantees. And then they offer estate owners cord and braid for their servants' liveries, and cinnamon, ginger, and preserved nutmegs for the gentlemen's kitchen, and silk fringes, crêpe and veils for their wives and daughters."

"So you see for yourself that thanks to the Jews trade flourishes," Peter Zaruba remarked. "Why not admit it?"

"My father of blessed memory told me that one should sell the Jews nothing," George Kapliř went on. "Each to his own, he always insisted. Jew should deal with Jew and Christian with Christian. And I've stuck to that all my life. If only those up at the Castle weren't such dilatory payers. Tell me, Peter, where does all the money go? What happens to all the revenue from the customs, the land taxes, the district taxes, the house tax, the poll tax, the town dues, the local rates, the excise charges, the beer duty, the road and bridge tolls? Where does all the Emperor's money go?"

They had reached the square in front of the Castle, where there was a great coming and going of footmen, chancery clerks, messengers, grooms and ostlers, persons of consequence, senior and junior clergy and officers on horseback and on foot. Crossbowmen of the Imperial Guards regiment were on duty at the gate.

"You must ask Philipp Lang that question," Zaruba said, pointing to the tall windows of the Castle. "He's the Emperor's valet and manservant, and he's said to have his fingers in all affairs of state. Perhaps he knows where the Emperor's money goes."

George Kapliř stopped.

"Listen, Peter," he said. "Won't you come with me when I do my business up there? I'll introduce you to Johann Osterstock, Second Secretary in the Master of the Household's office, it's he who pays me my money after the account has been checked and approved by the First Secretary. He's a very friendly gentleman, and he's a second cousin of mine on my father's side, he always talks about our family connections, and he'll end by inviting both of us to join him at the Emperor's table."

"At the Emperor's table?" Peter Zaruba interrupted. "Me at the Emperor's table?"

"Yes, Peter, if you'll come with me," Kapliř replied. "At the Emperor's table, as they say. We shall dine with the officers of the Imperial Guard, Johann Osterstock has always done me that honour."

"Listen to me, George," Peter Zaruba said after a brief silence. "How long is it since Anna Zaruba was married to your brother Heinrich?"

"It was a year on the Friday after Invocavit Sunday," Kapliř replied with surprise. "At the Chrudim church."

"And in all that time did no-one tell you that no Zaruba of Zdar has ever or will ever eat at the Emperor's table?" Peter

Zaruba went on. "And has no-one ever told you about Johannes Zischka's prophecy?"

George Kapliř shrugged his shoulders.

"She may have told Heinrich, but she never told me," he said. "You're behaving as if my ignorance in the matter was wronging you in some way. What sort of prophecy was it?"

"It was when Johannes Zischka was dying," Peter Zaruba explained, "in the camp at Přibislau, as you will remember. He summoned his commanders and beckoned to one of them, Lischek Zaruba of Zdar, my ancestor, to come close to him, and said: 'Yes, you're Zaruba, you're Lischek, I recognise you by your gait.' And he also said: 'I shan't be able to finish my work, that has not been granted me, but a member of your family, a Zaruba of Zdar, he won't be a fox like you, but a lion, he'll finish it, he'll restore the independence of Bohemia. But there's one thing you must always remember, Lischek. He must not eat at the Emperor's table, if he does, he's not the right man, the cause is lost, and bloodshed and evil days for Bohemia will follow.' "

"And then he turned his face to the wall and died?" Kapliř inquired.

"Yes, then he died."

"That's what they always do when they have made their prophecies," said Kapliř. "But look, Peter, every family in these parts has stories like that. The things my grandmother told me about the Kapliřs, for instance. How one of them spent three days and two nights drinking with King Wenceslas the Idle and drank him under the table; and another Kapliř killed the last dragon in Bohemia, the creature was said to have been living somewhere in the Saaz area, where they now grow hops. But even assuming that the story is gospel truth, what reason is there to suppose that Zischka was a great prophet? He was a great soldier and a hero of the struggle for independence, that I don't deny, but I've never heard that he was a prophet as well."

"But don't forget that Zischka was blind," Zaruba replied. "First he lost one eye in battle and then he lost the other. God sometimes gives the blind prophetic powers, enabling them to foresee the future with the eye of the spirit. And, like my

15

father and my grandfather, I believe in Zischka's prophecy. I believe that a Zaruba will restore Bohemia's ancient independence, and perhaps . . . In short, I will not eat at the Emperor's table."

"Believe whatever you like, and do as you think best," said George Kaplíř. "I don't have to restore Bohemia's independence, my attitude's different. I dance where the band plays and do the job that's in front of me. So goodbye for now, Peter, you'll see me tonight at my inn."

And off he went, leaving Peter Zaruba sadly disappointed, for he had counted on being taken to lunch at his inn by the wealthy Kaplíř, as was the custom with relatives. But now that was off. He, Zaruba, shared lodgings with two fellow-students, and a woman from the neighbourhood cooked for them. Their standard of living was far from luxurious. He knew that, if he went back now, minced steak loaf in brown sauce and small cakes or biscuits covered with plum purée and a sprinkling of white cheese awaited him. He was heartily sick of both these crude dishes, which reappeared with tiresome regularity on the same day each week.

On his way down to the bridge over the Moldau he passed an inn garden. The landlord was standing at the entrance, and he bowed and scraped and smiled at him. Peter Zaruba was a thrifty individual, and took no pleasure in handing over his money to innkeepers. But this one looked so friendly and inspired such confidence that it suggested he had nothing in mind but the comfort and well-being of his guests. Zaruba said to himself that it wouldn't cost him his head, after all, and he stopped and asked what was on the menu.

"I don't know yet what my French and Italian chefs have prepared today," the man replied, "but I can assure you, sir, that there will be four main dishes and eight others, beside an extra course, which is to be served last, as a surprise. And all this will cost you only three Bohemian groschen, sir. But I'm afraid you will have to be patient for a while, sir, because we shall not be ready to serve for half an hour."

A Bohemian groschen was not small change, but a big and heavy silver coin. But for a lunch of four main and eight side dishes, followed by an extra, surprise dish, three groschen was cheap, so Peter Zaruba went into the garden and sat at one of the handsomely laid tables.

Eight or nine other guests were already there. They all seemed to know one another, they talked from table to table and no-one showed any sign of impatience at the unseemly length of time they had to wait before the meal was served. For it was nearly an hour before the landlord appeared at Peter Zaruba's table and asked for permission to serve the distinguished gentleman in person. At the same time he placed on the table the first of the promised twelve dishes, saying:

"A fine game soup, or potage chasseur, if you please, sir."

He followed this with two kinds of omelette, one à la paysanne, and the other made with chives and chervil. Next came two more appetisers: carp's roe with truffles and chicken en gelée. Then there was a brief interval before the first of the four main dishes arrived. This was smoked stuffed pike, ceremoniously served by mine host. Then came sliced kidneys roasted on the spit, asparagus in consommé sauce, petits pois, and a cold dish – calves' tongues and stuffed pigs' trotters.

Peter Zaruba thought with a trace of sympathy of his two fellow-students who were having to make do with minced steak loaf and biscuit with plum sauce. He no longer regretted Kaplíř's failure to invite him to his inn, for he could not possibly have done better than he was doing now. He merely tasted the pheasant dish that the host offered him next. After this came the promised surprise: quails on toast spread with beef bone-marrow. The meal ended with small iced marzipan cakes, Italian grapes and sharp Hungarian buffalo cheese.

By this time Peter Zaruba had become rather drowsy. He sat there dreamily, thinking that perhaps it was like this that the Abbot of Strahov dined on Feast Days. But, in spite of his desire to nod off to sleep, he could not fail to spot George Kaplíř as he came down the hill, gesticulating and talking to himself, his face flushed with anger.

He called him.

"Hey, George, here I am, come in."

George Kaplíř stopped, and wiped the sweat from his brow.

Then he came into the garden, nodded to Zaruba and leaned heavily on the table.

"Have you been waiting for me?" he said. "I'm grateful to have someone I can talk to, Peter. I've had a terrible time with the people up there, I didn't get a penny out of them."

"What happened?" Peter Zaruba asked with a slight yawn.

George Kaplíř collapsed into a chair with a groan.

"I had a row with Osterstock. He said he couldn't pay me anything, because he didn't have it. He read me a long lecture about the Castle's money troubles, and he said I should be patient with him because of our close relationship and come another time."

"Is he such a close relative of yours, then?" Zaruba asked, drowsily.

"Relative?" Kaplíř exclaimed indignantly. "Relative? His grandfather's cock may have crowed once in my grandmother's chicken run, that's the extent of our relationship. And then he took me to the First Secretary, and the argument began all over again. They insisted that they had no money, and had nowhere to turn to get it. The First Secretary showed me for my benefit how overwhelmed the Emperor was with demands for money from all quarters, he showed me a whole file full of appeals and complaints – heavens, what a state they're in. Yes, Peter, where does the Emperor's money go? Herr von Kollonitsch, the commander-in-chief in Hungary, needs money to repair the frontier posts. The commandant of the fortress at Raab complains about shortage of supplies and has to be satisfied. The Pro-Cathedral of Linz needs money for maintenance of the imperial buildings, and has been told to wait. The three tigers that arrived from Florence last year for the Emperor's zoo haven't been paid for. Count Wolf von Degenfeld has applied for a grace-and-favour payment in recompense for years of loyal service, and has been told to wait. The imperial bodyguard at the Castle haven't been getting their pay and are beginning to get restive . . ."

"But," a man at the next table interrupted, "they say that three days ago the Bishop of Olmütz advanced eight hundred ducats for the imperial table, all of it can't have been used up yet."

"They say. They say," Kapliř mimicked him, for he disliked strangers intervening in conversations between him and his friends. "I take no interest in what they say. They say a deaf man heard a dumb man talking about a blind man who saw a cripple walking the tightrope."

He glanced contemptuously at the man at the next table, turned to Zaruba and went on:

"As I kept telling them, no cash, no lard, and, as they wouldn't give me a date for settlement of my account, the First Secretary asked me if on this occasion I would be satisfied with twenty gulden, and he wrote me out a chit to take to. . . ."

He stopped, shook his head, drew his hand across his brow, and said:

"What a farce life is."

"And where are you supposed to take the chit?" Zaruba asked.

"Now hold tight, Peter, or you'll fall off your chair," Kapliř said. "They said I was to take it to the Jew Meisl at his house on the Dreibrunnenplatz, and he would pay me the money. I, George Kapliř of Sulavice, am to take it to a Jew in the Jewish quarter. Would you believe it?"

He took the chit from his pocket, read it through, folded it, and put it back in his pocket.

"In the end," he went on, "Johann Osterstock took me to the officers' table, but I had no appetite left, I did little credit to the occasion. I took a few spoonfuls of the soup, it was game soup . . ."

Peter Zaruba interrupted him.

"I had game soup too," he said. "And then there were omelettes and chicken en gelée, and then another hors d'oeuvre . . ."

"Really?" said Kapliř incredulously. "So that's what you had, was it? And what else did you have?"

"Stuffed fish, and heaven knows what else," said Zaruba, struggling to stifle a yawn. "Twelve courses, it was too much."

"Was there a ragout of pheasant?" Kapliř wanted to know, "and quails on toast?"

"Yes," said Zaruba. "How do you know?"

"And you ended with marzipan cakes, grapes and Hungarian cheese?"

"Yes, how do you know?"

Kapliř leant back in his chair and summoned the landlord.

"How does it come about," he asked, "that today you offered your guests the same menu that I was offered up at the Castle?"

"Everything in this establishment is respectable and above board, sir, and there is no secret about how I conduct my business," the landlord replied. "A great deal of boiling and roasting takes place in the imperial kitchen, but not much is eaten, and the waiters sell the leftovers to the innkeepers of the neighbourhood, and I get my share. But only on weekdays, because my Sunday customers are less well off, and are unwilling to pay three Bohemian groschen for a meal."

Peter Zaruba blanched and his torpor had vanished. "George," he exclaimed. "I've eaten at the Emperor's table."

"So you have," said Kapliř laughing. "So what? Isn't life a farce?"

But Peter Zaruba felt as if a millstone lay on his chest.

"I've eaten at the Emperor's table," he muttered. "What will become of Protestant liberty? What will become of my beloved Bohemia?"

I was told this story of Peter Zaruba and the Emperor's table by Jakob Meisl, in his room in the Zigeunergasse when I was fifteen and he was a medical student and my tutor. "When Peter Zaruba walked into the inn garden, he thought it wouldn't cost him his head, but that is exactly what it did cost him," Jakob Meisl explained, "for after the Battle of the White Mountain he, with twenty-four other Bohemian noblemen, was executed on the Altstädter Ringplatz. And that is yet another example that shows the ignorance of school history teachers and the writers of school history books. They'll tell you, and prove in precise detail, that the Bohemian rebels lost the Battle of the White Mountain because Tilly was the commander on the other side and their general, Count von Mansfeld, stayed behind at Pilsen, or because their artillery was not positioned correctly and their Hungarian auxiliaries left them in the lurch. But that's just

20

rubbish. The Bohemian rebels lost the Battle of the White Mountain because that time in the inn garden Peter Zaruba didn't have the sense to say to the landlord: 'How can you provide twelve such courses for three Bohemian groschen? It's an economic impossibility, my good man.' And so Bohemia lost its independence and became Austrian, and we now have the imperial and royal tobacco monopoly, and the imperial and royal military swimming school, and the Emperor Franz Joseph and the high treason trials, all because Peter Zaruba was tired of his landlady's cooking, it wasn't good enough for him, and so he ate at the Emperor's table.''

DOG LANGUAGE

On a sabbath day in the winter of 1609 the Jew Berl Landfahrer was taken from his room in a house in the Ufergässlein in the Prague ghetto to the Old Town prison, which the Prague Jews called Pithom or Raamses, in memory of the bondage in Egypt. Next morning he was to be promoted from life to death by being hanged on the Schindanger between two stray dogs.

This Berl Landfahrer had been unlucky all his life. Everything he had tried his hand at since boyhood had ended in failure and, for all his efforts and exertions, he was still so hard up that he had to wear his weekday jacket on the sabbath, though others had a different jacket for every half-holiday. Recently he had started going round the neighbouring villages buying up the skins of slaughtered animals left over for him by Christian butchers, but this was just at the time when the peasants had taken it into their heads to ask twelve kreuzers for a skin that wasn't worth eight. His neighbours said that if Berl Landfahrer started dealing in candles the sun would stop setting, and that if it rained ducats he would be indoors, and if it rained stones he'd be out in the street. There wasn't a stick over which he didn't stumble, and if he had bread he wouldn't have a knife, and if he had both bread and a knife he wouldn't be able to find the salt.

His being arrested and taken away on the joyous day of the holy sabbath was typical of his bad luck. At the same time it couldn't be said that he was completely guiltless in the matter, for real misfortune does not come from God. He had bought from a soldier at an unusually cheap price, as he himself admitted, a sable-trimmed cloak and a silk robe with hanging sleeves, not knowing that two days before, Colonel Strassoldo, the commander of the imperial troops stationed in the Old Town, who, because of the unsettled times, had been given full powers by the Emperor, had issued orders forbidding anyone to buy anything from a soldier unless the latter could produce written authority signed by his company commander. The penalty for infringing this order was death on the gallows. For a number of burglaries had been carried out in the Old Town by unknown soldiers, and valuable materials, curtains and clothes had been stolen from aristocratic homes. In accordance with custom, the proclamation had been read out in all the houses of God in the ghetto, but just that day Berl Landfahrer had stayed at home in his room, so deeply immersed in the secret teachings of the book *Raya Mehemma*, or "The True Shepherd", that he missed going to synagogue. True, as soon as he discovered that he had been handling stolen property he had handed over the sable cloak and the silk robe to the head of the Jewish community. But it was too late. The commander of the troops in the Old Town was furious at his proclamation having been ignored, and he remained implacable. So Berl Landfahrer was to be hanged on the gallows between two dogs next morning as an example and a warning to others.

The Jewish elders and the Jewish council did everything in their power to save him, they went here, there and everywhere, they prayed, they promised, but all in vain. The powers of destiny seemed to be conspiring against Berl Landfahrer. An audience with the Emperor through the mediation of his stove attendant was unobtainable, for the Emperor was in bed with a fever and nine monks in the Capuchin monastery on the Hradschin were praying night and day for his recovery. The wife of Herr Czernin of Chudenitz was Colonel Strassoldo's sister-in-law, but she was on her estate at Neudeck, which was three days' journey from Prague. The prior of the Knights of the Cross monastery, who was well-disposed towards the Jews and had often intervened on their behalf, was on the way to Rome. And the Great Rabbi, the head and shining light of the diaspora, to whose words Christians too had listened, had long been in the next world.

The two stray dogs were not guilty of any crime. It was only to increase the Jew's disgrace that they were to suffer death by his side. They had no one to speak for them.

One of them was already in the prison cell when the warder opened the door and let Berl Landfahrer in. It was a big, wretched, half-starved, emaciated peasant's dog with bristly, reddish-brown fur and big, handsome eyes. It had probably lost or run away from its master, because for several days it had been wandering hungrily about the Old Town. Now it was gnawing a bone the warder had thrown it. When the warder came in with Berl Landfahrer it raised its head and growled at them.

Berl Landfahrer contemplated the companion who was to share his fate with considerable alarm. He didn't trust big dogs, which were his worst enemies on the peasants' farms and invariably grudged him the animal skins he took away.

"Does it bite?" he asked.

"No," replied the warder. "If you don't do anything to it, it won't do anything to you. You may as well make friends, because tomorrow the two of you will be going together to the Valley of Hinnom."

And he left Berl alone with the dog, and locked the door behind him.

The Valley of Hinnom is the Jewish term for hell. The warder was familiar with Jewish expressions, having had many Jews in his care.

"To the Valley of Hinnom," Berl Landfahrer muttered with a shudder. "What does he know about where I'm going? He said that out of sheer spite, if he looks into the water, it's enough to kill the fish. To the Valley of Hinnom. Eternal and righteous God – not that I'm criticising You, You know and You have seen that I have lived a life of prayer, fasting and study and honestly earned my crust of bread."

He sighed, and looked up at the sky through the barred window.

"I see three stars," he said, "so the sabbath is over. At home Simon Brandeis, the tapster, and his wife Gittel are now sitting in the room next to mine. He has said the Havdala, the prayer of discernment, and now he's singing the blessing for the week to come, wishing himself and his wife happiness and health, for

24

that alone is wealth, and, as on every sabbath evening, she chips in with her 'Amen, amen, and what we most desire, the year of the Messiah'. And now, while they light the fire and put the evening soup on the table, perhaps they're talking about me, calling me that poor Berl Landfahrer, or maybe that good Berl Landfahrer, because only yesterday I again gave Gittel oil for the sabbath lamp and wine for Kiddush, because she had no money to buy what was needed. Today people will be talking about me as that poor Berl Landfahrer or, perhaps, that good Berl Landfahrer, and tomorrow I'll be Berl Landfahrer of blessed memory, or Berl Landfahrer, peace be with him. Today I'm Berl Landfahrer, living at the house 'At the sign of the Cockerel' in the Ufergasse, and tomorrow they'll be calling me Berl Landfahrer who is living in Truth. Yesterday I didn't realise how well off I was in the world: I ate what I pleased, I read the Scriptures, and in the evening I went to bed. Today the hand of the Enemy is over me. Whom am I to blame? I can only blame the stones in the earth. What's the good of that? Praised be the Lord, the eternal and righteous Judge. I must accept what He has decided for me. You are the God of truth, Whose actions are without fault."

And, as it was dark by now, he turned his face to the east and spoke the evening prayer. Then he curled up on the ground in a corner of the cell in such a way that he could keep an eye on the dog, who growled again.

"It's as cold as if heaven and earth were trying to freeze together," he said. "The dog won't keep quiet either, it keeps growling and baring its teeth. Suppose it knew what's going to happen to it. But what has an animal like that got to lose? Man loses his *ruach*, his spiritual nature, and we Jews, when we lose our life, lose more than others, for what do they know of the sweet bliss we gain when we immerse ourselves in the *Book of Gleanings, The Book of the Four Rows*, or *The Book of Light*?

He shut his eyes and took off in thought to the heights and depths of the Secret Teaching, of which it is said that there are ten stages, up to that of God's angels. He did this because it is written: Busy thyself with the secrets of wisdom and knowledge, thus thou shalt overcome the fear of the morrow in thee.

And the fear of the morrow in him was great and almost not to be borne.

In his mind he explored the whole world of divine powers known to the initiated as Apiryon, that is, the Wedding Litter, in which the Eternally Shining Ones, who are also known as the Bringers of Insight, live – they are the supports and pillars of this world. He meditated on the motive forces that conceal in themselves the four-letter name of God, and on the Mysterious One who controls them and is called the Most Hidden of the Hidden, "He Who is Completely Unknowable". He let the letters of the alphabet, whose meaning is intelligible only to the Knowing, pass before his mind's eye, and when he came to the letter caf which, when it comes at the end of a word, is God's smile, the door was unlocked and opened and the warder let in the second dog.

It was a white poodle with matted hair and a black spot under its right eye and another over its left ear. Berl Landfahrer knew it, in fact the whole Prague ghetto knew it, because for years it had lived in the house of the wealthy Mordechai Meisl, who had died a poor man. Since Meisl's death it had wandered about the Old Town and the ghetto, getting its food where it could. It was on good terms with everyone, but refused to accept a new master.

"The poodle of Meisl of blessed memory," muttered Berl Landfahrer, who was deeply affected. "So they want him dead too. What would the blessed Meisl have said if he had known that the day would come when his poodle was to be hanged on the gallows?"

He watched the two dogs greeting each other in doggish fashion, scrapping and yapping. Soon, however, he began to find the noise intolerable, for the dogs wouldn't stop chasing each other round and round the cell, growling and yapping at the same time. Soon the dogs of the whole neighbourhood joined in, barking and howling from near and far.

"Quiet!" Berl Landfahrer shouted angrily. "Must you keep snarling and yapping? Can't you keep quiet? It's late, and people want to sleep."

But it was like talking into the wind, the dogs took no notice and went on scrapping noisily. Berl Landfahrer waited for a while, thinking the dogs would tire and lie down and go to sleep. He had no thought of trying to go to sleep himself, for he knew he wouldn't manage it. He wanted to spend the whole night immersed in sacred matters, but the dogs wouldn't let him.

But the Secret Teaching, the Kabbala, gives those who have penetrated to its deepest depths, plumbed its abysses and climbed its heights, great powers of a special kind. He could not use them to save his own life, for that would have meant infringing on the divine prerogative. But he could use them to control these two dogs that refused to obey him.

It was said of the Great Rabbi that he addressed the Melochim, the angels, as if they were his servants. But Berl Landfahrer had never in his life used the revealed secrets and their magic powers, for he was timid by nature and knew that the fiery flame of the Secret Teaching burnt and consumed everything that was not fire like itself. But now, trembling and in great anguish, he decided to try with the aid of the secret formula and magic spell to become master of these troublesome dogs that on his last night were refusing to allow him peace of mind and closeness to God.

He waited until the moon appeared from behind the clouds and then wrote the letter vav with his finger in the dust that covered the cell walls. Every conjuration has to begin with this sign, for in vav heaven is united with the foundations of the universe.

Below it he wrote the sign of the bull, for all the creatures that live among mankind in the world are included under that sign. Next to it he wrote in the dust the sign of the divine throne vehicle, and under it, in the prescribed sequence, seven of the Ten Names of God: the first that he wrote was Ehieh, 'the Always', for it is by the power of this name that the bull is guided and led. And under Ehieh he wrote the letter of the alphabet which conceals strength and power within itself.

He waited until the moon vanished behind the clouds again. Then he called by name on the ten angels, God's servants, who come between God and the world. These names are: the

Crown, the Essence, the Mercy, the Form, the High Court, the Strict Persistence, the Glory, the Majesty, the Primal Cause and the Kingdom. In a whisper he invoked the Three Heavenly Primary Powers. And finally he called aloud on the angelic hosts of the lower realms: the Lights, the Wheels and the Animals of Holiness.

At that moment the poodle said to the peasant's dog: "I don't know why he's shouting like that. One can't always understand them. Perhaps he's hungry."

Berl Landfahrer never found out what the error was that had crept into his magic formula. Under the first of the seven names of God he had written the letter theth, but in this his memory had deceived him. For the letter theth stands for discovery and knowledge, not strength and power, and the consequence of this change in the invocation formula was that, instead of attaining power over the two animals, he merely acquired knowledge of their language.

He didn't trouble his head about this, and he wasn't surprised at being able to understand what the poodle said to the peasant's dog. It was so easy and natural that it seemed a matter of course, and what he couldn't understand was why he hadn't been able to understand before.

He leaned back in his corner and listened to the dogs' conversation.

"I'm hungry too," the peasant's dog snarled.

"In the morning I'll take you to the meat stalls," the poodle promised him. "You country dogs don't know your way about. All you need do is walk upright on two legs with a stick in your mouth, and for that they'll give you a splendid bone with meat and fat on it."

"On the farm at home I was given bones without having to walk on my hind legs," said the peasant's dog. "And I was given groats too. All I had to do for it was to guard the farm and take care that foxes didn't get at our geese."

"What are foxes?" the poodle wanted to know.

"Foxes?" the country dog replied. "How can I explain to you what foxes are? They have no masters, and they live in the woods. They come at night and steal geese. That's what foxes are."

"And what are woods?" the poodle inquired.

"Really, you don't know a thing," said the country dog. "Woods are, not just three or four trees, but – I don't know how to explain it to you – wherever you look you can see nothing but trees. And behind those trees there are more trees. That's where the foxes come from. When one of them made off with a goose, I got a thrashing."

"I never had a thrashing," the poodle boasted. "Even when my master taught me to walk on my hind legs and dance. He was always friendly to me. We had geese too, but they were never worried by foxes, because there are no woods here from which foxes could come. If there were woods and foxes here, my master would have told me about them. He told me everything, he kept nothing from me. I even know where he hid the money that no-one was ever to find in his house and whom it belongs to."

"Yes, they bury money," the country dog agreed. "What for? You can't eat it."

"That's something you don't understand," the poodle pointed out. "It's clever to bury money. Everything he did was clever. I was with him on the night when they wrapped him in a linen sheet and took him away. But before that someone came with money in a bag, he said it was eighty gulden and it settled his debt. My master went with him to the door, he walked very slowly, because he was ill, and when he came back he said to me: 'What am I to do with this money? I've got rid of my money, but it runs after me. When they come here tomorrow, they mustn't find it, they mustn't find a single groschen, it must be out of here tonight. But where, tell me, where?' He coughed, complained about the pain, and held a handkerchief to his mouth. Then he said: 'I know someone who never had any luck, he could do with this money. I can't leave him luck, but this eighty gulden he shall have.' Just after that he struck his head with his hand, and coughed, and burst out laughing. 'Isn't that just like Berl Landfahrer?' he exclaimed. 'When it rains ducats here, he's somewhere else, travelling round the countryside

29

with his handcart.' He thought for a while, then took his stick and his hat and coat and the bag as well, and we went out and down the street to the river bank, where he told me to dig up the earth, and buried the bag. Then he said: 'When Berl Landfahrer comes back, take him by the edge of his coat and bring him here, the money's his, but it's too late for me to give it to him, for today I shall be going the way of all mankind. You know Berl Landfahrer – he limps slightly and three of his front teeth are missing.' "

"That's bad," said the country dog. "Tell him to give up gnawing bones and eat groats."

"But I didn't know him, and I still don't know him," the poodle explained. "I can't remember him at all, and the money's still buried. People don't go about the streets with their mouth open, so how can I see whose teeth are missing? How am I to tell which of them is Berl Landfahrer?"

Berl Landfahrer was taken aback when they started talking about him, and he began listening with tense interest. When he heard that Meisl's poodle had been looking for him for years, he came out of his corner and said, sadly and reproachfully:

"I'm Berl Landfahrer."

"What? Are you Berl Landfahrer?" the poodle exclaimed, wagging his tail excitedly and sitting up to beg. "Open your mouth and let me see. Yes, the teeth are missing, so you are Berl Landfahrer. That's fine, tomorrow I'll show you where your money's hidden." And he dropped back on to his front paws again.

"Tomorrow?" Berl Landfahrer exclaimed with a shrill laugh. "Tomorrow? Yes, I really am Berl Landfahrer. But tomorrow all three of us are going to be hanged."

"Who's going to be hanged?" the poodle asked.

"You, me, and him over there," said Berl Landfahrer, pointing to the country dog, who had dropped off to sleep.

"Why should I be hanged?" the poodle asked in surprise.

"It's orders," replied Berl Landfahrer.

"They may perhaps hang you," said the poodle, "but they won't hang me. Not me. As soon as they open the door I'll be out and away."

He started turning in circles, and then he lay down on the floor.

"Now I'm going to sleep," he said. "You put your head between your legs too. So you're Berl Landfahrer. No, they won't hang me."

And with that he fell asleep.

At first light the door was opened, but it wasn't the hangman come to take Berl Landfahrer to the gallows. Instead Rebb Amschel and Rebb Simcha, both members of the Jews' Council, walked in. Colonel Strassoldo had relented. He had yielded to the appeals and pressure put upon him, and had agreed to quash the death sentence provided the Jewish elders paid a fine of 150 gulden immediately.

"We bring release to the prisoner and freedom to the fettered," said Rebb Amschel.

Rebb Simcha said the same thing in less exalted language.

"You're free, Rebb Berl," he said. "The fine has been paid, and you can go home."

But Berl Landfahrer seemed not to have understood.

"The dog! The dog!" he yelled. "It was here a moment ago! Meisl's dog! It knows where my money's buried! Eighty gulden!"

"Rebb Berl, you're free," the Jewish councillors repeated. "Don't you understand? With God's help your sentence has been quashed. You can go home."

"The dog! The dog!" Berl Landfahrer wailed. "Didn't you see it? It went out through the door. Meisl's poodle. I've got to find it! Eighty gulden! Oh, wretched, unlucky me! Where's the dog?"

For many years after that he was to be seen in the ghetto and Old Town of Prague running after dogs, attracting and holding them and asking them whether they had seen a white poodle with black spots under one eye and over one ear, and telling them that if they met it they must tell it that he, Berl Landfahrer, had not been hanged, and that the poodle must take him to the Ufergasse, nothing would happen to it, it wouldn't be hanged, the fine had been paid for it too. The dogs would snap at him and struggle free, and Berl Landfahrer would run after them, and children would run after him, and grown-ups would shake their heads and say: "Poor Berl Landfahrer, that night in the prison cell he lost his human soul out of fright."

THE SARABAND

At a party in the city hall of Prague given by Herr Zdenko von Lobkowitz, the Privy Councillor and Chancellor of Bohemia, on the occasion of the christening of his first grandchild, one of the guests was Baron Juranic, a captain in the imperial army, who had arrived in the Bohemian capital from Croatia or Slovenia a day or two before. And while the other gentlemen were dressed in the manner that the occasion and fashion prescribed, that is, in a gold-embroidered silk coat trimmed with gold brocade, narrow breeches, silk stockings and satin shoes with silk rosettes, Baron Juranic appeared in travelling clothes, in leather breeches and high boots, which he excused on the ground that his baggage had been left behind at the last staging post and had not yet been sent on. Also, in accordance with the custom of officers serving on the frontier, he had rubbed lard into his hair and beard, but this peculiarity was not held against a man who, because of the continuing struggle against the Turks, the arch enemy of Christianity, had not had time to inform himself about what was permitted to a gentleman and what was banned and beyond the pale.

So Baron Juranic behaved with great aplomb at this party and enjoyed himself hugely. He drank and danced with inexhaustible energy and high good humour, though it must be admitted that the standard of his dancing was not very high. It made no difference to him whether the musicians played a jig, a courante or a saraband, he performed the same hops and skips at all three of these dances, demonstrating far more enthusiasm than skill. This brave officer's dancing, in short, was as graceful as a tame bear's. When the music stopped for a while, he drank to the newly christened child's health with everyone who crossed his path, he paid compliments to the ladies, assuring each one of them that he had heard her beauty praised by persons who were excellent judges in the matter. But his special attention was devoted to the youngest of Herr von Berka's three daughters; this very attractive but rather shy young lady was making her first appearance at such a big occasion, and he regaled her with stories of his deeds of arms, the successful raids, surprise attacks and other blows he had struck at the Turks, never failing to point out that, though they had made a great deal of noise in the world, in fact they were of no great significance. He also informed the young lady that in his homeland, where a bushel of corn was worth seven farthings and a barrel of beer cost half a gulden, he could be described as a rich man, and a woman sufficiently understanding to be ready to share life with him on his estate would live in abundance, for there were feathers, wool, honey, butter, corn, cattle and beer, in short, everything needed for an enjoyable existence. The only requirement was that heaven must have blessed her with a good figure, he added, glancing down at the young lady, for this last meant much more to him than noble birth and good breeding.

Now, one of the other guests was Count Collalto, of Venetian descent, a very fashionable young man, who thought he had certain claims on the youngest of the three Berka daughters, and he disliked the Croatian nobleman's manners as much as his appearance. And after the latter had danced yet another saraband with her, practising those odd little hops and skips of his, he went up to him with a bow and politely asked if he would favour him with some information: which celebrated dancing master had enabled him to reach such a high degree of perfection in the art of the dance?

Baron Juranic was able to take a joke with good humour even if it was at his expense. He laughed, and said he was well aware that he had little experience in the art of the dance and must therefore sincerely apologise. Nevertheless dancing gave him great pleasure, and he hoped the young lady and the other guests would not have found him too tiresome.

"Sir, you do yourself an injustice and you are too modest," said Collalto. "You manage the most difficult steps the way others sip hot soup. In the great pastoral ballet of the fountains that is shortly to be performed at the Castle for His Majesty, you could well play the part of one of the fawns, or perhaps even of Silenus himself."

"I am a soldier," the baron replied with complete composure, "and I am therefore more accustomed to the dance of battle than to any other kind, and in the course of my life I have listened more often to the roar of cannon than to the music of flutes and viols. As for Silenus, with his horns and his goat's feet, you, sir, must seek out someone else to play the part. And as for the hot soup, sir, you had better take care lest you be obliged to swallow what you have cooked yourself."

And with that he bowed, offered the young lady his arm, and they rejoined the dancers.

The young Collalto watched them go, and as this loutish baron refused to be parted from the charming young lady, and as he had found that taunts failed to disturb his composure, he decided to try something else. He approached the dancing couple and tripped the baron so neatly with his foot that he fell full length to the floor, bringing down as he did so, not the young lady, but a gentleman dancing next to him.

Confusion arose among the dancers, the music stopped, there was laughter, and questions and exclamations of indignation and dismay, but the bewilderment came quickly to an end when the baron stood up and went to the aid of the gentleman whom he had brought down. The latter at first looked very upset, but he recovered his composure when he realised that his finery had not suffered, and he turned to the baron and said, with perfect politeness in which only the slightest trace of irony was discernible: "I see, sir, that you manage to introduce a little variety into the dance."

Baron Juranic raised his hat and expressed his profound apologies. Then he looked for the young lady with whom he had been dancing, but she was nowhere to be seen; for, dismayed by the awkward mishap that had befallen her partner, she had left the hall in the general confusion. Meanwhile the music had struck up again, couples had rejoined each other, and Baron Juranic strode through the throng and went up to Collalto.

"You will please inform me, sir, whether you did that to me on purpose and with deliberate malice."

Young Collalto looked haughtily into space over Juranic's head.

"I demand to know," the baron repeated, "whether you did that deliberately to make me a laughing-stock in the eyes of the young lady."

"I am under no obligation to reply to a question put to me in such an insolent tone," Count Collalto replied.

"After such an insult you are under an obligation to give me the satisfaction due to me as a man of honour," the baron said.

"There are some here who call themselves men of honour, but at home follow oxen behind the plough in clogs," said Collalto, shrugging his shoulders.

Not a muscle moved in the baron's face, but the previously almost imperceptible scar of a sabre wound on his forehead reddened like a port wine stain.

"As you refuse me satisfaction, sir," he said without raising his voice, "and as you continue to insult me, I can no longer treat you as a man of honour. Instead I shall make you see sense by thrashing you like a common farm labourer."

Count Collalto raised his hand to slap the baron's face, but the baron caught and held it in an iron grip.

For the first time Collalto condescended to change his tone.

"This is not the right place or the right time to settle the matter," he said, "but you will find me in Kinsky's garden in front of the big circular lawn in an hour's time. The main gate is shut, but the side gate is open, and I shall be at your service there."

"That's as warming to hear as Spanish wine," the baron said with satisfaction, releasing Collalto's hand.

After agreeing that the duel should be with swords and without seconds they parted, and soon afterwards the baron left the party and the building without saying goodbye to the Berka young lady.

Meanwhile young Collalto went to one of the side rooms, where he found his host, Herr Zdenko von Lobkowitz, at a card table. He sat beside him and watched the play for some time.

Then he said:

"Do you know a person here who calls himself Baron Juranic?"

"Watch this, it's a game in which the seven of spades rules everything. I'm playing it for the first time in my life today. Juranic? Yes, I know him."

"Is he one of us? Is he of noble blood?" Collalto asked. "His manners are very crude."

"Juranic? He may have crude manners, but he's of good, genuine, noble stock," said Zdenko Lobkowitz, who knew everyone's genealogical tree by heart and was therefore an authority on such matters.

Collalto watched the game for a little while longer.

"It's absurd," said Zdenko Lobkowitz. "If someone has the seven of spades and the knave of diamonds at this game, he can't help winning, never mind how he plays. But, apart from that, even the Jew Meisl couldn't raise enough money to cover what you can lose if you're not very careful. What's this about Lorenz Juranic? Has he had too much to drink?"

"No, but I've had trouble with him," Collalto said. "I have an appointment with him tonight."

Zdenko Lobkowitz laid down his cards.

"What? With Juranic?" he said in hushed tones. "Then go and pray for divine protection. Juranic is a deadly fencer."

"I can use my sword with good effect too," said Collalto.

"What? Your sword? Juranic will cut your ears off," the elderly nobleman said. "Believe me, he's not a good man to quarrel with, I know him. Fence with the devil, but not with Lorenz Juranic. Go and settle the matter, there'll be no stain on your honour if you extricate yourself, or shall I do it for you?"

"I shall report to you when the matter has been settled," Collalto replied.

The big circular lawn in the Kinsky garden was one of the places to which the Prague nobility resorted to settle their quarrels with the sword. The lawn was surrounded by a gravel path. In the middle, between two lonely elm trees, there was a fountain, the splashing waters of which could be heard from a distance. A stone Neptune overgrown with moss lay outstretched on a rock, and the weather-worn sandstone mermaids, tritons and sirens that crouched round the edge of the pool sent criss-crossing jets of water to the reed pipe, the rocky reef and in steep arches up towards the sky.

It was here on the lawn that Collalto met the baron, who had brought with him two Croatian servants carrying torches, for the moon was in its last quarter. The two Croatians, who had swashbuckling moustaches and long hair gathered into a thick knot at the back, were standing with heads bent facing the stone figures of the fountain, crossing themselves and muttering prayers.

"My servants," the baron explained to Collalto, "have never in their lives seen anything like this fountain. To them it's a great miracle. In that Neptune they think they recognise St Laurence, my patron saint, and they think the mermaids and tritons are angels sent down from heaven to support the holy martyr lying on a grill by spraying him with water to cool him. Yes, my Croats are very religious and great venerators of the saints and, if there were no taverns here, they would crawl on their knees through all the churches in the town."

He showed the two servants where to stand so as to illuminate the lawn and path with their torches. The two duellists took up their positions facing each other at the prescribed distance, and saluted each other with their swords. Then Collalto, who had picked up a pebble, tossed it straight up in the air while the men stood motionless, listening, for when it touched the ground, that would be the signal for the duel to begin.

It did not last long. Collalto had holed many gentlemen's coats with his sword-point, but this time he was up against an opponent who could have taken on four swordsmen at once. He could, as they say, have stuck three of them in his hat and asked the fourth how many there were left. He really was what Lobkowitz had called him, a deadly fencer. At first he merely stood his ground and left all the lunging to Collalto. But then with his cuts and thrusts he drove Collalto down the path and across the grass all the way to the fountain, asking him as he did

38

so whether he didn't find the evening air too cool, and when he had last seen his cousin Franz Collalto. He drove him twice round the pool and then back across the grass to the gravel path and then back the same way to the fountain again. There the duel came to an end, for Count Collalto had reached the point where he could neither stand firm nor retreat. With his torso bent back over the edge of the pool, he struggled for breath with the point of the baron's sword at his chest.

"So that's that," said the baron. "Thrusting my sword through you would be as easy as drinking a glass of wine, and I should do so with as clear a conscience. All your worldly troubles and tribulations would be over."

Collalto said nothing. Cold drops from the jets of water proceeding from the tritons landed on his face; and the strange thing was that now, after what the baron had just said, he felt an agonising fear, a fear far greater than anything he had felt during the duel.

"What do you think of the blessed quality of mercy?" the baron wanted to know. "Haven't you been told how pleasing it is to God? Are you not aware of the great merit that is acquired by those who practise it?"

"If you spare me, you will have a true friend in me for ever," said Collalto in an agony of fear.

The baron let out a short, sharp whistle.

"I have not sought your friendship, sir, and would not know what to do with it," he replied.

At that moment Collalto heard the distant music of a flute, a violin and a drum. The stately pace of a saraband came from behind the bushes and slowly drew nearer.

"Perhaps your dancing is better than your swordsmanship," the baron went on. "By gambling with the latter you forfeited your life. With the former you may win it back from me."

"By dancing?" Collalto asked, and it suddenly seemed to him as if all this, the baron's voice, the splashing of the fountain, the sword-point at his chest and the music, which was now quite close, was only a bad dream.

"By dancing, yes. If you wish to survive, you shall dance," the baron said, the scar of the sabre wound on his brow reddening once more. "You made me a laughing-stock to the young lady."

He took half a pace backwards and Collalto straightened himself. He now saw that five more servants in addition to the two torch-bearers were standing behind the baron. All five wore the baron's livery. Three were musicians and the other two, who were glaring at him very threateningly, were holding pocket pistols.

"You shall dance from now until dawn," said the baron. "You shall dance through all the streets of Prague. I advise you not to tire, because if you stop you will get a bullet in your body. If you don't agree, say so. Well? Are you going to keep me waiting?"

The two Croats raised their pistols, the musicians struck up, and Count Collalto, driven by the fear of death, began dancing a saraband.

It was a strange nocturnal procession that made its way through the streets and across the squares of Prague. The torch-bearers led the way, next came the musicians with flute, fiddle and drum and Count Collalto dancing behind them, followed by the two men with pistols, who did not for a moment take their eyes off him. Baron Juranic, though he brought up the rear, was in fact the leader; for he showed the torch-bearers which way to go by pointing his sword.

They went through narrow, winding alleys, uphill and downhill, past palatial houses of the nobility, narrow, lopsided gabled houses, churches, garden walls, taverns and stone fountains. The people they met saw nothing surprising in the procession; they thought the gentleman dancing behind the musicians was in a happy mood, having had rather too much to drink, and that a friend of his had provided an escort of musicians and flunkeys to see him safely back to his quarters; no one suspected that he was dancing desperately for his life. And just when Collalto felt so exhausted that his heart was going to break into little pieces and he thought he could go no farther, but found no mercy and had to go on, they happened to have reached a little square in the middle of which there was a statue of the Virgin Mary. And no sooner did the Croats spot the stone carving than they went down on their knees, made the sign of the cross and began saying prayers, while Collalto collapsed to the ground and recovered his breath.

Baron Juranic burst into loud laughter.

"By my poor soul, this was not intended," he said, crossing himself like the others. "I should have realised it would happen. Yes, my Croats are very religious, they know what is due to Christ and his Holy Mother, and that tall fellow, the one with the pistol, is the most religious of them all. He'd rather cut his hand off than steal a horse on a Sunday."

Meanwhile the Croats had finished praying, all except the one who would never steal a horse on a Sunday and was still on his knees.

"Get up, damn you," the baron shouted at him. "Give the Holy Mother of God a chance to see something other than your face."

There were – and there still are – many hundreds of crucifixes and stone saints in the city of Prague. They stand suffering, blessing or imploring in the squares and niches and corners, outside church gates and hospitals and poor-houses and on stone bridges. And whenever the Croats came across one of them they went down on their knees and muttered prayers or sung litanies and gave Collalto a brief respite. At first Baron Juranic calmly put up with this, for he knew that in religious matters his Croats were not to be trifled with. But then he began getting more and more annoyed at the way in which the pious naïveté of his servants gave aid and comfort to his enemy, and he began thinking about how this could be prevented. And he ended by hitting on an idea that struck him as so tremendously amusing that he laughed aloud. To cap the ordeal he was inflicting on Collalto, he would make him dance his saraband through the streets of the ghetto, where there were no crucifixes and no sacred images.

At that time the Prague ghetto was not yet surrounded by a wall; this was not built until the time of the siege by the Swedes. It could be entered from the streets of the Old Town without first having to knock at a closed gate. So the baron took his little procession down the Valentinsgässlein into the Jewish quarter, down narrow, winding alleys and along the cemetery wall to the bank of the Moldau and back, past the Jewish baths, past the town hall and the bakehouse and the closed meat stalls and through the deserted flea market, and the musicians played and Collalto danced, and there were no sacred images to give him respite. Here and there a window would be opened when the procession passed by, and sleepy, anxious faces would look out, and then the window would be shut again. Here and there a dog would bark, suspicious of the procession. And when the two torch-bearers and the musicians behind them turned from the Zigeunerstrasse into the Breitegasse, just where the house of the Great Rabbi Loew stood, Collalto, who had reached the end of his tether, groaned, reeled, clutched his breast and weakly cried out for help.

The Great Rabbi, sitting over his sacred and magic books up in his room, heard his voice and knew that it came from the depths of despair.

He went to the window, leaned out, and asked who was calling and what aid he needed.

"An Ecce Homo," Collalto gasped in his extremity, dancing and reeling on and on. "An Ecce Homo, for the love of God, or it's all up with me."

The Great Rabbi took in at a glance the torch-bearers and the musicians, the dancing Collalto, the two lackeys with pistols and the laughing baron, and that glance was sufficient for him to see why the dancing man was crying out for an image of Jesus, and that here was a man in mortal danger to be saved.

On the opposite side of the street there was a house that had been gutted by fire; only a single wall, blackened with age and smoke, still stood. And the Great Rabbi pointed to this wall, and by his magic power he caused a picture to appear on it, made of moonlight, dust and decay, rain and soot, moss and mortar.

The picture was an Ecce Homo. But it was not the Saviour, the Son of God, the carpenter's son who came to the sacred city from the hills of Galilee to teach the people and to suffer death for his teaching. No, it was an Ecce Homo of another kind.

There was such nobility in his features, so appalling was the suffering that spoke from his face that the stony-hearted baron was struck by a lightning flash of self-knowledge and was the first to sink to his knees. And it was before this Ecce Homo that he arraigned himself for having been pitiless that night and without the fear of God.

My tutor paused briefly; he was the medical student Jakob Meisl, who told me this and many other stories of old Prague.

"There's not much more to say," he ended, "and if there were, it wouldn't be very important. Young Count Collalto is said never in his life to have danced again, and Baron Juranic is said to have left the service, and that's all I know about them. And the great Rabbi Loew's Ecce Homo? It was not Christ. It was the Jews, the Jews, persecuted and derided through the centuries, whose suffering was shown in that picture. No, don't go to the ghetto, you'd look for it there in vain. Time, wind and weather have destroyed it, and no trace of it remains. But walk the streets wherever you like, and if you see an old Jewish pedlar humping his wares from door to door, and the street boys running after him, shouting 'Jew! Jew!' and throwing stones at him, and he stops and looks at them with a look in his eyes that is not his but has come down to him from his fathers and forefathers, who like him wore the crown of thorns of contempt and suffered the lash of persecution, then perhaps you will have caught a glimpse, a slight and inadequate glimpse, of the Great Rabbi Loew's Ecce Homo."

EMISSARY FROM HELL

Rudolf II, Holy Emperor and King of Bohemia, was having a sleepless night.

His anxiety began as early as eleven o'clock, anxiety about something whose coming he foresaw but could not prevent, even by barring the doors and windows. He rose from his bed, put on his dressing gown, and paced quickly up and down his room. Every now and then he stopped at the window and looked across the gleaming ribbon of the river to where he could make out the roofs and gables of the ghetto. It was from there that the woman he loved, the beautiful Jewess Esther, had come to him, night after night. That had been years ago, and it had come to an end on the night when the demons of darkness had snatched her from his arms. There too, in one of the houses of the ghetto, lay his hidden hoard, his secret treasure, the gold and silver of the Jew Meisl.

The sounds that floated up to him from the deer park, the rustle of withered leaves carried by the wind, the whirr of moths, the sighing of the wind in the treetops, the nightly song of the frogs and toads – all these sounds bewildered him and increased his restlessness. Then, about one o'clock, came night terrors and ghosts.

At half past one he flung open the door and with a groan in his voice called for his valet, Philipp Lang.

But, as always at this time of year, Philipp Lang was on his estate at Melnik for the fruit harvest. The valet Červenka came hurrying along in his place, his nightcap askew on his head. He carefully wiped the perspiration from the Emperor's brow with a small linen cloth.

"I have often respectfully urged Your Majesty to take greater

44

care of Your Majesty's health and not to expose Your Majesty to the cold night air. But Your Majesty takes no notice of an old servant."

"Fetch Adam Sternberg and Hanniwald," the Emperor told him. "I have to talk to them. And tell Colloredo to bring me some strong wine, Rhine Falls or malmsey, I need it."

There were three cup-bearers and eleven carvers of the imperial table, and the Emperor knew very well which of them were due to serve him on every day of the week according to the duty roster, but he didn't know, or had forgotten, that Count Colloredo had died of a stroke several weeks before and that his successor as second court cup-bearer was the young Count Bubna.

The first to enter the room was Hanniwald, the Emperor's private secretary. He was a tall, lean man with silvery white hair, and Červenka had found him still at work. Soon afterwards Count Adam Sternberg, the Master of the Horse, appeared in his night clothes and only one slipper. The Emperor had been pacing quickly up and down the room, and his dressing gown had slipped from his shoulders, but now he stopped. His face betrayed agitation, helplessness and exhaustion. He took a deep breath and was about to begin describing what had happened to him that night and the two previous nights when the door opened and Červenka let in the young Count Bubna, followed by a flunkey with jugs of wine.

The Emperor looked Bubna straight in the face, stepped back in alarm, and exclaimed:

"Who are you? What do you want? Where's Colloredo?"

"Your Majesty will graciously remember," said Hanniwald, "that recently, in accordance with God's will, Count Colloredo went the way that we all must go. Your Majesty knows this, for Your Majesty was present at the Mass that was held in the cathedral for Your Majesty's loyal servant."

"And this," said Count Sternberg, taking up the thread, "is his successor, Vojtech Bubna, at Your Majesty's service."

"But he looks like Bernhard Russwurm," the Emperor exclaimed, again stepping back and raising his arm defensively. "Isn't he terrifyingly like Bernhard Russwurm?"

The Emperor was sometimes frightened by new faces. He thought he recognised in them the features of persons long dead by whom he imagined himself to be persecuted. Many years before, he had had General von Russwurm arrested and shot for duelling; he had ordered this in a fit of violent anger, and it weighed heavily on his mind. In every new face he saw Russwurm hatefully and derisively looking at him, and again and again Russwurm emerged from his grave and threatened him.

"Russwurm? Oh, no," Adam Sternberg said casually. "Russwurm was short, with a broad nose and a plump chin. I assure Your Majesty that I have known Vojtech Bubna ever since his shirt used to hang out of his knickers."

"But he looks just like Bernhard Russwurm," the Emperor exclaimed with his teeth chattering. "Who are you? Where do you come from? Do you come from hell?"

"I am here to serve Your Majesty, I come from Prastice, that's our small estate near Chotebor in the Časlau district," the young Count Bubna explained; he could not understand what was going on or why the Emperor was so hostile to him.

"If you're not lying, recite the Lord's Prayer, tell me the names of the twelve apostles, and recite the Creed," the Emperor said.

Young Bubna looked anxiously and inquiringly at Count Sternberg, who nodded vigorously, and so he recited the Lord's Prayer, followed by the names of the twelve apostles (he forgot St Jude, but made up for it by mentioning St Philip twice). Then he began reciting the Creed, but dried up and came to a stop. He was rescued by the valet Červenka, who was standing just behind him and gave him the cue in a whisper.

After the second Article of the Creed the Emperor had had enough.

"All right, all right," he said. "You're quite right, Adam, I made a mistake, he's not like Bernhard Russwurm. Russwurm can rest in peace, I forgave him a long time ago."

Červenka had gone behind the Emperor and laid his dressing gown round his shoulders. The Emperor took the wine jug from young Bubna's hands and emptied it.

Then he said:

"It's a merry life up here in the Castle, the strangest things keep happening. Someone came to this room and pestered me again tonight."

"Who came to see Your Majesty tonight?" Hanniwald asked, though he already knew the answer.

"One of his envoys," the Emperor, who disliked mentioning the devil by name, replied with a groan.

"And in the guise of a spice dealer again?" Hanniwald asked, putting his hand through his silvery white hair.

"No, not in human form," the Emperor replied. "Those envoys of his first came two nights ago, there were three of them, in the form of a crow, a cuckoo, and a bumble-bee, and they didn't screech like those birds generally do, but spoke to me with human voices and pestered me."

"God help us miserable sinners," the horrified Červenka muttered, and the flunkey who was holding the wine jugs tried to free one of his hands to make the sign of the cross.

"The cuckoo," the Emperor went on, "wanted me to abandon the Sacraments, the Mass, vigils, incense and holy water. The one in the guise of a bumble-bee whispered to me that the Lord Jesus, our hope, did not come in the flesh and that the Holy Mother of God was conceived in original sin."

"That makes the nature and origin of those birds clear beyond all doubt," Adam Sternberg observed thoughtfully.

"The third, who presented himself in the form of a crow," the Emperor went on, "tried to persuade me that the time had come, and that I must delay no longer, to abjure holy baptism and the holy cross, the Mass and holy water, otherwise he who had sent him would take the crown from my head and hand it over to the rogue and criminal, together with all my power."

When the Emperor spoke of the rogue and criminal, he meant his brother Mathias, the Archduke of Austria.

"God will not permit that," said Hanniwald. "Your Majesty's fortunes and those of the empire lie in His hands and not in that of the Enemy."

"And so it will be to all eternity, amen," Červenka muttered.

"Last night," the Emperor went on, "only two of his envoys

appeared, the one in the form of a cuckoo and the other in the form of a bumble-bee. The cuckoo called the Pope a dissolute Spanish chaplain, and the bumble-bee whispered to me that I should resist his master no longer, but do his will, otherwise I would suffer misfortune, the secret treasure would never come into my hands, it would vanish into nothing like snow in March, and I would be left desperate."

"Does Your Majesty know of a secret treasure?" Sternberg asked. "All I know of is debts here, there and everywhere."

"And tonight," the Emperor went on, "they came again, three of them this time, but the one in the guise of a cuckoo was the only one that spoke."

"Your Majesty will not have said the Benedictus," Sternberg suggested.

The Emperor drew the back of his small hand across his brow. His eyes were absent and in his soul there were terror and death.

"He said," he continued, "that he and his two companions had come and warned me for the last time; after them only one more would come and present himself to me in human form, and it was to him that I would have to give my answer. And I must consider it very carefully for, if it displeased his master, he would give my crown and imperial power to the rogue and villain and recreant, under whose sway war would come to all nations from the rising to the going down of the sun, with darkening of the moon and of the sun, and many fiery and bloody signs and portents in the heavens and on earth, and rebellion and bloodshed and pestilence and famine. And all men would despair and many would die, and everywhere there would be a huge demand for wooden boards for coffins. And I could take no more," the Emperor concluded his story, "but dashed from the room and found him there."

He indicated the valet Červenka with a tired and feeble movement of his arm.

"Yes," said the valet, "and Your Majesty was trembling in all his limbs and there were drops of perspiration on Your Majesty's brow, and I took the liberty of respectfully appealing to Your Majesty to take greater care of Your Majesty's health."

48

Sternberg signed to young Count Bubna to pass the Emperor the jug, for after the second jug his agitation generally subsided, his gloomy thoughts and melancholy ideas faded for a time and sleepiness set in. The Emperor called this forgetting his suffering.

Meanwhile Hanniwald said:

"Has Your Majesty yet graciously considered what answer is to be given to the ambassador from Satan who is expected?"

The Emperor said nothing, but drew his hand across his brow and through his ruffled hair. His breathing became audible and his chest rose and fell. The silence lasted for a minute. Hanniwald, who sometimes feared that the Emperor inclined towards the Utraquist heresy and might become disloyal to the Catholic faith, whispered to Sternberg:

"*Metuo ne Caesar in apostasiam declinet.*"

"*Optime, optime,*" replied Sternberg, who had totally failed to understand what Hanniwald said.

The Emperor now began to speak again. He spoke slowly and quietly, choosing his words carefully.

"You know, Hanniwald," he said, "how much unrest there is in Bohemia and how endangered the public peace and religion are here. We must therefore seek by temporal wisdom to appease the arch-fiend and enemy of mankind, and so avert the evil with which he threatens the countries entrusted to us by God. For I don't want war, that devastates and destroys the food of all men, their cattle and crops, their trade and commerce, and carries wholesale death under its mantle. What I want is peace, which I have sought all my life, a just peace that enables all mankind to flourish."

"Bravo!" exclaimed Sternberg.

"The power of which the arch-fiend and enemy of mankind so arrogantly boasts is actually not so very great," Hanniwald now said. "His power extends only to hell and not to the earth. His threats are idle, a tissue of diabolical deceptions and lies. In reality there is no need of worldly wisdom to avoid his snares and traps. All that is necessary is that we do not depart one finger's breadth from the Lord Jesus our Saviour."

"That is all that is needed," Sternberg repeated, once more

signalling to Bubna to pass the wine jug to the Emperor. "Well said, Hanniwald, well said."

"So it was nothing but a tissue of diabolical deceptions and lies," the Emperor whispered with a deep sigh.

"Hanniwald has an excellent mind, as I've always assured Your Majesty," Sternberg said, again signalling to Bubna, who was standing there as stiff as a ramrod.

". . . we must not depart by one finger's breadth from the Lord Jesus our Saviour," the Emperor murmured. "That is an excellent saying, it comforts the soul, it's as strong as Bezoar."

Now at last his eyes fell on Count Bubna. He took the jug from his hands and emptied it.

"So it was all deceptions and lies," he went on. "Amusing, amusing. So you're Vojtech Bubna. I knew a Bubna, I hunted wild boar with my beloved father of blessed memory on a Bubna estate. And you? How are things with you? How much money do you owe the Jew Meisl?"

Young Bubna flushed scarlet. Like most young Bohemian noblemen, he had secured a loan from Meisl on the strength of a promissory note, for the allowance he received from home was very meagre. He began stammering:

"Seventeen Rhenish gulden, Your Majesty will forgive me, it's not right, I know, but I had losses at cards, and I had nowhere else to turn."

This confession actually seemed to give the Emperor a kind of satisfaction.

"Never mind, never mind," he interrupted. "Valiantly got into debt and valiantly applied to the Jew. That's quite all right."

The valet Červenka now advanced stiffly upon the Emperor with slow and stately tread.

"Your Majesty," he announced, "it is my humble but imperative duty respectfully to call upon Your Majesty most graciously to go to bed."

"At the Prague court," the Spanish ambassador once wrote home to his King, "extraordinary things are ordinary and commonplace."

One of the extraordinary things that attracted little attention in Prague took place two days after this night-time episode. To the sound of bassoons, cornets, pipes and kettledrums, an envoy from the Emperor of Morocco proceeded in solemn procession from the quarters in which he and his escort had spent the night through the streets of the Kleinseite and the Hradschin up to Prague Castle.

This envoy had been negotiating in Venice with a view to procuring guns, gunpowder, ammunition and tackle for the Moroccan fleet, and he had come from Venice to Prague to deliver a message expressing his sovereign's respect and friendship for Rudolf II, through whose good offices he hoped to establish improved relations with the Spanish Crown, which had inflicted loss and damage on Morocco by cutting off its seaborne trade.

On his journey to Venice the envoy had been received at Liza Fusina by twelve Venetian noblemen clothed in silk and scarlet, who had delivered an address of welcome. A gondola adorned with embroidered cloths was provided for him, and fine carpets were laid out for him to recline on. He had then been wafted smoothly under a brilliant blue sky to the music of a lute, the sea was shallow and flat calm, and all sorts of fish were visible in the clear water. Then the city had risen out of the water before his eyes with its palaces, monasteries and bell towers. Outside the church of St Andrea he was again greeted by twelve noblemen, and he changed to another flat-bottomed but spacious vessel that they called the Bucentoro, and under a sun-blind of crimson satin he had advanced up the broad waterway of the Grand Canal. Here the houses were very big and tall; some were of stone and painted in bright colours, and others were of white marble. On the first day he had been shown the treasure of St Mark's, fourteen precious stones each weighing eight hundred carats, a great many golden trinkets, as well as vessels of hyacinth and amethyst, and there was even a bottle cut out of a single emerald. He was also shown the Arsenal, in which the Venetians manufactured everything required for a war fleet. Next morning he was taken with great pomp to the Signoria, where he handed his letter to the Doge.

Venice was palaces and golden domes, gliding gently to the inaudible rhythm of oars, the music of the lute and under blue skies. Venice was a triumphal city, governed with great wisdom, that knew how to honour its guests.

But here in Prague little honour came his way. The quarters allotted him were a house with damp, bare walls, its narrow, stuffy rooms meagrely furnished. A servant or secretary of the Chancellor of Bohemia had called on him in these quarters to inform him of the day and time of the audience to be granted him by the Emperor and to acquaint him with the ceremonial customary at such audiences. And two of the Emperor's gentlemen-in-waiting, ordinarily dressed, with no hint of splendour and only moderately well mounted, escorted him and his retinue up to the Castle.

Outside the gate he was received by a captain of halberdiers who led the way through the inner courtyard and up a wide staircase and then down several corridors to a room in which the Chancellor of Bohemia, Herr Zdenko von Lobkowitz, and the senior chamberlain, Count Nostiz, awaited them. A friar of the order of Friars Minor who was familiar with every African tongue acted as interpreter.

The two ministers and the learned friar led the ambassador and his retinue of mamelukes, footmen, attendants and musicians into the audience chamber.

In the middle of the hall there was a throne surmounted by a canopy. Carpets on the floor made footsteps inaudible. Tapestries on the walls showed mythological and hunting scenes. Cushions and a stool were provided for the ambassador, whose dark beard stood out sharply against his white silk clothing.

Three of his mamelukes took up their position behind him. The most distinguished of the three, an old man with but one eye, carried a crystal bowl covered with a gold-embroidered veil. This contained a message in the handwriting of the ruler of Morocco.

The musicians were ushered into the background. The hall filled with dignitaries, court officials and officers of the imperial bodyguard. The senior seneschal, Herr Karl von Lichtenstein, made a brief appearance. He seemed satisfied with the arrangements, greeted everyone, expressed his appreciation on all sides, and vanished again.

There was a brief roll of drums, a door sprang open, and behind the master of ceremonies, who knocked on the floor three times with his staff, the Emperor walked in briskly, looking round the audience chamber in lively fashion.

He raised his hat. The dignitaries and court officials who had bowed deeply, rose again and the officers of the bodyguard stood as motionless as statues. At a sign from the master of ceremonies the Chancellor of Bohemia stepped forward and presented to His Majesty the ambassador of the Emperor of Morocco.

The ambassador inclined his head, laid his right hand on his turban and bowed three times to the Emperor in the prescribed ceremonial fashion. Then he stepped one pace back and took his sovereign's hand-written message from the crystal bowl. He pressed it to his lips and handed it to the Chancellor of Bohemia, who handed it to the Emperor. The Emperor broke the seal and unrolled the scroll, which he handed back to the Chancellor of Bohemia, who in turn handed it to the interpreter to translate.

At that moment the bassoons, cornets, shawms and drums struck up a fanfare. One of the mamelukes made some dance movements and uttered some long-drawn-out cries. This was not foreseen in the official ceremonial. Then there was silence, and the learned friar began to read:

"I, Muley Mehemed, by God's will a powerful ruler and emperor in western Africa on both sides of the Atlas Mountains, king in Fez, Zagora and Tremissa, lord of Mauretania and Barbary, proffer my greetings to my brother, the Roman Emperor and King of Bohemia and wish him. . . ."

"It's Henry," the Emperor, who had been staring fixedly at the ambassador, suddenly exclaimed.

". . . and wish him," the interpreter continued, after a brief moment of embarrassment, "a long life and true knowledge of God, who alone . . ."

"Ask him," the Emperor interrupted, pointing at the

ambassador, "whether he believes and acknowledges that Jesus Christ came in the flesh to redeem us."

". . . who alone opens the gate of paradise so that he may dwell there for all eternity . . ."

"You are to ask him," the Emperor now said, raising his voice, "whether he believes that Jesus Christ came in the flesh."

A murmur arose among those present. The senior chamberlain and the Chancellor of Bohemia went up to the Emperor to try and pacify him. The learned friar stopped trying to read the missive and spoke a few words to the ambassador.

For a moment the ambassador stared silently into space. Then he made a gesture to indicate that he rejected the question addressed to him as if it were no concern of his.

"He refuses," the Emperor called out. "So tell him to recite the Creed."

The interpreter translated the Emperor's demand, but the ambassador indicated with a movement of his head that he was not in a position to comply with it.

"It's Henry," the Emperor then said, briefly and firmly. "Oh misery piled on misery. It's Henry, and he comes from hell."

The Chancellor of Bohemia, the senior seneschal and the master of ceremonies now realised that the Emperor took the Moroccan ambassador for a certain Henry Twaroch, who many years before had been a stable boy in the imperial stables, and they agreed that the audience must be ended as quickly as possible. For the mistake to which the Emperor had to all appearances succumbed was the more painful because this Henry Twaroch was not only of very humble origin but had also been convicted of theft. The Emperor was a great connoisseur of old coins and medals, of which he had assembled a fine collection, and Henry had extracted three Roman gold coins and a silver medal from his pocket. For this he would have been hanged had he not managed to file through the bar of his cell window and so escape at the last moment. The Emperor had been furious about the robbery, and the thief's escape from the gallows was concealed from him.

But before the Chancellor of Bohemia and the two other distinguished gentlemen could do anything to prevent the shocking scene that they feared and expected, the Emperor rose from his throne and walked up to the ambassador.

"Listen, Henry," he said, and there was anguish in his voice as well as repressed fear and horror. "I know from what realm you come and what you want to hear from me."

The Chancellor of Bohemia, the senior seneschal and the master of ceremonies breathed with relief, and all the other courtiers who were present looked amazed and put their heads together, for the Emperor had addressed the Moroccan ambassador in the Bohemian tongue.

"I shall not withhold my answer from you," the Emperor went on, raising his voice. "Go back to him who sent you, and tell him I will not depart by one finger's breadth from the Lord Jesus Who redeemed us, and I shall abide by that, even though I lose my empire and all my power in consequence."

He stopped, exhausted, his hands trembled, and there were drops of perspiration on his brow. The ambassador stood motionless, leaning slightly forward with his arms crossed.

"That time when I went to the stables to have a look at the Flanders stallion," the Emperor went on in muffled tones, as if what he still had to say to the man standing before him was for him alone, "you, thief that you were, took from my pocket three of my golden pagans' heads and sold them and drank the proceeds, and you paid the penalty and suffered a dreadful death. I have forgiven you, and I shall pray for God's mercy for you. And now leave us in peace, Henry. Leave us in peace and go away from here. Go to the place God has prepared for you."

The Emperor stepped back two paces, stopped, looked once more at the ambassador or devil's emissary, and as a parting gesture made the sign of the cross with two fingers of his right hand. Then he turned and walked out. The master of ceremonies, who had been standing there as if benumbed, seemed to wake up, and he struck the floor three times with his staff. There was a roll of drums, the door closed, the audience was over, and the incident had passed off so lightly that Herr Zdenko von Lobkowitz, the Chancellor of Bohemia, sent a prayer of thanksgiving up to heaven.

★

Shortly after dark that evening the ambassador left the house in which he was quartered by a back door, dressed like a Bohemian artisan on his way to the tavern. He wore a coat of thick cloth, grey woollen stockings, rough shoes and a broad felt hat.

He walked through the lower and upper New Town to the vineyards that lay outside the city area, followed the main road, and then took a path alongside a stream, the Bottič, until he reached the fields of flax and the fruit gardens that surrounded the little village of Nusle.

Here there was a cottage in the middle of a garden in which swedes, onions and mangel-wurzels were grown. A cat was asleep on the wall surrounding a well. There was a smell of cow-dung and damp earth.

The ambassador of the Emperor of Morocco walked into this cottage.

The gardener, a bald-headed old man, was sitting by the hearth looking at the milk soup that was simmering over the fire in the hearth. He didn't stand up. He drew his hand across his stubbly chin and nodded at the visitor.

"There you are again," he said. "You always come in the night like Nicodemus."

"I was up at the Castle today," the visitor said, looking round for a chair.

"That was very reckless of you," said the gardener. "It might have ended badly for you."

"He who serves must take such risks, and even bigger ones when his master's orders require it," said the visitor.

"Well, you've come back safe and sound," said the old man. "You've always been lucky. If they throw you in the river, you clamber out with a fish in your mouth."

He put the milk soup on the table, produced half a loaf from the bread bin, and they began to eat.

"Telling me you've become a great lord over in Africa doesn't take me in. The idea that your Moorish Emperor should seek your advice," the old man said, putting into his mouth a slice of bread he had dunked in the soup.

"But it is so," the ambassador replied. "I'm as close to my master as Peter was to the Lord."

"And the yarn that the duke who rules in Venice entertained you there at his expense for eleven days doesn't impress me either."

"But it's the truth," the visitor insisted. "What I had to spend there on trumpeters and drummers, door keepers and runners and oarsmen could have kept someone here in Prague for six months."

"And your hundred slaves and servants, and your I don't know how many wives? Am I to believe that too?" the old man went on truculently. "True, I've had several wives myself, but I had nothing but trouble with them, because none of the women here and around the Bottič are any good. If I ever take another wife I'll fetch her from some foreign place farther away, Michle or Jessenitz, for instance. But it was wrong of you to abandon the true faith and become a Turk, and I don't like it. There's no hope of eternal bliss for you."

"Whether your priests or ours possess the truth is a matter for God to decide," the visitor replied.

"You're an obstinate fellow," the old man said crossly.

For a while they ate in silence. Then the gardener said:

"Whom did you see up there in the Castle?"

"Zdenko Lobkowitz," the visitor replied. "He's aged a great deal."

"That's because of the way he lives. He ought to do as I do," said the gardener. "Swedes, radishes and red cabbage in the daytime, milk soup mornings and evenings with a slice of bread – that keeps you young. Did you also see His Majesty the Emperor?"

"His Majesty the Emperor received me," the visitor replied.

The old man glanced at the door to make sure it was shut. Then he said:

"He seems to be pretty weak in the head, according to what people say."

"He? Weak in the head? He's the cleverest of them all. He wasn't taken in for a moment by my silk apparel, my turban,

57

my Moroccan leather shoes, my beard or my emerald ring. Not he!"

The old man stopped eating and looked inquiringly at his visitor.

"Yes, father, he recognised me. After all these years he recognised me," Henry Twaroch said, half proudly and half ruefully.

THE FILCHED TALER

The young son of Emperor Maximilian II, the future Emperor Rudolf II, had just returned from Spain, where he had completed his education at the court of King Philip. One day, with no retinue, unaccompanied even by a servant, he rode from Prague to his small castle of Benatek, where he was to spend a few days. But when night fell he lost his way and found himself plunging deeper and deeper into a thick wood which seemed never-ending. Eventually he and his horse could go no farther, and he began to reconcile himself to the prospect of spending the night on damp moss under the fir trees. But then he saw the glow of a fire some distance away. Thinking that perhaps woodmen or charcoal burners were preparing their evening meal and that they would be able to show him the way to Benatek, he tethered his horse to a tree and made his way towards the fire.

He reached a clearing, and was suddenly confronted by two huge, red-haired men with thick staves in their hands, and what he had taken for a fire of wood or charcoal turned out to be three gleaming piles, one of gold coins, one of silver talers, and one of thick copper pfennigs; and there were enough of these gold, silver and copper coins to fill three corn sacks.

The young archduke thought he had come across two robbers who wanted to bury their treasure in the thick wood. But he did not feel afraid of them, for he saw that their only weapons were their staves, which he could easily evade with his sword, so he coolly asked them if they could show him the way to Benatek castle.

One of them pointed silently with his stave in an easterly direction. The young archduke was now beginning to enjoy this adventure, and instead of going he asked the two men who they were.

"My subordinates call me the Great and Powerful," the one who had shown him the way replied. "And my companion here is called the Terrible and Strong."

The Emperor's son immediately realised from this information, and even more from the informant's voice, that these two were not terrestrial beings, but ghosts or demons. At that time he still had the boldness and recklessness of youth. Nevertheless he now felt afraid and would have liked to be a long way away, but not for anything in the world was he prepared to let the two notice this, so he behaved as if he still thought them to be men of flesh and blood, and he asked them where all that money came from.

"One day, if you do not know it already, you, the first-born and heir to three crowns, will learn that gold comes from fire, silver from air and copper from water," said the one who had spoken before.

"And to whom does it belong? For whom are you keeping it?" the Emperor's son asked, trying to make his voice sound as firm and confident as possible.

"All this," was the answer, "is for one of the persecuted race, for Mordechaeus Meisl, your future domestic servant."

And the other one, who had not yet spoken, repeated in a voice that sounded even more terrifying:

"For Mordechaeus Meisl, your domestic servant."

In those days the Prague Jews were described as domestic servants of the Emperor, and for a moment the young archduke's indignation outweighed his fear.

"Is all this to belong to a Jew?" he exclaimed. "That won't do. I want my share."

And to prove his courage to himself he picked a taler, with his father's face on one side and the lion of Bohemia on the other, from the silver pile that was closest to him.

At this the taciturn demon, the Terrible and Strong one, raised his stave threateningly, but the other one stopped him.

"What are you doing, you hot-tempered one?" he shouted.

"You know it is written that hot temper and idolatry are the same."

Then he turned to the Emperor's son.

"Keep the taler, just keep it," he said. "You will have no good fortune or peace until it comes into the hands of him for whom it is destined."

A moment later everything – the men, the clearing, the three gleaming piles – had vanished, and the Emperor's son was alone in the dark wood.

At that he no longer tried to suppress his fear. He ran, stumbling over stones and the roots of trees. A branch snatched the hat from his head, and he left his coat hanging in the undergrowth. When he found his horse he felt better. He rode it in the direction he had been shown, and soon afterwards he found the road to Benatek.

Not till he had mounted his horse and ridden away did he realise that he was still clutching the filched taler.

Next day he learned that his beloved father, the Emperor, had been taken ill with a fever in Prague Castle. He set off for Prague immediately, but on the way his horse fell and broke a leg. He continued the journey in a peasant's cart, but the axle broke. And, when he arrived at Prague Castle after several more mishaps and delays, his father received him harshly and angrily because of his tardiness; he turned his face to the wall and would listen to no excuses.

And that was not all. During his absence a fire had broken out in one of his rooms in the Castle and ruined his finest Flemish carpet, a present from the King of Spain. Also his favourite dog, a small Spanish greyhound, had run away from the Castle and in spite of all efforts was never found.

The young archduke knew very well where all these misfortunes came from. He realised that he must keep the stolen taler no longer, but must hand it over to the person for whom it was destined.

One of the Emperor's two personal physicians was a baptised Jew who had been summoned to Prague Castle from Candia in Greece. He knew all the Jewish communities in the Levant, Italy and Germany and, though he was baptised, remained in contact with the Jews of Prague. The young archduke sought his help in tracing Mordechaeus Meisl.

The physician stroked his beard and pondered. Then he asked where this Jew lived and by what trade or occupation he made his living.

"I think he must be a great magician and alchemist and have great power in the invisible world, and he lives here in this country," the Emperor's son replied.

The physician shook his head. He knew of no Mordechaeus Meisl and had never heard the name.

The young archduke then sent two of his servants to the ghetto to inquire after Mordechaeus Meisl, but they came back empty-handed. One of them had applied to the Emperor's treasury officials and clerks who noted in their books all the tax and other payments made by the Prague Jews. But they too had no knowledge of a Mordechaeus Meisl.

In view of his failure to find him the Emperor's son decided to gamble with providence and put the power of destiny to the test.

One evening, unseen by anyone, he left the Castle, using a key he had procured to open a door that was nearly always locked, and went down the Hradschin and on to the stone bridge. He stayed there for a while, looking down at the river. Then he leaned over the balustrade and let the taler slip from his fingers.

He expected it to vanish into the waves for ever, but just at that moment a small fishing boat passed under the bridge, and the man in it dropped the rudder, put his hand to his head, and started swearing furiously, for he thought someone had thrown a stone at him. Then he spotted the taler in the circle of light thrown by the boat's lantern at his feet.

That is the work of divine providence, the Emperor's son murmured to himself, putting his hand to his heart, which was beating hard. He realised that the taler was now on its way and would perhaps pass through many hands before reaching its goal; and he also realised that he must follow it, or he would have no peace; and he must not lose sight of the man in the boat.

Meanwhile the man in the boat had picked up the taler. He

examined it carefully, rowed a few strokes, examined it again, threw it down to test its genuineness by the sound, picked it up again and, after looking all round, dropped it into his coat pocket.

The young archduke hurried from the bridge across the Kreuzherrnplatz and along the river bank, and just beyond the Mill he found his man. He had tied his boat to a post and taken a pail from under the thwart, and with the pail in one hand and the lantern in the other he was walking slowly up the Bethlehemgasse. He stopped outside a small house, one side of which faced on to a garden, and he was just about to knock at the door when a man appeared out of the shadow of the garden wall and took him by the arm.

"What have you got there? Fish?" he said in a curt and authoritative manner, and then added, like someone used to having his wishes treated as orders:

"I need your hat and coat and that pail of fish."

The astonished fisherman freed his arm and told the gentleman to leave him alone and go to the devil. But instead of going to the devil the gentleman put his hand in his pocket, produced a considerable sum of money and pressed it into the fisherman's hand. The fisherman examined it in the light of the lantern and then said, with a smile of satisfaction:

"Another ducat, sir, and I'll let you have my jacket, my shirt and my trousers if you like, sir, and I'll go home as naked as I was born."

He handed the stranger his coat, which was worn and shabby, besides smelling abominably of fish, his hat, which consisted of hardly anything but a broad brim, and his pail of fish. Then he picked up his lantern, wished the gentleman health and prosperity, and disappeared round the nearest corner. In his delight at the money he had been given he forgot all about the taler that was still in the coat pocket.

The stranger put the coat over his shoulders, pulled the remains of the hat right down over his forehead, picked up the pail, and knocked at the door. He told the maid who opened it that he had bought the fish that had been ordered.

She let him in, and he followed her up the stairs, at the top of which a very pretty young woman was standing. She put a handkerchief to her nose when she saw the alleged fisherman, who moved the brim of his hat up a little, whereupon she recognised her lover, who had thus gained entry to her house without rousing the maid's suspicions.

The young woman promptly sent the maid to the kitchen with the fish, and as soon as they were alone he whispered to her that he had been thinking for days about how to get to her but, damn that fishmonger, his coat smelt so horribly that it was intolerable, and she took his hand and pressed it and took him into the bedroom, where they spent the night.

The young archduke had seen the coat with the taler in it pass into other hands, he had seen it vanish into the house, and now he waited for it to reappear. He walked up and down, up and down, he was tired, and the hours passed slowly.

Towards morning, when it began to get light, he saw the new owner of the coat emerge feet first from a window; he clung with both hands to a thick branch of a pear tree and then swung down from branch to branch until he finally landed on the grass like a ripe pear. A young woman in night attire appeared for a moment at a window. She blew the owner of the coat a kiss, and threw the coat after it. The kiss reached its objective, but the coat got caught in the branches of the pear tree. Its owner rose to his feet, climbed with some difficulty to the top of the garden wall and, after some hesitation and thought, jumped down on the other side. After rubbing his knee and feeling his ankle, he quickly made off, dragging one foot slightly. The coat was left hanging in the branches. It smelled foul and billowed in the wind.

The archduke did not doubt that it would soon find a new owner and, sure enough, a cart heavily laden with wine casks soon appeared. The driver spotted the coat hanging in the branches, drove quite close to the wall, pulled up, and brought the coat down with the stock of his whip. He put it on the wine casks behind him and drove on. The Emperor's son followed.

He didn't have far to go. The cart stopped outside a tavern on the Kleine Ringplatz, the casks of wine were unloaded with a great deal of noise, the horses were put in the stable and the cart was put in the shed. The driver picked up the coat, took it across to the ghetto, and went into an old clothes dealer's shop in the Breitegasse, which in spite of its name was a narrow street, though a busy one.

The Jews' strange faces and behaviour, their busy activity, and the fact that he was standing and waiting and being pushed about by the crowd outside an old clothes shop made the Emperor's son feel he was having a bewildering dream. His disappearance must certainly have been noticed by now up at the Castle, and there was bound to be a great to-do as they searched for him everywhere, but here in the ghetto nobody bothered about him, and he cursed the hour when he had helped himself to the taler, prompted solely by curiosity. He was exhausted after being up all night, he was hungry, and he felt dreadful. But he had to stay and see what happened to the taler.

At an itinerant food stall, of which there were many in the ghetto, he bought a boiled egg, an apple and some bread. He had had enough of standing and waiting in the noisy street, so he walked into the old clothes dealer's shop.

The dealer, who was holding the coat while the driver talked to him about it, appreciated at a single glance the expensiveness of the newcomer's hat, ruff, clothes and shoes. He saw immediately that this visitor to his shop had come, not to buy or sell, but for some other, not yet apparent purpose; and he asked in what way he could be of service to him.

The young archduke asked if he might rest in the shop for a short while and eat his breakfast there. He had been on his feet all night and still had a long way to go. Then he moved aside a pair of shoes and a belt on a bench up against a wall, sat down, and produced the egg and the bread he had bought. The dealer turned back to the coat and the driver.

"What am I to do with it?" he said, turning it this way and that and showing the holes and patches. "The shop's full of such stuff, and I can't sell it."

"But it's worth twelve pfennigs," the driver insisted. "Everyone needs a coat, and if he can't afford a new one he buys an old one."

"But not one like this," the dealer replied. "Not nowadays, when joiners and brushmakers wear lined coats with slashed sleeves just like the nobility and gentry."

"All the same, it's worth twelve pfennigs," the driver insisted. "Even if the brushmakers and the gentry won't buy it, there are poorer men who will."

The dealer resumed turning the coat this way and that. His expression was sorrowful.

"It's no use for Kiddush and it's no use for Havdolo," said the dealer, using a Jewish expression meaning that it was of no use to anyone. "It's worth a blown egg. It's a fisherman's coat and you can't get rid of the fishy smell."

"It may be a fisherman's coat," the driver admitted, "but all the same" – he thought for a moment – "it's worth ten pfennigs."

"Eight pfennigs, Guv'nor," the dealer declared, counting out the money on the table. "Eight pfennigs, and I'm losing on the deal. But as it's you, and as this is the first business I've done today, and I want you to come back another time. . . ."

After some hesitation and grumbling the driver pocketed the money and walked out.

The young archduke, who was sitting on a bench eating his bread and egg, was delighted at the outcome of the bargaining, because he had been afraid that the driver would reject the offer and take the coat away, in which case his rest would have been over and, in spite of his tiredness, he would have had to continue his pursuit of the taler in the pocket.

The dealer threw the coat on a pile of old clothes in the corner. The young archduke took a knife from his pocket and began peeling his apple; and while he was so engaged a man, evidently a clerk, came in and wanted to buy a black coat with brass buttons and puffed sleeves. The dealer produced a number of such coats and tried to convince the clerk of their excellent value, but none of them suited the man. They were either too long, or too tight, or the cloth was of inferior quality, or they were too expensive, and so, after a great deal of haggling, in the course of which the dealer in his enthusiasm went so far as to claim that when the Lord Mayor himself came to the Old Town he wore a coat of not half the quality, the clerk left the shop and no business was done.

"Yours seems to be wretched business," the young archduke remarked, biting into his apple.

"Yes, that's the right word for it," said the dealer, "it's full of worries and troubles. For every twelve who come and bargain, there's only one who buys. We also suffer from dealers who have no stalls but carry their goods on their arm and sell them on market days, thus spoiling prices. Also there are the taxes that prevent us from selling cheaply, and there's as much that could be said about that as about the exodus from Egypt. But worst of all is not being allowed to trade in the Christian part of the city."

Aha, so that's what he's getting at, the future Emperor said to himself. Stay in your ghetto, my man, or there'd be unrest and trouble instead of peace and order. To calm down the old clothes dealer, he quoted aloud a jingle that was often repeated by one of his servants up at the Castle: "The world is full of trouble; trouble afflicts us all. But if you have strength and health, then you have real wealth."

"I'm in good health, praised be the Holy Name," said the dealer. "To be ill you need time, and I don't have any time. But I do know that this trade was laid on me as a punishment for my sins."

"No, not as a punishment for your sins but, as I have reason to believe, because you are descended from Reuben. For members of the tribe of Reuben – so I was taught in Spain – threw dice for our Saviour's clothing; and for that a curse was laid on their descendants, condemning them to dealing in old clothes for the whole of their lives with no benefit from it but worries and troubles and cares."

"There's nothing about that in the books written and handed down to us by our wise men," replied the old clothes dealer, shaking his head. "Also I am not of the tribe of Reuben, but of priestly lineage, of the tribe of Levi."

But the young archduke was well informed about the tribe of Levi too.

"Those of the tribe of Levi have their share too," he said. "One of them gave our Lord Jesus vinegar and gall to drink, and

67

those who belong to that tribe therefore suffer thirst for all time, but cannot drink properly."

"Is that so?" the old clothes dealer said with a trace of sarcasm. "I get a great deal of pleasure from drinking half a pint of wine when I'm thirsty."

The young archduke was not to be put off.

"Then you're saved, and the curse has been lifted from your shoulders," he assured the dealer.

And to show that he was well informed about the Jews and their story he changed his ground.

"You Jews," he said, "boast of and glory in having had a wise man, King Solomon. But he had seventy wives, and over and above that three hundred concubines. That wasn't so wise."

"He knew how much sweetness and bitterness is concealed beneath a woman's skirt," the old clothes dealer replied. "But there's one thing I'm sure of, and that is that, in comparison with the majesty of King Solomon, all the kings of the present age, including the Roman Emperor himself, are but a feeble spark."

This was too much for the young archduke to swallow. In his eyes his beloved father was far superior to King Solomon.

"You speak with little respect of His Majesty the Holy Roman Emperor," he said.

"I am his loyal domestic, and I have always paid my taxes and other dues punctually," the dealer replied. "May the Lord increase his might, and may an enemy sword never invade his territory."

The door opened gently, and a strange small form entered the shop, a boy wearing shoes much too big for him; his coat was patched all over, and his hat had had all the colour washed out of it. He was carrying a coarse linen bag with hardly anything in it.

"Here I am," he said, laying two copper coins on the counter. "Praised be the Holy Name, I'm able to pay you again today."

"Blessed be your coming," the old clothes dealer said, taking the copper coins, and the boy went and busied himself with the pile of old clothes in the corner.

"He pays me," the old clothes dealer explained to the young archduke, who looked at him inquiringly, "he pays me two thick pfennigs when he has them, but that isn't every day. That entitles him to whatever he finds in the pockets of the clothes I've bought that day or the day before. He always finds the same things; a bit of bread or biscuit, an apple or a swede, a bit of string, a button, a nail, or a small empty bottle – all that goes into his bag. Sometimes he finds nothing, for there are people who empty their pockets before taking their clothes to the dealer's. But sometimes he finds treasures; a ribbon, a glove, a ball of wool or, on a really lucky day, a tin spoon or a handkerchief. And you won't believe it, sir, but on that he keeps his mother and two younger children. Money? No, he has never yet found money. People who sell their clothes never leave money in the pockets."

The boy's voice came suddenly from the cloud of dust that rose from the pile of old clothes.

"Almighty God, raise me not up and cast me not down," he exclaimed.

"What is it? What have you found?" the old clothes dealer asked.

"Blessed be the day," said the boy, emerging from the corner with the taler in his hand.

The sight nearly took the dealer's breath away. "A taler!" he exclaimed.

"Yes, a taler, really!" the boy panted, pale and then red and then pale again with excitement, fear and pleasure. There was a question in his eyes.

"Why are you looking at me like that? It's yours," the old clothes dealer said. "The fool who left it in his pocket will never come back, he knows nothing about it, he thinks he drank it long ago. Don't worry, I know my people."

The boy nearly jumped out of his shoes, and then began dancing round the room.

"Hey, you, what are you going to do with the money?" asked the young archduke, fearing that he might have to follow the taler still further. "Will you buy yourself new shoes, or a new hat or coat?"

The boy stopped and looked at him.

"No, sir," he replied. "My father – blessed be his memory –

taught me that you can't make two shoes out of one, and a hat will never be anything but a hat. But if you have one taler it's easy to turn it into two."

He picked up his linen bag, and a moment later he was out of the door.

"What's your name? Where are you going?" the Emperor's son called after him, but the boy was out of earshot.

"His name is Mordechai Meisl, and where he's going to I've no idea," said the old clothes dealer. "He's always in a hurry. He may even turn that taler into two this very day, or even this very hour."

BY NIGHT UNDER
THE STONE BRIDGE

The evening wind swept smoothly over the waves of the river, the rosemary flower snuggled closer to the red rose, and the dreaming Emperor felt the kiss of his beloved on his lips.

"You're late," she whispered. "I lay and waited. You made me wait such a long time."

"I was here all the time," he answered. "I lay looking out into the night, watching the clouds and listening to the rustling of the trees. I was tired after the burden and noise of the day, I was so tired I felt my eyes were closing. Then at last you came."

"Did I? And am I here with you?" she asked. "But how did I get here? I don't know the way, I've never been this way before. Who brought me to you? Who brings me to you night after night?"

"You're with me, and I hold you in my arms, that's all I know," said the Emperor.

"So I walked through the streets, unaware of myself, and climbed the steps, and the people I met looked at me in surprise, but no-one got in my way, no-one stopped me. The gate sprang open, doors opened, and now I'm with you. It's not right, I shouldn't do it. Do you hear the murmur of the river?"

"Yes. At night, when you're with me, the murmur's louder than usual, as if it wanted to sing us to sleep. The first time you heard it you wept with fear. You wept, and called out: 'What has happened to me? Where am I?'"

"I was afraid. I recognised you, and couldn't grasp the fact that I was with you," she said. "The first time I saw you, you were riding a milk-white horse, and behind you was a procession of men in armour, the armour flashed and glittered, the horses' hooves clattered and the trumpets played, and I hurried home and called out: 'I've seen the Emperor in his majesty' – and I thought my heart was going to stop."

"And the first time I saw you," said the Emperor, "you were standing against the wall of a house with your shoulders raised slightly as if you wanted to run away and hide, you looked timid and nervous like a little bird, that's what you looked like as you stood there with your brown curls tumbling over your forehead. I looked at you and knew I would never forget you, but would think about you day and night. But the nearer I got to you the farther away you seemed, you moved farther and farther away from me every moment, you were as unattainable as if I had lost you for ever. And then, when you came here and were with me and I held you in my arms, it was like a miracle or a dream. My heart was full of joy, and you wept."

"I wept, and I still want to weep today. Where are we, and what has happened to us?"

"How fragrant you are," said the Emperor. "Like a small, delicate flower whose name I don't know, that's what you smell like."

"And when I'm with you I feel as if I were walking through a rose garden," she whispered.

They fell silent. The murmur of the passing waves of the river grew louder. There was a gust of wind, and rose and rosemary met in a kiss.

"You're weeping," said the red rose. "Your eyes are wet, and there are tears like dewdrops on your cheeks."

"I weep," said the rosemary, "because I have to come to you and yet don't want to, because I have to leave you though I want to stay."

"You mustn't go. You're mine, and I'm holding you. I've prayed to God for you on a hundred nights, and God has given you to me, and now you're mine."

"Yes, I'm yours. But God didn't give me to you, it wasn't His hand that led me to you. God is angry with me, and I'm afraid of His anger."

"He's not angry with you," said the Emperor. "How could

He be angry with you? He looks at you, and smiles and forgives."

"No," she whispered. "He doesn't smile. I have broken His commandment. He is not a God that smiles and forgives. But, whatever happens, even if He rejects me and casts me out – I'm with you and can't leave you."

And rosemary and rose clung fearfully and blissfully together.

"What sort of day did you have?" the rosemary asked.

"My day was a poor man's day," said the rose, "full of worries, troubles and cares. Great lords and little lords, rogues, chatterboxes, charlatans, great fools and wretched little fools – they were all there, and that was my day. They came and spoke words into my ear, evil, stupid or empty and idle words, they wanted this or that, and they were tiresome. But when I shut my eyes I saw you. That was my day, and what was yours?"

"There were voices and shadows all round me, that was my day. It was like walking through a mist, I wasn't sure where I was, it wasn't real, it was deception and illusion. Phantoms called, I heard myself speak and didn't know what I was saying. Then the day faded, blew away like smoke, vanished like a spectre, and I was with you. You alone are real."

"In the dark hours of the day, when the chaos of the age weighs on me like a nightmare and the noise and bustle of the world is about me with all its perfidy and cunning, its lies and treachery, my thoughts fly to you, you are my comfort and consolation. With you there's clarity, when I'm with you I feel as if I could understand the way of the world and see through the lies and penetrate to the truth behind the perfidy. Sometimes I feel lost and call you, call you aloud, though in such a way as not to be overheard – but you don't come. Why don't you come? What holds you back when I call you? What prevents you?"

No answer came.

"Where are you? Do you hear me? I can't see you, are you still there? A moment ago I held you in my arms, felt your heartbeat and your breath – where are you?"

"I'm here, I'm with you, for a moment I felt I was far away, as if I were at home in bed, there was moonlight on my pillow, a bird fluttered through the room and out again, and there was the cat, it climbed in from the garden on to the window ledge, and there was the sound of something breaking, and I lay there and listened, and then I heard you calling out: 'Where are you?' And I was with you, and the whole thing, the room, the moonlight, the cat and the frightened bird, was only a dream."

"You had a child's dream," said the Emperor. "When I was a boy I dreamt of fields and woods, hunting, dogs, birds and all sorts of animals, and I woke up happy and cheerful, ready for anything. Later I had bad dreams, dreams that frightened me, and I often wished that night was morning. And yet night is better than day. Human noises are stilled, the sounds to be heard are the ringing of a bell, the soughing of the wind, the rustle of trees, the murmur of a river, the wing-beat of a bird, and over us are the eternal stars following their courses according to their Creator's will. I often think about God's creation of men and how he made their brains. While above us, order and obedience prevail eternally, down here below there is unrest, strife and chaos – where are you? Why are you silent? What are you thinking about?"

"I'm thinking about how I used to be able to live and be happy without you, and I can't understand it. I'm thinking about how the stars follow their courses though they should stop, time should stop while I'm with you."

"Time doesn't stop, and just when someone is happy it races like a hunted animal, and hour after hour plunges into infinity. Come and kiss me. Where are you?"

"I'm at your lips, I'm at your heart, I'm with you."

Drunk with reverie and happiness, the rosemary flower freed itself from the red rose.

"I must go," she whispered. "Farewell, I can't stay, I must go."

"Where? Where? Don't go, stay. Why must you go?"

"I don't know. Don't stop me, let me go. I can't stay, I must go."

"Stay. Where are you? I can't see you. Where are you? I was just holding you in my arms, where are you? Where has she gone?"

"Where has she gone?" the Emperor called out, raising his head and looking about him.

The valet Philipp Lang was in the room.

"I heard your Majesty groaning and calling out, so I came in," he said. "Your Majesty must have been having a bad dream, that's why Your Majesty was groaning and calling out. Perhaps I should have awoken Your Majesty to prevent *male di testa* from setting in again. A number of persons outside are craving an audience. Shall I order Your Majesty's breakfast?"

"Where has she gone?" the Emperor murmured.

The beautiful Esther, the wife of Mordechai Meisl, awoke in their house on the Dreibrunnenplatz. The morning sun on her face put a reddish gleam in her hair. The cat moved noiselessly about the room, awaiting its saucer of milk. A small flower pot that had stood on the window ledge lay broken on the floor. In the next room Mordechai Meisl was walking up and down, chanting a morning prayer.

She sat up and pushed her brown hair from her brow.

"A dream," she whispered, "and the same dream night after night. A lovely dream but, praised be the Lord, only a dream."

WALLENSTEIN'S STAR

His Bohemian brain was his joy and pride,
So wining and dining he left aside.
In his campaigns in west and east
He gave no quarter to man or beast;

Gave much money and land away,
And hanged many innocents on the way;
Owed his military renown
To victories for the imperial crown.

Now that he's dead it's safe to remark
That the cocks can crow and the dogs can bark.

From an epitaph on Wallenstein

In 1606 the great mathematician and astronomer Johannes Kepler, whose intellect embraced the whole visible world, was living in the most abject poverty in a dilapidated house in the Old Town of Prague, from the windows of which the only view was of a blacksmith's and nail-maker's workshop, a tavern frequented by drunken, rowdy soldiers, and a wooden fence behind which there was a pond full of croaking frogs. Great promises had been made to him when, after the death of Tycho Brahe, he was offered the post of astronomer to the imperial court at a salary of 1500 gulden a year but, as was usual at the Prague court, the promises were forgotten and the salary unpaid and, when he applied for a few gulden on account, he was kept hanging about for days at the Prague treasury before his application was attended to. Often he did not know where the money was coming from to buy food for himself and his sick wife and three children next day. Also things were expensive at the time and, as Kepler himself predicted in his calendar for 1606, early and severe cold set in that autumn.

Thus on a gloomy, rainy November day Kepler had once more been to the deer park up on the Hradschin to draw his entitlement of firewood from one of the imperial gamekeepers – a task that, not being able to employ a servant, he had to perform himself. But the load he had to carry home was not heavy – the wood was just sufficient to bring the pot of soup to the boil and to take the chill off the room in which his sick wife lay. And now, wrapped in his rain-sodden coat, he was sitting in the big unheated room listening patiently to the reproaches of the Emperor's private secretary Hanniwald; the astronomical tables, to the compilation of which, by His Majesty's express wish and will, it was his duty to devote most of his time, had not yet been completed.

"You are well aware," Kepler said when Hanniwald had finished his lecture, "what dire, troubled, difficult times these are, and I have no desire to make matters worse. I should much prefer not to have to mention this, but I hope to be excused if I point out that I, together with the whole of my family, would have starved to death if I had carried out his Majesty's command for, unlike the chameleon, I cannot live on air. So, to save his Majesty's honour, instead of preparing the tables with the production of which his Majesty graciously entrusted me, I have been obliged to produce predictions and worthless calendars that will do no good to my reputation. Nevertheless they have served to feed me and my family, which is, after all, rather better than troubling his Majesty every day with petitions, complaints and protests."

"That would have done you no good, even if you had appeared only once and never again in his Majesty's presence," said Hanniwald, who was not well disposed to the Protestant Kepler.

"That made it all the more necessary for me to take steps to procure the meagre nourishment that I and my family require in order to survive," Kepler continued, with no sign of indignation and no bitterness in his voice. "That was by no means easy and, to tell you the whole story, today happens to be one of the days on which I have not two groschen at my disposal. I put my trust in God, who can change everything. But, in short, it's a wretched life."

He stopped, exhausted, put a handkerchief to his mouth, and coughed.

"His Majesty," Hanniwald went on, ignoring Kepler's complaints, "His Majesty is also highly displeased at your having so completely ignored his commands in connection with the conflict between his Holiness the Pope and the Republic of Venice."

"His Majesty," replied Kepler, who was still troubled by his cough, "recently sent his valet, Philipp Lang, to me with a lengthy explanation of why I was to prepare an astrological report on the future course of that conflict and its likely outcome. I explained to Philipp Lang with all due respect why I was unable to comply. For an astronomer who undertakes to announce, not only the movement of the stars and their future configuration, but also the future destiny of men and nations, which God alone can foresee, is a common liar."

"So I am to conclude," Hanniwald said, "that you totally reject astrology, a discipline and science which has come down to us from ancient times, and has been tried and tested a thousand times, and has been used by many princes and great lords to their temporal advantage as well as their eternal salvation."

"No," said Johannes Kepler, "I do not totally reject it. I do reject the division of the heavens into twelve houses, the domination of the trigon and all similar fantasies and inventions of petty minds. But the harmony of the heavens I accept."

"And the configuration of the stars? What do you think of that?" Hanniwald wanted to know.

"I accept that too as a factor of some importance, though with a number of reservations," Kepler replied. "For the life of a newborn child takes this form or that according to the stars' rays at the time of his birth. If the configuration is harmonious, a good disposition results."

"Thus, if I have understood you correctly," Hanniwald said thoughtfully, "astrology emerges as a basically greatly altered though not entirely new discipline. Have you sought to bring your hypotheses into harmony with the doctrines of the Church?"

"God forbid that I should ever do such a thing," Johannes Kepler exclaimed. "I refuse to get involved in theological disputes. What I say, write and do I say, write and do as a conscientious mathematician. I leave Church matters strictly alone."

The Emperor's private secretary shook his head.

"Your answer worries me, and I strongly disapprove of it, Master Kepler," he said. "You speak humbly, but what you say sounds arrogant and unChristian. In fact, what you just said seems to me to be horned and cloven-hoofed. But it's not my business to examine you in these matters. My most gracious master sent me to you because you have repeatedly given him cause for displeasure. I have heard what you have had to say in your defence, I have heard that and nothing else. When I report to His Majesty I shall not omit to mention the wretched circumstances of which you complain. And so, Master Kepler . . ."

He had risen and pushed his hat back slightly, thus showing Kepler the respect to which he was entitled; and he was just about to walk out stiffly, with a look of disapproval on his face, when Johannes Kepler stopped him.

"After five years in this city I'm still a stranger here," he said. "I have hardly any contact with the nobility of the country and know few other persons of consequence. Do you, Mr Secretary, know of a young nobleman and officer of the name of . . ."

He glanced at a slip of paper on his desk on which something was written. A stone on it acted as a paperweight.

". . . of the name of Albrecht Wenzel Eusebius von Waldstein?" he said. "Do you know of him?"

"The Waldsteins," Hanniwald began, and warmed to his theme as he developed it – Kepler's 'horned and cloven-hoofed' reply went quite out of his mind, "the Waldsteins are an old

Bohemian family descended from two brothers, Havel and Zavic, who lived in the twelfth century, and they are also known as Valstein, Wallenstein or Wartenberg. I know three of them. The one at Krinic, Heinrich, is a Utraquist. The one at Slowic, in the Rakonitz district, was born with only one arm, and Ernst Jakob, of Zlotic in the Königgratz district, is an imperial councillor and is known as the Turk, because in his youth he was a prisoner of the Bey in Algiers, where he was made to weave linen. And I used to know another one, Wilhelm, who lived on the Hermanic estate, also in the Königgratz district, his wife was a Smirzicka, they're both dead. But an Albrecht Wenzel, and what did you say? Eusebius? No, I've never heard of him."

The idea that there was a member of an old Bohemian family of whom he had never heard left him no peace. He sat down, rested his head on his hand, and racked his brains.

"Albrecht Wenzel Eusebius von Waldstein," he repeated. "Now I remember. I must have heard the name some time – no, not heard it, seen it on a document, and it can't have been very long ago. Perhaps he submitted a petition to His Majesty and it passed through my hands. An officer? Didn't you say he's an officer? Didn't he apply for a posting with the troops in Hungary? Or to be put on half-pay while his services were not required? Or for some other recompense for meritorious conduct on active service? I think I must have read something of the kind. Was his petition supported by a recommendation? Did he secure a recommendation from his uncle, the imperial court councillor, or someone else? Otherwise Philipp Lang will have written 'must wait' on the petition and put it aside."

"I know nothing whatever about that," Kepler replied. "The young nobleman sent a message asking me to note his desire and intention to wait upon me today in connection with a 'heavenly matter'."

"A heavenly matter?" Hanniwald said in surprise. "Is he a member of the clergy, then?"

"No," Kepler replied. "On a heavenly matter means that he wants me to work out the state of the planets at the time of his birth and forecast his future on the strength of it. I think he's faced with important decisions, perhaps a turning point in his life, and he wants my advice."

"He who is arrogant enough to predict the fate of human beings, which God alone can foresee, is nothing but a common liar. Isn't that so, Master Kepler?" Hanniwald said sarcastically.

"Yes, that is so," said Johannes Kepler, who was so wrapped up in his thoughts that he didn't notice the sarcasm. "For he who predicts things solely from the heavens comes to no correct answer or, if he does, has luck to thank. To me men's nature and inclinations, their mentality and reason, are more important than any star. But all that . . ."

He took Waldstein's note from the table and contemplated it in silence for a while.

"All that is reflected in their handwriting," he then said.

"Do I hear rightly?" Hanniwald exclaimed. "You believe you can read a person's nature and inclinations and mentality from his handwriting? Master Kepler . . ."

"All that and a great deal more," Kepler interrupted. "If I look very carefully at a person's handwriting for some time, it comes to life and talks to me, it reveals his innermost thoughts and secret plans. I then know that person thoroughly, I know him as well as if I had shared salt with him for many years."

These last words were drowned in Hanniwald's peals of laughter.

"That I didn't know," the Emperor's private secretary exclaimed. "By my immortal soul, I didn't know that if you hold a note like that under your nose it will begin confessing to you. By my soul, Master Kepler, if I didn't know you were a dreamer and a fantasist I should take good care to see that nothing I wrote fell into your hands. But tell me, what did Herr von Waldstein's letter tell you about him?"

"Great things, Mr Secretary, great things," Johannes Kepler replied. "A great deal of evil, a great deal that frightened me, but by and large great things. He's restless, this Herr von Waldstein, he wants change, he's prepared to resort to unusual means to achieve his ends, he's suspicious, sometimes melancholy, he despises human laws, and will therefore often come into conflict with authority until he learns to dissimulate and conceal his real opinions. He lacks pity and brotherly love – and yet: his unusual nature, that today makes him aspire to rank and power, will one day, when it attains maturity and full development, make him capable of high and noble deeds."

"Good gracious, so this Herr von Waldstein will be heard of again," said Hanniwald. "So far, of course, he hasn't been talked about very much. And you've discovered all this from that note. Now, Master Kepler, I am not one of those who have learnt to dissimulate and conceal their real opinions, and so I tell you frankly that I consider all this to be the by-play of a learned mind. Your servant, Master Kepler, your most humble servant."

Johannes Kepler accompanied the Emperor's private secretary down the stairs and opened the door. It had begun to snow; it was the first snow of the autumn.

When Kepler was back in his room he thought no more of Hanniwald and the conversation he had had with him. He had noticed a snowflake that had clung to the sleeve of his coat, and he examined it through a magnifying glass. Then he picked up a pen and, with the smile of one who has once more found an idea of his confirmed, began writing on a sheet of paper the words: "*De nive sexangula*. Of the remarkable, multiform but always hexagonal nature of the snowflake."

He really is a restless soul, or something is worrying him and making him impatient, Johannes Kepler said to himself when he noticed that the young officer who had come to see him "on a heavenly matter" could not sit still for half a minute, but kept shifting in his seat and then sprang to his feet and began pacing up and down the room.

"So today you are thirty-two years, two months and six days old," he said, once more turning to his visitor.

"Yes," said the young nobleman, walking from the window to the stove and holding out his hands to warm them, only then noticing, or perhaps not noticing, that the stove was cold. "Yes, sir, and if by that you mean to say that others have done memorable deeds at that age and caused their names to be inscribed on the roll of honour of history – if that is what you mean, you are perfectly right. I can only claim to have studied military science at Padua and Bologna and to have subsequently served under General Basta against the Turks. I kidnapped a *bassa* or *bey* in his quarters, but that is all I have to boast about. After the Gran affair I left the service, and then . . . it's intolerable," he broke off, and pressed his hand to his temple as if he felt a dreadful pain there.

"Don't you feel well, sir?" Kepler asked.

"It's intolerable, that noise down there in the street," said the young nobleman, in a voice that now sounded angry rather than complaining. "Don't take it amiss, sir, but I cannot understand how you can read your books and collect and arrange your thoughts with that noise going on."

"Noise? To me it seems very quiet now down in the street," Kepler said. "The nail-maker has shut his shop and the soldiers at the tavern don't start singing, swearing, making a din and brawling till late in the evening."

"I'm not talking about the soldiers," the young nobleman explained. "I'm used to their noise. I'm talking about the godless croaking of those frogs, there must be a hundred of them down there, can't you hear them, sir?"

"I hear them and yet I don't," Kepler replied. "It's said of the Nile Falls that the roar of the waters has made the inhabitants of the neighbourhood deaf. But I don't think that's the case. They are used to the noise and don't notice it. In the same way I don't notice the croaking of the frogs, which I wouldn't call godless, for like all other creatures they raise their voice to the glory of God."

"If I were God, I'd see to it that I was glorified in some other way. I wouldn't allow myself to be troubled by frogs," the young nobleman said peevishly. "I can't stand it, I can't stand any animal noises, whether they're dogs, cats, donkeys or goats, they're a torment to me. But it's time we got down to business," he said, changing his tone. "*Hora ruit*, time flies, I mustn't take too much of your time, sir."

"You want your horoscope?" Johannes Kepler asked.

"No, not this time, I'm very much obliged to you, sir, but it's not a horoscope I came for," said the young nobleman, "but there is just one brief question that I would like to put to you, sir: Is fiery Mars in the ascendant tomorrow night in the domain of Charles's Wain?"

"Is that all?" said Kepler. "In that case I can give you the answer straightaway. Tomorrow night not Mars but Venus will be in the ascendant, or will be in the domain of Charles's Wain. Mars, whom you call fiery, is moving into the domain of Scorpio."

The young nobleman was taken aback. "Is that possible?" he exclaimed. "Venus? Not Mars? Venus? It can't be. Sir, you must be mistaken."

"No, I'm not mistaken," Kepler assured him. "It's Venus, not Mars, you can be sure of that."

For a while the young nobleman stood in silence. Then he went on, talking to himself more than to Johannes Kepler:

"Then it's lost before it's begun. All the same it's got to be done. *Errare humanum est*, too much depends on its success."

He fell silent again. He looked at Kepler as if he wanted to ask him something else, but he did not. He shrugged his shoulders, and a movement of his hand seemed to indicate that he must make up his mind himself. He turned to go. Downstairs in the doorway he paid his respects to Kepler by bowing and raising his hat.

"I am greatly obliged to you for your kindness, sir," he said, "and, sir, you will hear from me again very soon, the day after tomorrow, I think. If you are right, sir, and the thing fails, I shall still have the ring, a rare prize I brought back from the Turkish war. We'll see what I manage to do on the strength of it. Until then, sir, I am your humble and obedient servant."

He raised his hat again and then set off up the steep street and past the wooden fence behind which the frogs croaked more loudly than ever as if to spite him.

An old man named Barvitius, who had once been a great lord in the kingdom and had even been a privy councillor, but had been dismissed from the service because he fell out of favour with Philipp Lang, the Emperor's valet, was living at the time in a house in the Jakobsgasse, not far from the Altstädter Ring. Also he had lost his money and his property, partly at cards and partly in unsuccessful speculations. Thus he would have ended his days in poverty and want if he had been an honest man. But he went on living as he had always done. He entertained, kept servants, a carriage and horses – though he generally preferred to walk, for his health's sake, as he said – and was to be seen at the card table in many noble houses, and he liked good cooking and fine wines.

However, he was not an honourable man. It would never have occurred to those who saw him going to the church of the Holy Spirit or the Tein church on Sundays or holidays, leaning on his stick – it would never have occurred to them that this respectable and indeed venerable-looking man was actually the leader of a gang of thieves.

Most of the followers whom he had recruited and used for his criminal purposes were corrupt and debauched riffraff of murky origin who would have sold God and His saints for half a gulden – they were real candidates for the gallows, in fact. But among them there were also the sons of honourable citizens who had gone astray because they shunned honest toil as the devil shuns holy water. Indeed, for money they were ready to do anything, not excluding using a knife if there were no alternative. One of them was Georg Leitnizer, the son of a goldsmith on the Kleiner Ring and a former student, who because of his good manners and lively intelligence enjoyed Barvitius's special confidence. Barvitius sent for Leitnizer practically every day, while the others saw him only rarely, and then only at night by candlelight with his face muffled or otherwise made unrecognisable.

But they were all completely devoted to Barvitius, whom they obeyed blindly. They knew they could do nothing without him, for it was he who spied out opportunities and made plans that took account of all eventualities; and he made his preparations with such care that only rarely did a coup of his fail.

Early one November day Leitnizer called on Barvitius and found him playing cards with himself, staking one or two gulden now on one card, now on another, and cursing loudly when he lost. This displeased Leitnizer, for it was generally known that this was how Barvitius spent his time when he was in a bad mood or had met with unexpected difficulties in one of his undertakings; or sometimes it was because his gout was troubling him, as it often did.

The reception he gave Leitnizer on this occasion indicated a very bad mood indeed.

"What? You again?" he snapped. "Did I send for you? Can't you leave me in peace for a single day?"

"It's raining and my feet are cold," said Leitnizer, who sat by the fire, took off his shoes and stretched his legs as if he had come only to warm his feet by Barvitius's fire.

Barvitius resumed his game of cards, cursing, moving the gulden from one card to another, banging his fist on the table, throwing in his hand and shuffling the cards, and then dealing and laying them out again. For about a quarter of an hour he took no notice of Leitnizer, but then he put the cards aside, pocketed his winnings as well as the money he had lost, and called himself a blockhead who, never mind how he began, invariably ended by making a fool of himself at the card table for someone else's benefit. Then he turned to Leitnizer with an expression of surprise but not displeasure at seeing him there.

"I'm glad to see you, Georg, I want to talk to you," he said. Leitnizer rose, slipped into his shoes and went over to the table. "I can't conceal from you any longer, Georg, that things are not going well at the moment."

"That's true," Leitnizer replied, looking at his shoes to see if they were dry. "In the last few weeks we've burned the midnight oil but made no money."

"It's not that," Barvitius went on. "If only it were. Listen to this, Georg, but don't tell the others, keep it to yourself. One of my good friends up there" – he pointed over his shoulder with his thumb, and Leitnizer realised that "up there" meant Prague Castle – "one of those who wish me well, took me aside a short time ago before we sat down at the card table and started talking about Philipp Lang. He mentioned among other things how dangerous it was to have him for an enemy, and he said that he had his fingers in everything, and at the moment the town captain was so tremendously busy – and then, while we were sitting at the card table, he said how advisable travelling was, it was so good for the health."

"That may have been just idle talk," Leitnizer said.

"It was a warning, Georg, make no mistake about it," Barvitius replied. "Philipp Lang has always had his eye on me. It was a warning from someone who wishes me well. And I've had no peace ever since, I feel as if I were being trailed, in the street I hear footsteps behind me, and when I look round nobody's there."

"Well, then, that's it," said Leitnizer. "Nobody's there."

"And last night I dreamt I saw the hangman whipping you up one street and down another, Georg. And your hands were tied behind your back."

Leitnizer suddenly became very animated.

"We ought to look it up in the dream books," he said. "Was it a long whip? I mean, did it crack properly? A whip that cracks means something. I think it means money is coming into one's house. We ought . . ."

"Listen to me, Georg," Barvitius interrupted. "Think of our people one by one, examine each one of them in your mind very carefully, examine them all and think about them very carefully indeed, and then tell me whether there's one among them who you think might have been capable of playing a double game."

"Boss," Leitnizer said solemnly, "there's not one of them who wouldn't let himself be burnt, flayed and broken on the wheel for you."

"Don't talk to me about breaking on the wheel," said Barvitius. "You know I don't like it. I have enough with my gout, which daily breaks me on the wheel like any hangman."

For a while he sat silent, with furrowed brow. Then he said:

"Shall I one day have to tell myself that I ignored good advice, dismissed it, and got what was coming to me? I think I shall go abroad. But first . . ." He broke off. "And you, Georg? Wouldn't you like to see France and the Low Countries, or St Mark's in Venice?"

"I know St Mark's," Leitnizer replied. "I've seen it on a copper engraving. There's a shop on the Niklasgasse that has copper engravings on sale. But shouldn't we take one of our people abroad with us, Smutny or Reissenkittel, for instance, to clean the room for us, make the beds and keep the stove alight?"

"One can get servants anywhere," Barvitius replied. "But before we go, before I leave Prague. . . ."

He fell silent and remained lost in thought for a few moments.

"Before we go," he went on, "there's something I want to do that I've had in mind for some time – something that will leave our busy town captain with nothing to do afterwards but wipe his mouth, it's something that will be talked about for years, Georg, in Prague and throughout the kingdom."

"And what sort of thing is it, boss?" Leitnizer asked eagerly.

Barvitius leant back in his chair and folded his arms across his chest.

"You know that I have my eyes and ears everywhere – including in the ghetto," he began. "And there's someone there whose closer acquaintance I've been wanting to make for a long time. Jews and Christians swarm round his house like flies round a milk jug. He succeeds in everything he touches. The Jews say of him that if the whole town has a bad year, he'll still be in clover. And they say he's so rich that he spreads sugar on his honey. Do you know the Jew, do you know his name?"

"He's Mordechai Meisl, he also calls himself Marcus Meisl, and he lives on the Dreibrunnenplatz," Leitnizer replied.

"That's the man I'm talking about. He started by pawnbroking, lending money to small tradesmen on the security of all sorts of rubbish that others wouldn't accept, like the copper beam of a balance or a worthless goat skin or a buckled brass pan. Also he used to go to the markets at Jičin and Chrudim and Welwarn and Časlau where wool is traded, and he bought as much wool as he could, bartered it for fine cloth from the weavers in the Old Town, and sent the cloth to the St Bartholomew's fair at Linz, thus profiting twice. He succeeded in everything. If he loved money, money loved him even more, it seemed to seek him out and run after him. His business kept expanding, and the Emperor has extended his patronage to him by royal charter, encouraged him, and given him many privileges. And there are people up there," – once more he pointed his thumb over his right shoulder – "who say, who whisper, who murmur that His Majesty the Emperor is secretly associated with him."

"The Emperor? With Meisl? With a Jew in the ghetto?" exclaimed Leitnizer, who was shocked and indignant.

"So they say," said Barvitius, shrugging his shoulders. "They also say that since that royal charter the Emperor has always had money in his coffers. People complain that old debts are not paid, though the Emperor keeps acquiring treasures from all over the world for his art gallery and his collection of curiosities. Mansfeld buys paintings for him in the Netherlands, and Khevenhueller in Madrid and Harrach in Rome and Florence do the same. Marble statues and reliefs come from Mantua. The abbot of St Moriz at Besançon sends him rings and stone carvings found in Roman tombs. The Welsers and Hochstaetters send him marvellous birds from the New World. The Elector of the Palatinate sent him an ivory altar decorated with scenes from the life of Christ, and a monk in Alexandria sent him Moses' staff, together with a document proving its authenticity, but the Emperor wouldn't accept it, he said the staff had once been a snake and might turn back into a snake again. Antonio di Giorgio provides him with spherical and parabolic mirrors and Miseroni with crystal goblets – and for all those things there's money. The question is, where does it come from?"

"The Emperor associated with a Jew in the ghetto? I can't believe it," Leitnizer muttered.

"What do you know about what goes on in the world? What do you know about the world? You know nothing," said Barvitius. "We are not concerned with His Majesty the Emperor, but with the Jew Meisl, and we have to act quickly or we'll be left with nothing, because he has gone mad and is giving his money away."

"I know a madman who goes about the streets in nothing but his shirt, shouting to people to pour water over him because he's a soul in the fires of purgatory, and I know another who believes he's a fish and sits in a tub all day long, and at bedtime has to be pulled out with rod and line. But I've never heard of a madman who's giving his money away, and I've been wanting to meet someone like that for a long time."

"He may or may not be a madman, but he's giving his money away," said Barvitius. "He's doing it in great secrecy, and doesn't seem to want it to be publicly known; and he doesn't just give it away, he scatters it widespread, throws it into the street. He lends money without security, without an IOU, without sureties, all he requires of borrowers is silence, none of them is supposed to know about any of the others. Poor girls who want to get married are given money for their trousseau without knowing where it comes from. It was he who had the old bath-house pulled down and a new one built, the old one wasn't grand enough for him. And a new town hall is to be put up in the ghetto, and an infirmary and an orphanage. And with whose money? With Meisl's money. And, as if his money wasn't running through his fingers fast enough with all this, I'm told that he now proposes to have every street and corner and puddle in the ghetto paved with fine cobblestones."

"So that's what you meant, boss, when you said he was throwing his money out into the street."

Barvitius rose to his feet and chuckled to himself.

"He won't be doing it much longer, because it's time I intervened," he said. "I'm going to take him from his house to a safe place, where he'll stay until he has bought himself out. And he'll do so with a sum so huge that we shan't be able to spend it all during the rest of our natural lives . . . I shan't leave him with very much, the ghetto will remain unpaved."

Leitnizer nodded, this suited him. He began working out in his head how much would be needed to keep him and Barvitius for the rest of their lives, but he did not finish the calculation, because Barvitius, who had spread out on the table a plan of the Meisl house and the surrounding Jewish streets, now looked up and asked:

"How many men have you who could be used for this business?"

"There are eleven of us, and if necessary there could be fourteen," Leitnizer replied.

"Whether it's eleven or fourteen, it's one too few," Barvitius announced. "Yes, one too few," he repeated emphatically as Leitnizer looked at him in surprise. "You won't be in charge of this operation, and none of the others is suitable either. For this is an operation of a kind that is normally carried out only in wartime. It can't be done without a certain amount of noise and violence, and so I need someone who has learnt in war how to carry out a raid with a handful of men and capture someone in his quarters and get him away safely – someone who, if he runs into an obstacle, will know what to do without coming to me for orders. In short, I need someone who knows the business of war from the ground up, and is willing to be used in an affair that won't earn him military credit or promotion, but . . ."

He went through the motions of counting out money.

"I know such a person," Leitnizer said. "Yes, boss, I think I know the man you want. He's a young nobleman, one of the Waldsteins. He fought with distinction against the Turks, then quarrelled with his commanding officer, resigned from the service, and is now living in Prague and studying, his room is full of books. . . ."

"Studying what?" Barvitius wanted to know.

"How to storm the town and castle of Peterwardein or the fortress of Raab. He deploys troops, lays mines, puts artillery in position. He can also explain to you exactly how the Romans at Cannae should have manoeuvred to beat Hannibal."

"Good. Go on," said Barvitius.

"He believes in the star-gazing superstition," Leitnizer went on. "He says that Mars and the constellation of Charles's Wain are his patrons in the sky and that when Mars is in the realm of Charles's Wain, that would be his day, and he would be successful in whatever he undertook. But in spite of this heavenly patronage he's so poor that he can afford a roast and a pint of wine at a tavern only once a week. He's dissatisfied because, he says, no great enterprise can be undertaken without money, and he has several times asked me what one would have to do to get hold of money quickly, and he indicated that to get it he was prepared to do anything, even if it was dangerous or unlawful, for in these times it was hard to achieve anything honestly."

91

"All that sounds very promising," said Barvitius. "And how old is this nobleman?"

"Not much over twenty."

"Oh, dear," said Barvitius. "Green wood . . ."

"Yes, I know," said Leitnizer, ". . . makes plenty of smoke but not much fire. But that doesn't apply to Waldstein. He's the man you want. No ditch is too deep and no wall too high for him. With half a dozen of his dragoons he kidnapped a vizier in a Turkish camp and came away safely with him."

"Then perhaps he is the right man," Barvitius admitted. "Go and talk to him. But be careful, don't tell him too much, because a young fellow like that often still has a conscience that's like a colt; if you go too close it kicks out."

"Don't worry," said Leitnizer. "I'll put it to him in a way that appeals to him."

Young Albrecht von Waldstein, who in Leitnizer's opinion was the right man to carry out Barvitius's coup, was lodging at the time with a tailor's widow in a small and rather lop-sided house below the Hradschin in a part of the city known as the Kleinseite. From the window of his narrow attic he had an extensive view right down to the Strahov monastery. But the first thing that caught his eye when he went to the window in the morning was the widow's small kitchen garden in which, much to his fury, her two goats, her chickens and her dog Lumpus roamed, bleating, clucking or yapping as the case may be. But it was her cock that irritated him most; this was a battered-looking creature, whom the tailor's widow called her Jeremiah, because its crowing sounded as pitiful and sad as if it were bewailing all the world's sorrows. When the noise was too much for him he dropped the Polybius he was immersed in and dashed downstairs to the kitchen, where the widow would be busy with her skimming ladle and pots and pans. It was hell, he shouted, he could stand it no longer, if the noise wasn't stopped he would have to leave; and the widow laughed, and said she didn't keep the chickens for the sake of their clucking, but if the gentleman wanted milk soup and pancakes he'd have to put up with the goat and the chickens, and, as for Jeremiah, his days were numbered in any case, for he was soon going to serve as a Sunday roast.

In the afternoon the kitchen garden was quieter, Lumpus was not there to chase the goats and the chickens, for he would be out roaming the streets. He came back at night, always at the same time, that is, when the bell of the small Loreto church struck twelve. He yelped and whimpered outside the door, demanding to be let in, and this woke Jeremiah, who began lamenting the world's miseries, whereupon the goats joined in, while Waldstein put his hands to his temples and groaned and yelled that this was hell, he wouldn't spend another night here, there was no peace and quiet in the daytime, and there was none at night either. Meanwhile the tailor's widow had opened the door and let in Lumpus, who crept quietly to his corner, the goats were happy again, and last of all Jeremiah went to sleep too and forgot the world's sorrows.

But while the kitchen garden with its chickens, goats, Lumpus and Jeremiah were hell for Waldstein, just beyond hell lay paradise. This was a big park, surrounded by handsome wrought ironwork and yew trees, and behind the old trees the gables, chimney and weather vanes of a small pleasure palace were visible. In this park quiet prevailed, nothing stirred, and only the wind whined plaintively through the leafless treetops, and occasionally the distant call and gentle hammering of a woodpecker were to be heard.

The park and the pleasure palace belonged to Lucrezia von Landeck, a young widow, who was said to be one of the richest heiresses in Bohemia. It was said that many noblemen had sought her hand, but she had rejected them all because she wished to remain unmarried, so that she could bequeath the whole of her wealth undiminished to the Church, for she was very devout. She was said to attend Mass every day in the Loreto church and always to carry about with her a small Bible, so that she might have God's word before her eyes wherever she went. She took little part in the diversions the big city had to offer, and was hardly ever seen in high society. Her friends were a canon of St Vitus's, who was a relative, two elderly spinsters from the aristocratic home for gentlewomen on the Hradschin, and a Jesuit priest from St Salvator's.

Albrecht von Waldstein often stood at his window looking at the park, he did not know why. Sometimes he was overcome by melancholy, and could not help thinking about the small estate inherited from his father that had had to be sold off during his boyhood because of accumulated debts. He had once seen Lucrezia von Landeck talking to a gardener's boy who was carrying an armful of freshly cut roses. She struck him as not tall but as having a good figure, and he had not been able to make out her features. Afterwards it struck him that this might not have been Lucrezia von Landeck, but one of her ladies-in-waiting. Thus Albrecht von Waldstein lived, looking alternately at hell and heaven until the day when Leitnizer walked into his attic.

Leitnizer had worked out what he thought was the best way of presenting the project to Waldstein, and he began by lauding Barvitius, his "boss", to the skies, pointing out what a remarkable man he was. He enjoyed the respect of everyone at court, all doors were open to him, he was able to use his influence at any time to his friends' advantage, and it was highly desirable that Waldstein should try to make his acquaintance.

"And who is this gentleman of whom you speak?" Waldstein asked. "Has he a position at court? Or in the royal administration?"

Leitnizer made a dismissive gesture.

"I'll tell you about that later," he said. "But I can assure you of this. He is his own master. For the moment his name is irrelevant. We never call him anything but the boss. I am speaking of some of my friends who have also devoted themselves to his service. And, to tell you the whole story right away, I have already talked to him about you and convinced him that you are the very man he wants to help him in a project."

"And what sort of project is it?" Waldstein inquired.

"I'll tell you about that later," Leitnizer replied. "But perhaps I can tell you right away that it's an operation that the Bohemian party at court wants to carry out against the Spanish party, because the head of the Spanish party . . ."

"Thank you, but I'm afraid that doesn't appeal to me. I don't want to have anything to do with court intrigues or questions of politics," Waldstein interrupted, for he had his future to think about, and did not want to antagonise any of the parties struggling for influence at court, neither the Spanish, nor the Bohemian, nor that of the Austrian archdukes.

Leitnizer realised at once that he had made a bad mistake and hastened to make it good.

"A political matter is just what this is not," he assured Waldstein. "It is perhaps too early to talk about it, but, believe me, the man who is to be taken from his house and put in a safe place has as little to do with court and national politics as the chickens down there in the garden."

"Who is to be taken from his house and put in a safe place?" Waldstein asked. "I don't much like that either."

"There are things that perhaps don't sound very well when you say them, but have to be done all the same," Leitnizer replied. "And then, consider this, a chance like this to earn five or six hundred ducats by a single coup won't occur again in all eternity."

"Six hundred ducats?" Waldstein repeated in astonishment. With a sum like that he could raise and equip a light cavalry squadron, and with a light cavalry squadron he could undertake a raiding and plundering expedition into Turkish territory and thereby perhaps lay the foundations of a career.

He did not show his astonishment. Instead he said:

"Six hundred ducats isn't much for an enterprise which, it seems, won't succeed without lighting a candle to the devil."

When Leitnizer heard Waldstein talk of lighting a candle to the devil he knew that the young man was as good as won over to the project, even though he considered it an evil one, and that all that remained to be settled was the amount he was to be paid.

"You say six hundred ducats is not a great deal?" he said. "Well, sometimes one has to be satisfied with a good start. But you needn't worry about the devil, the affair enjoys high patronage. In two days your star, Mars, will be in the ascendant in the realm of Charles's Wain, so I have been told, and so you can't fail."

"Is it to take place in two days' time?" Waldstein asked. "And who is the man . . ."

"More about that later," said Leitnizer, very satisfied with what he had achieved. "Now I must go, the boss is expecting me."

He came a second and a third time. On the third occasion there was no more talk of "more about that later" and the two reached complete agreement in every respect.

"The boss," Leitnizer said before he left, "wants to talk to you himself tonight, and that is an honour he doesn't grant everyone. Walk up and down outside your house when it begins to get dark, and you'll be picked up. But don't be surprised if a number of ceremonies have to be gone through, for the boss doesn't like anyone seeing his face and doesn't like people knowing where he lives. He's very particular about that."

Waldstein began pacing up and down outside his house long before dark. An hour previously Johannes Kepler had told him that not Mars but Venus was going to be in the ascendant in the realm of Charles's Wain on the night of the coup. That made him uneasy, but it was too late to draw back now.

As he was walking up and down and beginning to get impatient, a coach made its way down the bumpy road and stopped outside the house. The coachman got down from the box and opened the coach door. His hat was drawn right down over his face. "At your service, sir," he said. "You are expected."

Young Waldstein got into the coach. As the door was shut behind him and he took his seat, a voice said to him out of the dark beside him:

"The gentleman will please oblige by permitting me to blindfold him. Those are my orders."

The coach had already moved off.

It was a long drive.

Soon, after a quarter of an hour perhaps, Waldstein noticed

with surprise that the coach was no longer travelling on the paved streets of Prague, but on a rain-soaked main road in open country. The man sitting silently beside him now opened one of the coach windows. There was a gust of cold autumn air and a smell of damp plough land. The wind whistled and an owl hooted in a nearby wood. They seemed to be approaching a village or a manor house, for the barking of dogs and mooing of cattle became audible. It was a village, for as they went on they heard country tavern music, a fiddle and a bagpipe.

"This is Vlasic," said the man beside him, closing the window again. "We're going through Vlasic. They grow bilberries and mushrooms here for the Prague market."

"Is it still far to the boss's billet?" Waldstein asked.

"To where?" the man beside him replied.

"To the boss's place," Waldstein repeated. "I thought he lived in the city."

"We still have four or five miles to go," the man said.

"That's strange, I can't really understand it," Waldstein said, half to himself.

Silence prevailed once more. Waldstein wrapped himself tighter in his coat. The rain splashed more violently on the roof of the coach and the water in the puddles rose in cascades under the wheels and the horses' hooves. When another half-hour had passed under the drumming downpour the man turned to Waldstein again.

"We're now at Hochauz," he said. "They brew a strong beer on the Schlick estate here of which everyone speaks highly. We're now half way."

Waldstein did not hear him, for he had rested his head on his arm and was fast asleep.

He started awake when the coach stopped and wanted to rub his eyes, but he couldn't because of the blindfold, and then his memory came back. He got out of the coach. The rain had stopped. Gravel crunched under his feet, and a hand took his.

"Go straight ahead, sir, you're expected," said a voice which was not that of the man who had sat beside him in the coach.

He walked along a gravel path. There was an autumnal smell of late roses and yellowed foliage.

97

"Steps," the voice warned him.

He went up some steps, and then the hand led him over tiles first to the right, then to the left, and then to the right again. Then the guide's hand dropped his and he stopped. In spite of the blindfold he knew he was in a brightly lit room. Behind him there was a whisper:

"The gentleman's here."

At the same time he heard a restrained laugh, and a clear voice said:

"There's no need for the gentleman to look as severe as Themis himself. Let him at last remove his blindfold and step nearer, he is welcome."

Waldstein removed the blindfold. The room was not so brightly lit as he had supposed. The only light came from the fire in the hearth and from two wax candles in a silver candlestick on a table that was laid for two. By the fire a lady was sitting; she wore a deep violet velvet dress that was not in the least fashionable but displayed the outline of her body in an attractive manner. There was a trace of red in her hair, her hands were small, her ankles slim. That was all that Waldstein could make out, for her face was hidden behind a black silk mask.

Just imagine it, the boss is a woman, would you believe it? Waldstein said to himself as he made his bow.

"I find it charming that you have come, I didn't dare hope for it," the lady said from behind her mask. "For my sake you have had a tedious journey in bad weather and on muddy roads."

"Not at all," young Waldstein assured her, "I'm used to travel, though it's true I prefer horseback to sitting in a coach."

"I know you were a captain of dragoons," said the lady.

"At your service," Waldstein said, bowing once more.

Meanwhile two man-servants, masked like their mistress, entered with the first course: wine soup, stuffed breast of lamb, suckling pig, red cabbage, chicken wings, chicken livers and haunch of wild boar, and the lady invited Waldstein to join her at the table.

"Please put up with such humble fare as the house and kitchen are able to provide," she said while the servants filled the glasses.

"Only to oblige you," young Waldstein said as etiquette required, helping himself to some lamb's breast, two chicken wings, some red cabbage and two slices of boar.

When the second course with its veal and venison was over and dessert was served and the servants withdrew, Waldstein thought the time had come to discuss with the boss the enterprise that was to earn him six hundred ducats.

"I drink," he said, raising his glass and looking at the mistress of the house straight in the eye, "to the success of tomorrow night's enterprise."

"I join you with pleasure," the masked lady replied, "even though I don't know what you have in mind for tomorrow night. But I hope you are not forgetting tonight, to which I am looking forward with some pleasure. Or are you one of those who, when they are involved in an affair, are already thinking about the next one?"

"I beg your pardon? Do I understand you correctly? Is the thing to go ahead tonight?" Waldstein asked in grave concern. "I'm afraid there won't be enough time, as . . ."

"Why won't there be enough time? Are you in such a hurry to go back to your tailor's widow?" the masked lady asked rather sharply.

"No, boss," Waldstein replied, "but if the thing is to take place today . . ."

"What do you call me?" the mistress of the house exclaimed. "Boss? None of my – none of the gentlemen who have been my guests here have ever called me that. Boss? Is that the way to talk to a lady? A lady who, moreover, yields to none of you in birth and position?"

"I beg your pardon," young Waldstein muttered in consternation. "But one of your servants told me that that was how I should address you."

"Really!" the lady replied indignantly. "And which of my servants was crazy or stupid enough to put that over you?"

"The one who came with a message from you this morning and yesterday also," Waldstein replied. "I know his name, though I can't remember it at the moment."

"Such heights of rubbish are climbed by this liar, that without a ladder he can't hope to get higher," the masked lady hummed, while she rose and prowled round Waldstein like a cat. "Let me assure you, captain, that I don't believe a single word of your story. For neither yesterday nor this morning did I send a servant of mine or anyone else with a message to you."

"But he said that you had sent him and that I should hold myself in readiness, because you wanted to talk business with me."

"Business?" the woman exclaimed with a laugh. "This is getting better and better. No, captain. I don't want to praise you too highly to your face, but that I should send for a handsome young officer such as you are to talk business with him – no, captain, whoever says that doesn't know me. I'm afraid you're entangled in a concatenation of errors."

"I'm afraid so too," young Waldstein said in dismay, for he saw his six hundred ducats floating away. "But won't you tell me why you brought me here?"

"One might really believe that your mouth still smelled of wet nurse's milk," the masked lady said with a laugh, and once more she started prowling round Waldstein like a spoiled cat and looked at him, now from one side and now from the other. "Why I brought you here? Is that so difficult to guess? Just think."

Nothing was farther from Waldstein's mind at the moment than an amorous adventure, for Leitnizer's assurance that never again in his life would he have such an opportunity of earning six hundred ducats still rang in his ears. He sat there gloomily and said nothing.

"You are said to be highly intelligent," the lady went on, "but you seem to make use of your intelligence only with moderation, because otherwise, captain, you would have noticed my situation. I have met you several times before, and there seemed to me to be something about you, something that differentiated you from the other men I know. Am I mistaken? But that is something you don't know yourself. I like you, and I should like you to like me a little too."

She spoke these last words not hesitantly or shyly, but as if what she wanted was the most natural thing in the world.

Young Waldstein smiled, his gloom had vanished, and he couldn't help thinking of Johannes Kepler, who had told him that not Mars but Venus was going to preside over his adventure.

"As the loveliest of all women has been pleased to choose me as her lover," he began, taking her hand . . .

"Don't misunderstand me," the loveliest of all women interrupted. "For one night," she said, freeing her hand and starting to fumble with her dark violet dress. "For one night only, captain, please note. Because I want to be free and to do what I choose with myself. But that one night will be worth a hundred to you."

"If," said young Waldstein, without showing much disappointment, "if you have decided to make me your lover for tonight, why will you not show me your face, so that I may caress it?"

"Because," said the lady, still fumbling with her dress, "I am more concerned than you think with my reputation, and don't trust men. They are only too fond of boasting about their love affairs and can't keep their mouth shut."

"Perhaps that's the difference between me and other men," said Waldstein. "I can keep my mouth shut."

"Perhaps," the lady admitted. "But even men who can keep their mouth shut often make the most surprising mistakes, so that the whole world guesses their secret. No, my dear. You can ask anything of me tonight, but the mask stays on."

She threw back her head, dropped her arms, and the dark velvet dress slipped to the floor.

When they were lying together in a close embrace after taking their pleasure the lady was overcome by a desire to talk, she could not keep quiet, but began talking about everything that came into her head.

"I'm wide awake, darling, but you must go to sleep, because when the sun rises tomorrow morning you must be three miles away, you must go home, where everything will be as it was before, and you won't think about me. One of the things they say about you, so I've been told, is that you sit over your books night and day. Is it the Holy Scriptures that you read so zealously?"

"No," replied Waldstein. "I read Latin and Greek authors who have written about military science."

"Then you're a real storehouse of learning," the lady said, half teasingly and half admiringly. "I know Latin too. Would you like to hear how good I am at Latin? *Hodie*'s today and tomorrow is *cras*, there's *aliquid* floating in the butter-tub, alas. Yes, darling, *hodie* you're with me, and tomorrow, alas, you'll have gone, everything doesn't happen as one would wish; and I used to know what the *aliquid* floating in the butter-tub was, but I've forgotten, can't you remind me, you who are so learned?"

"Show me your face and I'll tell you," said Waldstein.

She shook her head, let herself be kissed and kissed him in return, and her thoughts went off in another direction.

"Tell me, my dear, as you're so learned, why do women so often and so gladly fall into sin? If you don't know, if the answer isn't in your books, let me tell you. The reason why I sin is that I have three weighty reasons for doing so. The first is, because it's hidden from the world, nobody knows or meddles in my affairs. The second is because God is merciful, He gives sinners time to repent and change their ways, as my chaplain has assured me; and the third is because other women do it too, but you know that better than I do. Or don't you?"

Strokes of a bell came from a church tower, Waldstein counted them, and there were twelve. After the last one died away there was a quiet barking and whimpering in the distance, it was so quiet that at first Waldstein could hardly hear it and took no notice, but then, in addition to it, there was the bleating of a goat, and then – could it be possible? Wasn't that just like Jeremiah's mournful crowing? There was no doubt about it. It was Jeremiah bewailing the world's sins.

For a moment Waldstein was as bewildered as if he had been struck on the head, but then he realised where he was and who was lying by his side.

"It's twelve o'clock," she said. "You must go to sleep, darling, you have a long drive in front of you, you must leave early."

But she went on talking and wouldn't let him sleep.

"Six miles from home, five miles, and you're still thinking about me," she said. "Four miles, and you've forgotten me. Three miles, and you're getting impatient. Coachman, get a move on. And the coachman cracks his whip, the geese get out of the way and stretch their necks and cackle behind you, two miles, and then another mile, and there's Prague New Town.

"When you get to the gate prepare for shocks,
In front of it stands a stony ox.
One, two, moo,
The ox is you."

"Be quiet, Lucrezia, that's enough tomfoolery," young Waldstein said. "I don't have a long drive in front of me, and I shan't be going through the New Town gate."

She raised her head and looked at him with frightened eyes, and hid her dismay behind a laugh.

"What did you call me?" she asked. "What new name have you thought up for me? First you call me boss, and then – what was it you just called me?"

"Oh, stop it," said Waldstein. "I knew who you were from the first moment. No, my dear Lucrezia, I have no intention of spending another two hours in your coach. All I have to do is to walk through the garden, climb over the fence, and I'm home."

Lucrezia von Landeck sighed, looked at him, sighed again, and removed her silk mask, revealing a small, pale, frightened face with big eyes and long lashes, a pointed nose and the mouth of a woman with a will of her own. Her lips were trembling.

"'Oh, darling, what have you done?" she said. "What have you done? Oh misery, it's all up with me, you've got to die, and I'll never again be happy in my life."

She got up, went to a wardrobe, rummaged in it, and when she returned she had in her hand a pocket pistol, which she pointed at Waldstein.

"Look," she said, "I've often thought about what would happen to a man who discovered my secret, how I mustn't let him leave the house alive however much he pleaded, there would be no mercy for him. It's easy to imagine all that, but when it comes to the point – I don't know what to do with this thing, I don't know how to handle it, I've never studied military science."

"Shall I show you what to do with it?" Waldstein suggested. "It's not difficult. First of all you prime it, taking care the powder doesn't blow away."

She laid aside the pistol, and looked at Waldstein helplessly.

"What am I to do?" she said. "Tell me, darling, what am I to do?"

"I should never have met you, Lucrezia," young Waldstein said. "But now it's happened, and I shall love you as long as there's any breath left in my body."

Her face brightened, as if those were the words she had been waiting for.

"Yes, that's the only way," she said firmly. "As my husband you'll keep silent and guard my honour with your life. In birth and position we are equals, and we also know each other as man and wife. Does that please you? A chaplain and two witnesses are close at hand."

"Yes, it pleases me, how could it do anything else? Here with the chaplain and the witnesses," he exclaimed so loudly that Lucrezia started back in alarm.

"Quiet!" she whispered, and laid her finger on his lips. "Don't make such a noise. Don't forget that you're in bed with a lady who isn't your wife yet. Do you want the whole town to come dashing in?"

When Waldstein returned to his attic after the marriage ceremony next morning, he found Leitnizer waiting for him in a corner. He was in a pitiful state, tired and distressed, looking as if he had spent the night in a haystack, for there were bits of straw in his hair, his shoes and his crumpled clothing.

"Where were you last night?" he exclaimed as soon as Waldstein had shut the door behind him. "You didn't sleep here? Did someone warn you?"

"Warn me? What about?" Waldstein wanted to know.

Leitnizer put his hands to his face and began to sob.

"They've arrested him," he wailed. "Do you hear? They've arrested him. I waited for you, I waited for you for two hours. You didn't come, I went back to tell the boss, and when I got there the house was surrounded, and when they took Barvitius away his feet were shackled and his hands tied behind his back."

"Barvitius? Who's he?" asked Waldstein, not greatly concerned.

"He's the boss," Leitnizer groaned. "And he foresaw it. He foresaw it, and I wouldn't listen to him. And how will it end up? Prison, chains, the gallows or the galleys. And me? What am I to do without him? Where's France? Where are the Low Countries?"

He looked angrily at Waldstein.

"You must be made of stone and marble if you feel no sympathy," he said.

"All this has nothing to do with me," Waldstein said.

"You don't feel quite so sure about that or you wouldn't have spent the night out of the house," said Leitnizer. "And you were quite right to do so, for they're sure to have been trailing me and to know that I came to see you here several times. I'm clearing out, I shan't be seen in Prague again, and I advise you to find other lodgings quickly."

"I've already done so," said Waldstein.

Later the same day Johannes Kepler received a letter from Herr Albrecht Wenzel Eusebius von Waldstein in which he expressed "due thanks for the valuable information graciously given". He added that Venus must already have been in the domain of Charles's Wain the night before, for the "most obedient" signatory who described himself as "ever at your service" had triumphed in the most glorious fashion.

Enclosed with the letter was a sealed bag containing five Hungarian ducats.

Johannes took it to the room in which his sick wife lay. He sat on the edge of the bed, gave her a spoonful of medicine, and wiped the perspiration from her brow.

"You know, and I have often told you, that astrology, which is so highly prized by the injudicious, is the bad and degenerate daughter of the noble science of astronomy. But, like many a child who has gone astray, its charms help to keep its mother, of whom no one else thinks."

And he laid the five ducats on the sick woman's bed.

"A dog that barked and a cock that crowed were the foundation on which Wallenstein's fortunes were based," my private tutor, the medical student Meisl, said on a rainy, misty November day when he told me this story instead of introducing me to the mysteries of calculating with sines and cosines. "You will, of course, have been told nothing of all this at your high school, where they do nothing but stuff you with dates. Heaven forbid that I should say anything bad about Wallenstein, but he was a good calculator, in war as in love, and I therefore doubt whether Venus alone was in the domain of Charles's Wain at the time. Remember what I told you at the outset about Lucrezia von Landeck. She was one of the richest heiresses in the kingdom of Bohemia. She died young. But when war with Venice broke out her wealth enabled Wallenstein to raise two regiments of dragoons and offer them to the Emperor. And that was the beginning of his meteoric career, which ended when he was struck down by a halberd at Eger."

The medical student Meisl filled his long student's pipe, the porcelain bowl of which displayed a portrait of Voltaire, with some cheap product of the imperial and royal tobacco administration. Then he went on:

"Johannes Kepler, who had such insight into the laws of the universe, certainly made no mistake. Venus was dominant that night in the realm of Charles's Wain. But I think there was another, smaller and more inconspicuous star quite near, and that that was Wallenstein's real star, Mercury. And even if you're bad at Latin and can't even construe an easy passage from Ovid decently, yet you know that to the ancients Mercury was the god of money."

THE PAINTER BRABANZIO

Prague was the home of a painter of whom little is known to posterity. His name was Vojtech or Adalbert Brabanec, but he was by no means averse to being addressed as Signor Brabanzio. He could certainly have been called a rogue and vagabond rather than a painter. Every year he used to go on his wanderings through Bohemia, Austria, Hungary and Lombardy, but he never accepted work with a recognised master and never stayed anywhere for long, for he had his own views about the art of painting and would not adapt himself to a master's instructions. He was of a restless disposition in other ways too, for wherever he went he made rebellious speeches against authority and showed his contempt for respectable and responsible people, and even for those who were merely decently dressed. So he spent his time in peasants' beer houses, harbour taverns and houses of disrepute, where his rebellious speeches were enjoyed and his ability to draw likenesses of his boon companions with a few strokes was appreciated. Even when he was not drunk, and even on Sundays, he looked like someone who had just been picked up out of the gutter, and his face bore traces of affrays and brawls in which he had been involved, for when trouble broke out he and his companions were always ready with their knives.

When he had had enough of brawling and wandering for the time being, he would come back to Prague, shirtless, in tattered shoes, without a kreuzer in his pocket, and sometimes actually without the tools of his trade, and he would stay with his brother, who was a jobbing tailor and lived on the bank of the Moldau not far from the convent of St Agnes. The two brothers got on badly, though they were fond of each other. The tailor deplored the fact that he did not paint respectable people, or madonnas and saints, but only common people and shady characters: drunken soldiers, gipsies, dog catchers, pickpockets, the washerwomen on the banks of the Moldau with their baskets, quacks, tooth extractors, all sorts of characters from the streets of the ghetto, and the women who sold their home-made plum cakes on the Kleine Ringplatz. He also took amiss his brother's failure to be sensibly economical with the money he occasionally earned with his daubs, for, as the saying is, a fool and his groschen are soon parted.

Now, some of his little pictures, hasty sketches and drafts, came into the hands of persons who knew, or claimed to know, something about art; and one of his products, showing a bearded, rather awkwardly built Capuchin friar rapturously contemplating a cheese that had been either stolen or scrounged, had been seen by the Emperor.

At the time Rudolf II was passionately devoting himself to the enrichment of his picture gallery and his collection of rareties, and he scraped together the money to pay for these things from wherever he could, with the result that the treasury had a great deal of difficulty in paying his debts. He was taking little interest in affairs of state at that time, for he lived only for his beloved arts; and, though from the Church point of view he disapproved of this artist's choice of subject matter, it nevertheless seemed to him remarkable, indeed almost incredible, that among his Bohemians, who had produced so little good painting, there should be living in a squalid corner of the Old Town a painter who was in no way inferior to the Italian or Netherlandish masters of his time.

The Emperor still occasionally left Prague Castle at that time, for he was not yet perpetually haunted by fear of murderous attacks by his brother Mathias and other persons hostile to him. So one morning he dressed like a public letter writer, i.e., in worn shoes and a shabby coat, with two quill pens and an inkpot in his belt and a chain round his neck to which a medallion with a portrait of St Catherine, who is the patron saint of all writers, was attached; and in that disguise he left through a side door of the deer park and was led by his valet Červenka through narrow, empty streets and across the river to the house 'At the sign of the bass fiddle', at the back of which was the tailor's workshop.

It was a February day, an icy shower of rain had just fallen, and the Emperor shivered as he said goodbye to Červenka. He adjusted the chain round his neck – he regarded this as an essential part of his disguise – and walked cautiously across a rain-soaked and pitifully bare little garden, in which a cat was chasing the sparrows, and entered the workshop.

The room was fair-sized, and three men were in it. The tailor, wearing a pair of spectacles that he kept continually adjusting, was sitting on a stool warming each of his feet alternately over a brazier in which coal was glowing. Spread in front of him was an old coat of the kind known as a *surtout*, for which he was making a new lining. In the middle of the room a giant of a man, a Moldau raftsman in his Sunday best, was sitting on two chairs placed side by side. His portrait was being painted by Signor Brabanzio, and he looked very unhappy about it, and seemed not to know what to do with his great horny, hairy hands. At the moment he was holding them out a long way in front of him, folded as if in prayer. The painter had insisted that he must not move, with the result that he was terrified of spoiling or breaking something in the workshop by a clumsy movement of his hands. It was this childishly awkward and slightly anguished expression on his bearded face that the painter wanted to capture. While the raftsman sweated with fear, Signor Brabanzio moved round him with his reddle in his hand, looking at him now from one side and now from the other, adjusting the man's face by pulling his ear or his beard, moving closer again and adding a stroke to the portrait, which seemed to be practically finished.

The Holy Roman Emperor Rudolf II shut the door behind him and raised his hat. Uncertain and embarrassed as he always was when confronted with strange faces, he tried to bow exactly as his privy councillor Hegelmüller did when he entered his room with calculations or a bundle of documents. But all he managed was a slight nod and a raising of his left shoulder. He then apologised for his intrusion by asking whether he might be allowed to warm himself a little for, so he said, he suffered from an obstinate chest complaint and the cold weather and the damp outside were very bad for his health. To demonstrate the truth of this statement he coughed slightly into the hollow of his hand.

The tailor cordially invited him to sit beside him by the fire. "So your trouble is your chest, sir," he said. "Mine's my digestion. Bread and dripping and a slice of sausage – that's perfectly all right. But a sip of beer with it, and I'm subjected to all the sufferings of the holy martyrs." "What do you need beer for?" the painter remarked. "A real tailor gets drunk on a bit of cheese."

"Can I get up sir?" the raftsman asked.

"And *his* trouble," the tailor went on, pointing his needle at his brother, "is his head, as you can see. He's a fool. And so each of us has his cross."

He again gestured to the guest to take a seat, and only then realised that the raftsman was sitting on two chairs and that there were no others in the shop.

"Get up, you kneading trough, you hogshead," he shouted angrily. "Can't you see that other people want to sit down?"

The raftsman to whom these unusual expletives were addressed rose clumsily to his feet, delighted at no longer having to sit still, and pushed one of the two chairs in the direction of the supposed public letter writer. Meanwhile the artist had finished his portrait, which he held in his outstretched hand, looking at it appraisingly, shaking his head and grimacing as if he were not totally satisfied with his handiwork. Then he handed it to the bearded giant, who carefully and expectantly took it with two fingers.

He saw a face that seemed familiar to him and might very well be his own. He also recognised the handkerchief round his neck. But there was no trace in the picture of his new Sunday coat.

He was disappointed. A strong wish, and disappointment that it had not been fulfilled, struggled for expression in his brain.

"Why, sir," he asked, "why did I put on my Sunday coat?"

"That's what I want to know,' said the artist. "Also I don't understand why you shortened your beard. As it was yesterday it suited you better. Now go, I've no more time for you."

The artist pushed him towards the door, though he kept stopping in the hope of getting at least a small part of his Sunday coat into the picture, but the artist kept pushing him step by step until he was out.

The Emperor had been sitting by the brazier and was warming his hands. He now turned to the tailor and said:

"Stomach trouble, did you say? And the doctors can't do anything for you? I wonder whether you have ever prayed for the deliverance of a damned soul."

"What? Me? Whom should I pray for?" the tailor replied, adjusting his spectacles.

"St Gregory," the Emperor explained to him, "once prayed very ardently that the soul of the pagan Emperor Trajan, whose portrait he saw on a marble tomb and who appeared to him several times in dreams, might be delivered from damnation. His prayer was granted, but in return the saint had to suffer from stomach trouble for the rest of his life."

"You're not right in the top storey either," said the tailor, pointing his needle at the Emperor's brow.

The Emperor fell silent. He had been struck by a small picture in water colours that was fixed to the wall. It was of the small garden through which he had walked shortly before, without taking any notice of it. Hardly anything was to be seen in the picture but a blackthorn bush and a leafless tree with thin branches, a patch of snow and the rails of a fence, but it was suffused in a magic that was inexpressible in words – the melancholy of winter and the hint of spring to come, or perhaps only the charm that is sometimes peculiar to the poor and unpretentious.

It was the work of a great master, as the Emperor saw, and it was clear to him that he must possess it and that it must be given the place it deserved next to the works of other masters, and he already visualised it next to a landscape by Lukas van Valkenborch that he specially loved. At the same time it struck him that he had omitted to provide himself with money when he left the Castle with Červenka in the guise of a public letter writer. But never mind, never mind, he said to himself, I'll send Červenka early tomorrow morning with two, three or perhaps four gulden. Červenka's very good with people and knows how to handle them, he doesn't give a damn for anyone, he'll get this masterpiece for a song, he always gets things cheap.

But then he thought of a way of acquiring other fine works by this master.

"That's good work and a pleasure to look at," he said, pointing to the picture.

"What? That one?" the tailor said in surprise, adjusting his spectacles.

"You should take it up to the Castle," said the Emperor, turning to the artist, "to show them what you're capable of."

"Thank you for your advice," said the painter, who was busy sharpening his reddle and his chalks. "If it was a gulden, I'd pocket it."

The Emperor was not to be put off.

"You should enquire about the possibilities of an appointment at the imperial court," he said.

"I have no such lofty ambition," the artist replied. "I'm content with my present position in life."

"There you see it," the tailor exclaimed indignantly. "It just shows you the limits of his intelligence. A regular income, a settled existence, doesn't appeal to him. He says he likes to feel a cold wind whistling round his nose. When he isn't staying with me he often doesn't have a crust of bread to eat."

"If I haven't any bread I eat butter on its own," said the painter, still sharpening his chalks.

"His Majesty," said the Emperor, rising slightly from his chair as he said those two words, "would certainly show you every favour and appreciation of your rare talent."

"And go on owing me the pay, just as he owes it to Miseroni, imperial courtier and stone carver, who has nothing left in his house that he can call his own. His Majesty's hand is always a long way from the purse in his pocket."

"The devil —" the Emperor blurted out, but he suppressed his indignation and annoyance, and said in a voice in which there was a trace of guilt:

"He authorised a payment of twelve gulden to Miseroni a fortnight ago."

"Yes, twelve of the hundred and twenty that he owes him,' the painter pointed out.

"To a tailor, twelve gulden is a good sum of money," said his brother, who regarded the stone carver as a kind of fellow craftsman. "But as for the Emperor and King of Bohemia, people say that those who want to see him have to dress up as stable boys, grooms or gardeners, for his pleasure garden and his stables are the only places he goes to every day."

"Perhaps," said the Emperor, and furrows appeared on his brow, "he avoids people who say the same thing to him every day: Help me, Emperor, give me, grant me, make me happy, make me rich."

"And they also say," the tailor went on, "that there are three men up at the Castle, a valet, an astrologer and an antiquarian, who govern the country in the Emperor's place and decide on the taxes."

"If you go to the imperial pleasure garden at this time tomorrow, you will meet His Majesty and be able to present your petition," the Emperor said, turning to the painter.

"My petition?" the artist exclaimed in surprise.

"Yes," the Emperor replied. "Your petition to be allowed to serve his Majesty with your art."

The painter Brabanzio took his pencils and chalks and arranged them in a row on the window ledge.

"Those who serve kings are fools," he said. "Also it is written: 'Put not your trust in princes, for there is no help in them.' No, sir, I shall serve neither this king nor any other."

"And there you have it," the tailor exclaimed excitedly. "As I've told you, he's a fool. Good advice is as helpful to him as cupping is to a corpse. I pray to God for him every day. Lord, I say, let him be halt, let him be lame, but give him a morsel of commonsense, don't let him be an idiot any longer."

"Here comes the Jew again," said the painter, who was standing at the window. "The one with the goat's beard. This is the third time. I wish I could help him, but I can't."

The Jew with the goat's beard whom the painter Brabanzio could not help was Mordechai Meisl.

He came because of his dead wife Esther. Three years had passed since the night on which Melach Hamoved, the angel of death, had taken her away. But time had not diminished his pain. She was always in his mind, and he wanted her portrait painted.

He had heard of painters who made life-like portraits of persons long dead: the patriarch Moses with the tables of the law in his hand, Susanna, the wife of Joiakim, Roman emperors and kings of Bohemia in past times, and he himself had seen in a nobleman's castle a picture of the youthful Absalom hanging pitifully by his hair; and he had developed a fixed idea that the painter Brabanzio would be able to paint a portrait of Esther, whom he called his darling, his beloved, his innocent one, if he could only describe her to him correctly; and he was convinced that he could describe her to him as graphically as if she were standing in front of him in the flesh.

True, it was written: Thou shalt make no image. But the head of the diaspora, the Great Rabbi Loew, who was a gaon, a prince among the wise, had made it clear to him that this was not one of the seven Noachian laws, and that those who obeyed the Noachian laws were assured of their part in the kingdom of God.

"May long life and blessing from the Governor of the world and peace be with you," he said in accordance with the Jewish practice as he entered, and he did not recognise the Emperor, and the Emperor did not recognise him.

The painter looked bewildered and distressed, like someone completely at a loss.

"Sir," he said, "you have come here in vain. No one can do what you ask, it's impossible."

"You can do it if you want to," Mordechai Meisl replied. "It can't be so difficult. Be patient with me, try again. Your trouble will be well rewarded."

"I know," replied the painter. 'You promised me eight gulden. But they are not for me and I must remain poverty-stricken."

"Eight gulden?" the tailor exclaimed. "Do you suppose a Jew produces eight gulden from his sleeves every day? Do what he wants, get on with it, don't let me be disgusted with you."

And, as if to set the painter a good example, he settled down to work on the new lining for the coat more industriously than before.

The painter had joined the alleged public letter writer by the fire and was warming his hands.

"When I paint someone's portrait," he said, more to himself than to him, "it's not enough to see the person's face, which is changeable, and looks like one thing today and tomorrow looks quite different. I ask him questions, and don't stop until I've seen into his heart. Only if I've done that can I do good work."

"That does you honour and will perhaps one day be the basis of your fame," said the Emperor.

The painter Brabanzio made a dismissive, contemptuous gesture, as if he regarded honour and fame as a fistful of wind.

"I'm interested in the eight gulden," he said. "He wants me to paint his beloved dead wife. I can't go down to the dead like Ulysses. But perhaps I can conjure up her shadow like the witch of Endor."

And he turned to Mordechai Meisl as if he had made up his mind.

"You say she was so beautiful. What kind of beauty was it?"

"She was as beautiful as the silver moon, she was as beautiful and devout as Abigail," said Mordechai Meisl, his eyes gazing into the past. "God took from me the crown of my head. He must have found many and great sins in me, and so I had to lose her. I can no longer laugh with the cheerful, grief and pain have descended on me like armed myrmidons . . ."

"That shows the fickleness and inconstancy of fortune," remarked the tailor.

"I asked you to tell me what kind of beauty was hers," the painter reminded Meisl.

"She was like a perfect sacrifice, so lovely and without

blemish she was," Mordechai Meisl went on. "She was like a flower of the field, so sweet was she in the eyes of the beholder. Yes, and she could read, write and calculate, and she used to make little things of silk, and when I was at table with her she waited on me so beautifully. She was so clever that she could have spoken in the Emperor's presence. She had a cat she was very fond of, and she used to give it milk every day. Sometimes she was sad. She said the time passed so slowly that she wished it was night."

"Sort that out with your Creator," the tailor said crossly. "Who can do anything against misfortune?"

"We had our evening meal, and then we went to bed," Mordechai Meisl went on. "She went to sleep and she breathed quietly. During the night I heard her groaning and crying for help. Yes, she cried for help. I bent over her . . ."

He fell silent, and some time passed before he went on:

"The neighbours came, and I don't know what happened then. When I came to my senses I saw a small oil lamp burning on the east side of the room, and then I knew she was dead."

The Emperor quietly spoke the words of the Preacher:

"The children of men are vanity, to be laid in the balance they are altogether lighter than vanity."

". . . altogether lighter than vanity," Meisl said after him, and he glanced at the Emperor as if he were surprised to hear these holy words from the mouth of a nescient who had never attended a cheder, a Jewish children's schoolroom.

"The Highest had decided," he went on, "and what happened was in accordance with His will. She is dead, and I have no more pleasure in the world. The days pass in care and worry. Night sometimes brings forgetfulness, but in the morning the old pain returns."

And, as Mordechai Meisl said that, something strange happened to the Emperor. It was as if he and not the Jew had spoken. With every morning the old pain returned – his own fate was contained in those words, that was what had happened to him ever since the night when the beloved of his dreams was snatched from him.

He sat lost in thought, and no longer heard what the painter and Meisl said to each other. He forgot where he was. The image of the beloved of his dreams conjured up by those words rose before his eyes, he saw her more clearly and distinctly than ever before. He was completely carried away and, to hold the vision fast, he took his silver pencil from his pocket and seized a sheet of paper.

When he had finished the drawing the spell faded. Under the drawing he wrote in tiny, untidy, hardly visible handwriting *Rudolfus fecit*. He looked at it again, but the longer he looked at it the less satisfied he was. He sighed, and shook his head.

No, it wasn't she. It was someone else, it was like her in many ways, but it wasn't she. It was a Jewish girl with big, frightened eyes, whom he had perhaps noticed that time when he rode through the streets of the ghetto. But it wasn't she, it wasn't the beloved of his dreams.

Perhaps, he said to himself, I looked too much at her face and too little into her heart, and so could not bring it off. Heedlessly he dropped the drawing on the floor and rose to his feet. He was shivering, and for the first time felt he had lost her for ever.

The Jew was still talking to the painter, who shook his head and shrugged his shoulders. The Emperor glanced again at the picture with the patch of snow and the blackthorn bush. Then he inclined his head and raised a shoulder, and with that farewell he walked to the door, and no-one took any notice.

When he opened the door and shut it behind him as he left, a gust of wind swept through the workshop. It whirled the piece of paper on the floor into the air, and then deposited it at the painter's feet. Mordechai Meisl picked it up, held it in his hand for a moment, and exclaimed:

"This is she. Why didn't you tell me you'd already done it? Why did you say nothing and let me talk? Yes, this is she, this is she. My darling! My beloved!"

The painter took the picture from Meisl's hands, looked at it, turned it this way and that, twisted his mouth a little, and handed it back to him. He was astonished and incredulous.

"Do you really think it's she?" he asked.

"Yes. Thank you, sir. It's she. As I described her to you,"

Meisl said, hiding the picture behind his fur coat as if he were afraid the painter might take it away from him again.

Then he counted out eight gold gulden on the table.

The painter picked them up after Meisl had left. He let them clink in his hands, and was delighted by the unfamiliar music. He tossed two of them up in the air and caught them, did the same with three, then four and then five, and finally, with the skill of a fairground juggler, kept all eight in the air simultaneously, while the tailor watched open-mouthed.

Then, when he tired of this little game, he dropped the gulden one after another into his pocket.

"Yes, money's good stuff," he said with obvious satisfaction. "In summer it doesn't spoil, in winter it doesn't freeze, and sometimes it's easy to get. I don't know, I can't remember doing the drawing the Jew took away with him. I can't understand it. It didn't look to me as if I'd done it."

"The same sort of thing often happens to me," said the tailor. "In the street I meet a pair of trousers I've mended, I look at it, because that's my custom, but I don't recognise it. You can't keep everything in your head, you see."

"Yes, my dear fellow," my tutor, the medical student Jakob Meisl, ended his story. "I've always regretted those eight gulden that my great-great-great-great uncle, Mordechai Meisl, paid for a drawing signed by the imperial amateur, not for my sake, you can take that from me, for not a single kreuzer of Meisl's wealth, his legendary wealth, came down to me – you know what happened to it. But those eight gulden were responsible for the fact that the little painting the Emperor liked so much never reached his picture gallery and that the name of Brabanzio is not recorded in the history of art. For with those eight gulden in his pocket Vojtech Brabanec, alias Brabanzio, could not face staying any longer in his brother's workshop. He succumbed once more to the lure of distant lands and set out on his travels again, taking all his possessions with him. When Červenka, the Emperor's valet, called next morning, both the picture and the painter had gone. Brabanzio was on his way to

Venice, where an epidemic awaited him of which he died. Only one picture survives that is signed with the words *Brabanzio fecit*. It is hung in a small private gallery in Milan, and it shows a man sitting in a harbour tavern, perhaps Brabanzio himself, and two ugly old women are pressing forward to embrace him. One of them, I think, is Pestilence and the other, who is as grey as a winding sheet, is Oblivion."

THE FORGOTTEN ALCHEMIST

In the course of years a new guest had crept into the heart of Mordechai Meisl, which had for so long been filled with nothing but grief and sorrow. This new guest was ambition. Money and property, his wealth that grew from day to day, meant nothing to him. The primacy that he enjoyed in the Jewish community did not satisfy him. He aspired to freedoms, rights and privileges that would elevate him above his station, and he wanted to be helped and protected in all his aims by a royal charter. And so he got together with the Emperor's personal valet, Philipp Lang who, for all his plebeian origin, had enormous influence over the Emperor, but was hated and feared by the common people, Christians and Jews alike, for he was blamed for everything that went wrong in the state. He was said to be practised in evil ways and highly skilled in every kind of fraud and deception, and it was claimed that never before had a scoundrel at a royal court had such calamitous effects on ordinary honest citizens. And now he was sometimes to be seen making his way through the streets of the Jewish quarter and disappearing into Mordechai Meisl's house on the Dreibrunnenplatz.

The Holy Roman Emperor up in Prague Castle was in dire straits at the time, for he was more impecunious than ever. The greatest necessities for the imperial household could not be afforded, the treasury that was responsible for checking the bills that came in and dealing with and settling the imperial debts was at its wits' end. And so His Majesty's trusted counsellors, Strahlendorf, Trautson, Hegelmüller and several others, got together to devise ways and means of coping with the financial crisis. A number of proposals were made, only to be dropped after their pros and cons had been debated. Also there was no lack of rhetoric, but the fine words and phrases served for nothing more useful than blowing on hot soup. His Majesty's trusted advisers eventually agreed on a resolution declaring that there could be no remedy to the situation so long as His Majesty the Emperor persisted in living, acting and spending his money in accordance with his pleasure and not in accordance with the advice of his servants.

When this resolution was brought to the Emperor's notice he flew into a rage. He stormed through the halls, chambers and corridors of the Castle brandishing a rapier, declaring that Hegelmüller must never again appear in his presence, he had forfeited his life, and that applied to Trautson too, for both were in the pay of his brother Mathias and wanted to swindle and betray him, but, in spite of all scoundrels, brothers, poisoners and archdukes, he was not going to be swindled and betrayed. And, while shouting and raging like this, he reached the great dining hall, where he swept the crockery from the table and shattered the cut glass.

The rage subsided and gave way to deep depression. He complained that no ruler of any country in Christendom led a life as wretched as his. He was surrounded by enemies, he had nothing but cares, worries and troubles, and all temporal pleasures were denied him. He forgave Trautson and Hegelmüller, and even his brother Mathias, who in such unbrotherly and unChristian a manner wanted his life. In an emotional voice he prayed to God for forgiveness and turned his rapier against himself, trying to stab himself in the throat. Philipp Lang, who had hurried after him upstairs and downstairs, through long corridors, chambers, rooms, galleries and halls, arrived just in time to snatch the weapon from him.

Then, in his bedroom, when he was in a calmer frame of mind which, however, was more like total exhaustion, Philipp Lang began talking to him, for he thought this a favourable opportunity to mention a plan he had concocted. He wanted to make the Emperor, not just a secret partner in Meisl's widespread and multifarious business activities, but the heir and sole beneficiary of his wealth. Philipp Lang knew that Meisl could not expect to live for long, for he was often feverish, coughed, and spat blood into his handkerchief. He would be compensated and rewarded by rights and privileges and a royal charter that put him and his property under imperial protection and patronage, but in reality cheated him of everything. Meisl's riches would flow into the Emperor's pockets and he, Philipp Lang, hoped to do not too badly out of it himself. He expected no great difficulty in persuading his imperial master of the benefits that would flow from his plan, for the Emperor was desperate for money and indifferent to where it came from. All the same, he must be tackled very carefully.

"Your Majesty must not lose heart," he began. "Things are not so bad that a way out cannot be found. True, debts are a bad thing, and not for anything in the world must they be allowed to increase and multiply. They are like snake bites. At first you think they're nothing, but they end by being fatal."

The Emperor said nothing. His debts, great though they were, worried him only slightly, for it was the treasury's business to deal with them. What drove him to frenzy and despair was his counsellors' refusal to approve the money he needed to pay for a number of precious paintings that had been offered him through his agents in Rome and Madrid, Count Harrach and Count Khevenhueller. Among them were important works by Roos and Parmigianino, two masters who were not yet represented in his gallery; and the idea that they might fall into other hands gave him sleepless nights.

"Your Majesty set your hopes on alchemy," Philipp Lang went on. "I have seen alchemists, adepts and initiates, coming to court one after another with great acclaim and then ingloriously disappearing. There was Ezekiel Reisacher, of whom one could not decide whether he was a man or a woman; there was Geronimo Scotto, of whom I alone have a pleasing memory, because he prescribed me a cure for buzzing in the ears and watering eyes, there was Thadaeus Krenfleisch, who was a pastry cook before he became an alchemist, there was Edward Kelly . . ."

At the mention of this name the Emperor grimaced and put his hand behind the back of his head.

"Yes, his hair was as bright red as coal in a smelting oven," Philipp Lang went on, "and he roused your Majesty's displeasure by spending his night carousing with the officers of the bodyguard. The next was Count Bragadino, who wasn't a count but a bosun's mate from Famagusta. And then there was Vitus Renatus, who claimed that for lack of practice he had forgotten his Bohemian mother-tongue, because he spent the whole of his life in the company of scholars and men of learning and therefore could speak nothing but Latin. Six of them were here in the Castle, and two were convicted of fraud and hanged."

The Emperor made an involuntary movement as if he wanted to drive away an unpleasant memory, but Philipp Lang interpreted it correctly. His Majesty felt tired and wanted to go to bed.

A little later, while he was helping the Emperor to undress, Philipp Lang went on:

"And now it's two years since your Majesty took Jakobus van Delle into your Majesty's service. He chose the stove-attendant Brouza, the jester, as his friend, and that's all I know about him. But I don't believe he'll ever catch the dove of Trismegistos, by which, as Brouza says, he means the powder or elixir with which he hopes to turn thick leaden plates into the finest gold."

The Emperor angrily stamped his foot.

"I know Your Majesty has grown tired of waiting and has given him a time limit," Philipp Lang went on, handing the Emperor his gold-embroidered but slightly worn silk nightshirt. "How it will end time alone will show. But I believe . . ." He shrugged his shoulders.

". . . I believe there's only one real alchemist in the kingdom, and that's the Jew Meisl."

"What Jew?" asked the Emperor. He knelt in front of the big, cast-iron crucifix, lowered his head, prayed and made the sign of the cross.

"The Jew Mordechaeus Meisl in the ghetto," Philipp Lang explained when the Emperor had finished his prayer. "He has no need of the bird of Trismegistos that van Delle seeks so frantically. Everything that passes through his hands turns into gold for him. If through Your Majesty's gracious generosity I had a hundred gulden, or even fifty, and gave them to a peasant, he'd buy himself a plough and oxen to pull it, and what would he gain by it? A bit of bread with salt on it every day, and that's all. If I gave it to the tailor down below in the square, he'd send for some fine cloth from Malines, and with it and his needle and scissors he'd earn himself a helping of roast or boiled meat every day and a jug of wine to go with it. But if I gave a hundred gulden to Mordechaeus Meisl he'd turn it into two hundred in no time at all. And that, Your Majesty, is the real art of alchemy."

"That Jew's a very dangerous man," said the Emperor. "He's in secret communication with evil spirits and demons, and they bring him the gold."

"I know nothing about that," Philipp Lang hastened to assure his master. "There are a great many rumours about him, people envy him and talk a great deal. But it is his humble wish that he may be permitted to support and serve your Majesty with everything that he possesses."

"Is he willing to accept baptism?" the Emperor asked.

"No, he is not," Philipp Lang replied, adjusting the Emperor's pillow, for he had gone to bed. "On that point he is like other Jews, who are a stiff-necked, evil and vexatious people, as is testified by holy scripture and the Book of Chronicles."

"And yet our faith and salvation came to us through the Jews," the Emperor said.

"Yes, and therefore they must be accepted as they are, with Christian charity," said Philipp Lang. "I wish your Majesty a restful night."

And at a sign from the Emperor he blew out the candles.

There was another alchemist in Prague Castle besides van Delle. This was the illiterate Anton Brouza, who was an adept in the art of transmuting blows with a stick into gold coinage. He had a pointed chin, a flattened nose, and a grey, bristly moustache that had once been red. He had been court jester to the late Emperor Maximilian, who so much enjoyed his simple jokes, smutty speeches and strange ideas that he had made his son Rudolf, the heir to the throne, promise never to dismiss him from his service or from proximity to his person. But Emperor Rudolf II was unwilling to tolerate the proximity of any court jester, so he had Brouza appointed stove-attendant in the Emperor's quarters. Brouza's reason for adapting himself to the situation was – as he explained to the Emperor – that it would never do to have two fools under the same roof. But he went on calling the Emperor young master, young gentleman, or even godfather, and bickering and arguing with him, and the Emperor, when this got too much for him, would give him a thrashing with his stick. When this happened Brouza was delighted and kept still, for it gave him an excellent excuse for asking the Emperor for money or other gifts to compensate him for the pain of the beating. As soon as he saw that the Emperor's anger had subsided he would start wailing and lamenting, and he would swear that, when he eventually rejoined his dear departed master in the next world, he would complain to him about what was done to him in this building, which was worse than any hangman's vault in which people were tortured and put to death. These threats and lamentations would go on and on until the Emperor, for the sake of peace and quiet, and because he really believed that Brouza might one day denounce him to the late Emperor, put his hand in his pocket and ended the matter by resorting to his purse.

Jakobus van Delle had not brought a servant of his own to the Castle, and one of Brouza's daily tasks was to bring him big loads of wood and coal and light the two furnaces, the big one, which was called Athanor, and the small one, which was called the Imp. When he had finished the job he often squatted in a corner of the workshop, for the alchemist's many strangely shaped glass tubes, bottles, crucibles, phials, stills and retorts fascinated him. Sometimes he watched with horror and amazement when the alchemist's hand glided over a flame, causing it in unintelligible fashion promptly and obediently to change colour and flash now blue, now saffron yellow, now green, now violet. He saw that the blazing tongues of flame did not burn the alchemist, but that he played with them, his eyes tamed them, they were subject to his will. The alchemist's small, delicate and clever hands impressed Brouza, as did his beard, which was trimmed in the French fashion, his flame-coloured coat, and the white locks that protruded from under his silk cap. Brouza tried to make himself useful in the workshop so that he could stay there longer; he used the bellows, stirred the molten lead with an iron rod and pounded sulphur or phosphorus in a mortar. He also brought van Delle food from the kitchen and, when the clock struck one a.m., his sleeping draught made of spices.

Van Delle at first took practically no notice of him and rarely spoke to him, but he succeeded in gaining the alchemist's confidence. Brouza's total devotion was bound to give pleasure to a man who felt himself to be surrounded by mistrust, who had no real friends at the Castle, and had grown almost completely unaccustomed to contact with people. Only on Sundays did he leave the Castle to attend Mass at the Barnabite church, and only rarely did one of the Emperor's gentlemen-in-waiting call and listen loftily to an account of the progress of his work and then ask sarcastically how much longer he was going to take cooking his soup.

Thus in the course of time a relationship developed between van Delle and Brouza that could not be called friendship, for the two were too different for that, apart from their inequality in birth and station; nevertheless a kind of understanding grew between them. Brouza's veneration of van Delle was reciprocated with an indulgent fondness such as one might have for a rather scruffy but good and obedient dog.

To Brouza the normally taciturn alchemist was sometimes communicative, and Brouza kept his folly and his smutty talk under strict control while they were together. Among the many things on which they agreed was that the imperial court was a happy home only for those who were good for nothing or had nothing good in mind. Brouza told van Delle about everything that went on in Prague Castle. He described to him how money and other things were filched from the kitchen, as well as from the clothes and silver stores and even the court chapel, and told him that Philipp Lang knew about it all and said nothing, because he had his finger in every pie. He described how Eva von Lobkowitz, an attractive young woman, after she was refused an audience, entered the Castle grounds disguised as a stable boy, threw herself at the Emperor's feet and appealed for a pardon for her father, who was in strict confinement in the tower of Elbogen castle. The Emperor had raised his hat, addressed her by name, told her to rise to her feet, agreed to grant her appeal, and actually noted the matter in his notebook. But several days later he had sent for Count Sternberg, the Master of the Horse, and rebuked him severely for allowing stable boys to approach him in the Castle grounds and trouble him with trifling matters; he ought to have better control of his people. Brouza also described how a cook had dashed from the kitchen, spit in hand, and had turned round and round a dozen times and shouted for help for Christ's sake, for his belly was behind him and his back was in front. Cold water had been poured over him, he had come to his senses and found that his belly and his back had returned to their proper places. In the late Emperor's time, Brouza told van Delle with tears streaming from his eyes, he had been the only fool among a hundred sensible men, but now there wasn't a single man of sense among a hundred fools and there wasn't an honest man among a hundred thieves.

Jakobus van Delle talked to Brouza, to whom the world did not extend beyond Heraun and from there beyond Pisek and Rakonitz, about his travels in foreign countries. He described how he had gone to Istanbul, the metropolis of learning, to study fine old manuscripts. There he had come across Jews who had renounced their faith and worshipped a god whom they called Asmodai, the lord of the spirits. He described how he had met the Wandering Jew, who had given him marvellous and very secret information about the future of the universe, but had then asked him for a small contribution to his travelling expenses. He told Brouza that it was possible to see Mount Sinai, but not to climb it, for it was surrounded and guarded by huge white scorpions. He also said he was confident of being able to discover a way of artificially producing saltpeter, but the Emperor was not interested in saltpeter, he wanted gold. He, van Delle, had gone to Venice to discover the secret of the ruby-coloured glass that the Venetian glass blowers possessed but refused to reveal. This had exposed him to grave dangers, and in the end his project had failed, but he still hoped one day triumphantly to solve the problem of producing ruby-red glass. His life had always been subject to great vicissitudes – and Brouza translated this into his own terms. Yes, he said, he had experience of that himself, one day a good, rich roast and meagre fare next day, that had happened to him too since the departure from this world of his most gracious Majesty the Emperor Maximilian; and calling to mind his former master caused him to snivel and weep, and he had to wipe the tears from his eyes, and van Delle had to comfort him. The situation in this world, he explained, was such that the wearer of the crown of crowns lasted no longer than a farm hand.

Now, Jakobus van Delle had once violently contradicted the Emperor, who in a bad mood had derided alchemy and denounced its practitioners as frauds. He had told him that on St Wenceslas's day, which is celebrated as a joyous festival in Bohemia, he would hand him a twelve-pound bar of solid gold as a first and small example of what he could do. The Emperor had sarcastically asked him whether he was prepared to stake his head on this, and van Delle had said he was, and they had agreed on the deal. Van Delle had done this because he felt his honour had been challenged, because after so many years of toil he believed himself to be at last on the right track towards transmuting base metal into gold and, above all, because he foresaw in the weeks ahead a constellation of heavenly bodies that had rarely occurred in the past but had always been extremely favourable to him and his work.

But this constellation came and went, Saturn, which is unfavourable to everything new, returned to its old realm from the remoteness of the scaly tail of Hydra, and van Delle's great master stroke, the transmutation of the elements, had failed to occur and actually seemed farther away than ever. The pledge he had given the Emperor weighed heavily on his mind. He had acted like someone who clinks his spurs without having a horse in the stable. And the closer St Wenceslas's day came, the greater grew his anxiety and gloom. Sometimes he got to work as frantically as if the furies were behind him. He began one thing and then another without finishing anything, and sometimes he sat idly, staring into space, for hours or even days.

Brouza noted with concern the change that had come over him, which he could not explain; and when the alchemist yet again left untouched the meal he had brought him from the kitchen he could stand it no longer and appealed to him to tell him what was wrong.

Van Delle did not reply and went on staring into space, and Brouza persisted until the alchemist admitted his plight. He had failed in his work, he had pledged his head to the Emperor, and he now feared he was going to lose it.

"I must leave, I must get away, but how can I?" he said in conclusion. "I'm being kept under guard. You must have noticed that for several weeks past two arquebusiers have been posted in the corridor not far from my door, one on the right and the other on the left, and on Sundays when I go to Mass they follow close behind me and don't lose sight of me even in church. Cursed be the fate that led me to this house."

Brouza was dismayed and bewildered on hearing this, and at first he could say nothing, he could only croak and grind his teeth, there was a painful knot in his throat. Eventually, when he was able to collect his ideas and find words to express them again, he told the alchemist to try again, for he would succeed, he always succeeded, and he must not give up hope.

"That hope," said van Delle with a sad smile, "is a vain hope, and those who nurse it bake bread with corn that is not yet sown. No, Brouza, I'm a lost man."

"Then you must go down and throw yourself on the Emperor's mercy."

The alchemist shook his head.

"Have you ever seen the Emperor laugh?" he asked. "No," Brouza replied. "I've often seen him angry, but I've never seen him laugh."

"No mercy is to be expected of someone who cannot laugh," said the alchemist. "More pity is to be expected of the Cyclops and the wild beasts in the deepest depths of the forest than from His Majesty the Emperor."

Brouza asked whether by Cyclops van Delle meant charcoal burners. But van Delle was in no mood to tell Brouza about Ulysses and his adventure in the cave of Polyphemus, and so he merely said that the Cyclops were not charcoal burners but goatherds, savage and dangerous, wicked men. And then he again said that he was lost.

"You certainly are not," exclaimed Brouza, who had recovered his composure. "Just put together what you want to take with you and leave the rest to me," he said. "I'll smuggle you into the deer park without being seen and get you away from there. And if you want to join the Cyclops in the forest, I'll come with you, I'm not afraid of goatherds."

The alchemist explained that he didn't want to join the Cyclops, but to go to Bavaria, where he had friends. But for that he would need money, and he knew of no way of getting any.

When it's a question of money, and one party has some and the other wants it, it's often the end of a friendship. But not in this instance.

"Is it only a question of money?" said Brouza. "That's no obstacle. I have my savings, and I'm going to increase them by several gulden this very day."

With that he left van Delle, and for the last time, or so he believed, went to see the Emperor to put to the test his own alchemical skills.

When Brouza entered the gallery the Emperor was looking at one of the paintings he had paid for with money derived from Meisl's business transactions. He was in a good mood, and he beckoned to Brouza.

"Come here and look at this picture. What do you see in it?" he said.

The picture was a *Last Supper* by Parmigianino. Brouza went up to it, rubbed his nose, making it flatter than ever, furrowed his brow and stuck out his lower lip, thus assuming the air of a man determined to get to the bottom of something.

Then he announced:

"Those are the twelve sons of the patriarch Jacob. I could swear they're talking Hebrew."

And he made some guttural sounds in imitation of the Hebrew tongue.

"But there are thirteen of them, not twelve," the Emperor pointed out.

"Jacob and his twelve sons, that makes thirteen altogether," Brouza replied.

"Don't you recognise Christ?" asked the Emperor, using his knife of brightly coloured agate to point out the Saviour.

"Yes, now that you point Him out, young master, I do recognise Him," Brouza said. "God bless You, Christ." Then he said resentfully: "Sits at table enjoying Himself," as if in his opinion Christ should always be on the cross.

"He's talking to Judas, who has sold and betrayed Him," the Emperor explained.

"What do I care if he betrayed Him? I don't get involved in gentlemen's squabbles. I leave everyone to his own affairs and don't care about any of them."

He thought this blasphemous enough to make the Emperor pick up his stick and start beating him immediately. Instead the Emperor gently chided him.

"You ought to talk respectfully about sacred matters, you're a Christian, after all," he said.

"And you? You a Christian and call it a sacred matter when you make Christ the subject of commercial transactions? You yourself trade in Christ."

"What? You say that I make Christ the subject of commercial transactions?"

Brouza behaved as if it were his duty to call the Emperor to account.

"What Judas sold you this Christ and how much did you pay for Him?" he wanted to know.

"No Judas, but Granvella, the cardinal's nephew, sold me this fine picture, and I paid forty ducats for it, and now go away and leave me in peace," said the Emperor.

"Forty ducats?" Brouza exclaimed. "Now you see, young

master, that as I've always said, you conduct your affairs like a proper fool. You pay forty ducats for a painted Christ when the price of the living one was only thirty pieces of silver."

"Are you calling me a fool? Just wait, I'll teach you manners and respect for your royal master," cried the Emperor, who had now lost patience, and Brouza knew that only a minimum extra effort was now necessary to make sure of the beating he wanted. He acted as if he were trying to pacify the Emperor.

"Why are you shouting? Why are you angry?" he said. "You know how much I respect you. I respect you far more than the king of diamonds."

This was too much for the Emperor, and anger got the better of him. Brouza's simple, snub-nosed face dissolved into a diabolical, savage mask, and the Emperor flung at it the nearest objects at hand, first of all the agate knife and then a plateful of cherries, and when the latter missed its target he went for Brouza with his stick.

Brouza took the beating like a field takes rain after a long drought. And when the Emperor, panting and exhausted, sank back into his armchair and his anger died away, Brouza knew the time had come to moan, snivel and complain violently.

"Help me, O God," he wailed, rubbing his back. "What hellish torment you have inflicted on me, young master. Never would I have believed that such a thing would happen to me in your house. And one day, when I return to the service of your blessed and gracious father up above, he will learn that you tried to stone me."

And he pointed to the broken plate, the cherries scattered about the floor, and the agate knife that had scratched his brow.

The Emperor handed him his handkerchief to wipe away the drops of blood. Then he asked to be forgiven in a spirit of Christian charity; he had acted in anger, and he was sorry. But Brouza went on raging and storming. Anger was a deadly sin, he declared, this time his torment had been too great to be cancelled out by words, and he demanded seven gulden for the beating, and one extra for the knife, which had nearly deprived him of the sight of his eyes.

The Emperor said eight gulden was much too much, he couldn't possibly give him that.

Brouza was willing to discuss the matter, for he didn't know how well provided with money the Emperor now was.

"Well, let me have something on account, young master," he suggested, "and the rest can stand over, but I want security for it."

The Emperor handed over three gulden, but when Brouza wanted to take the Parmigianino as security for the other five the Emperor's anger flared up again and he picked up his stick; and Brouza, who had had enough beating for one day, decided that three gulden would do and took his departure.

He had found a silk rope-ladder in the bedroom of Count Colloredo, who had held the office of imperial cup-bearer. The count had used it in the course of his amorous adventures, most of which took place in the neighbourhood of Prague Castle. However, in the course of years he had become a very corpulent gentleman, and nowadays he was rather short of breath, comfort was more important to him than anything else, and he had long ceased to be a threat to the virtue of the daughters of the worthy citizens of the Kleinseite and the Hradschin. But the rope-ladder was still in good condition, and Brouza put it in the basket he generally used for carrying wood and coal on his back up the steps and took it to the alchemist's workshop.

Here it lay for three weeks, for the escape had to be postponed several times. First van Delle had a sore throat and was feverish. Then there was a spell of bad weather, and it rained heavily and continuously for two days and nights. This was immediately followed by a heavenly constellation that van Delle thought not sufficiently favourable for such a hazardous enterprise, and this caused another postponement. In the end they fixed on the eve of St Wenceslas's day, and no further postponement was possible, however much van Delle, who regarded the venture with apprehension and foreboding, would have liked one.

On the eve of St Wenceslas's day Brouza brought him a plate of meat soup, a helping of chicken pie, hard-boiled eggs, cheese, a slice of honey cake, a fig cake, and a jug of wine.

"Set to and fortify yourself, sir, and eat your fill, for we don't know what we shall be getting to eat and drink tomorrow," he said, and then advised him to rest for an hour or two before they left.

"You'll need all your strength," he said. "At daybreak we must have half a dozen miles behind us."

Van Delle ate with little appetite. He talked sadly about the high hopes with which he had arrived at the Emperor's court.

"I relied far too much on hypotheses in my work," he said. "I allowed myself to be carried away by pure imagination, with the result that I'm now reduced to leaving ignominiously, in darkness and mist."

"Whether we shall be having any mist is very doubtful," said Brouza. "A little mist, not too much of it, would be no bad thing, but it doesn't look as if we shall be having any. But I think we'll manage very well even if we have to do without it, particularly as there's a new moon."

"In my heart fear and hope are in balance," said the alchemist. "But, as the poet Petrarch said, in human life fear turns out to be justified by events far more often than hope. So what is left but to face the bitterness of fate with a firm brow."

He had decided with a heavy heart to leave his books behind. Now he went to the huge pile, picked out a slim volume and put it in the pocket of his flame-coloured coat. It was Seneca's *De tranquillitate vitae*, "On a quiet life", which he wanted to take with him on his arduous way.

Meanwhile Brouza said:

"An enterprise like this cannot be carried out without difficulty and danger. You have the advantage that never before in my life have I helped anyone to flee."

"And what advantage do I derive from that?" the alchemist wanted to know.

Brouza had relapsed for a moment into his old jester's role.

"You know the saying that a priest is never again so good as at his first Mass. So be of good cheer. You'll see that, as in the rosary, the Gloria comes at the end."

When the clock struck one, Brouza fixed the rope ladder to two iron hooks he had driven into the bay windowsill and secured with two wedges. Then he showed van Delle, who was trembling with fear in all his limbs, what to do. He climbed on to the windowsill and down the ladder until his snub-nosed face was out of sight, and then he reappeared and asked the alchemist to hand him the bundle with his belongings and his own knapsack.

"It's not difficult, and there's nothing dangerous about it," he said. "The only thing to remember is to look up and not look down. Take one rung at a time and don't hurry. If you hear footsteps or voices or anything else, stop and don't move. When I'm down you'll hear me whistle."

And with that he disappeared.

When van Delle had his feet on the rope-ladder, one of the Emperor's lions, which were kept in cages in the deer park below, started roaring, and soon afterwards the silence of the night was broken by the melancholy cry of an eagle which was chained to an iron bar. These noises, wild as they sounded, did not alarm van Delle, who was used to the roar of lions and the cries of eagles. But when a bat whirred past close to his head he failed completely to suppress a startled cry.

As he went down one rung at a time his fear diminished. He discovered that what he was doing was not difficult or dangerous. The rustling of the trees below him grew louder, birds startled from their sleep whirred past him and flew away. Above him were the familiar stars: Auriga, the Great Bear, the Crow, the Ox's Head, the Crown of Ariadne and Orion's Belt.

When he was nearly down he was so over-confident that he let go of the ladder and jumped too soon. He was near the ground, but he landed so clumsily that he staggered and fell.

Brouza bent over him, and he heard his voice.

"Get up, sir, get up," he said. "All's well, and there's no time to lose."

With Brouza's help he tried to get up, but couldn't. Instead he sank back again with a cry of pain. He had injured his leg.

There could be no more question of flight, but Brouza did not lose his head. He carried, dragged and pulled van Delle to a remote part of the deer park where a hut leaned against the perimeter wall like a drunk leaning against a doorpost. Here he made van Delle, who did not stop groaning, as comfortable as possible on a sack of feathers. He lit an oil lamp, carefully took off van Delle's shoes, and brought him a pair of Turkish slippers which, though worn, were made of the finest gazelle leather.

"Where am I?" van Delle asked.

"In my house," said Brouza, "and everything here is at your disposal. No-one will look for you here. Let them chase you down all the main roads in the country, you're safe here. This house was given me by the late Emperor, as well as the two apple trees outside and the little garden in which I grow vegetables."

He wiped tears from his eyes.

"Now you see the troubles and woes that threaten this wretched life of ours," the alchemist said in a weak voice, "and how fortune has once more shown me her wiles and her inconstancy."

"When you jumped from the ladder you relied excessively on God's aid," said Brouza. "It might have been even worse."

The alchemist pointed to a whip with a short stock and long leather thongs that was hanging from a nail on the wall.

"What's that for?" he asked. "Do you keep a dog?"

"No," Brouza replied. "The late Emperor sometimes whipped me with it if I upset him. It's what's called a relic. I also have other relics from him. He honoured me with those two chests over there, the copper wash-basin, stockings, shirts, handkerchiefs, a small prayer book, a ring with a blue stone, a cupping glass and many other things. Those slippers are from him too. Bear in mind that you are wearing sacred relics on your feet, sir. Never again will there be a master like mine was, alas."

He looked as if he were again going to burst into tears at the thought of the dead Emperor. But time was pressing. He said he must go and get rid of the rope ladder and try and find, somewhere outside the town, a surgeon or leech who would not be too inquisitive. He produced a key from his pocket with which he could open one of the small gates in the wall, and he told van Delle not to be afraid, to wait patiently, and not move his foot.

An hour later he returned with a village barber-surgeon who

claimed to know sixty-two ways of correctly treating broken bones and also to be an expert on burns. Brouza had found him in the tavern in the little village of Liben, which was too far away for local gossip and rumours to reach Prague Castle.

The man, who was slightly drunk, felt the foot, the ankle and the leg, and said it wasn't serious, but he would be obliged to cause the gentleman some pain.

"One must pass through the sea of pain as the salamander passes through fire," the alchemist said.

Immediately afterwards he let out a piercing shriek, causing Brouza to lay his hand on his mouth. By violently pulling his foot the barber-surgeon had set the dislocated ankle before he expected it. That left not much more to do. The barber-surgeon asked for two small boards or sticks to act as splints. The patient would have to stay in bed for twelve days or a fortnight with these on his leg before he tried to walk. The barber-surgeon prescribed cold compresses, and asked how the accident had happened.

Van Delle explained that it had not been his fault, but was to be attributed to a specific quadrature of the most important planets.

"Sir," said the barber-surgeon, "you're not trying to persuade me that the planets up there conspired together to dislocate your ankle?"

"They inflict both good and evil on us," the alchemist explained, "and we are more subject than you believe to their position in relation to one another. But," he added, "if you have no objection, I would rather not discuss this matter with you any further."

The barber-surgeon had no objection. Experience had taught him that when patients were feverish or in pain it was better not to upset them by contradicting them, even when he believed them to be totally wrong. Meanwhile Brouza had produced from his chests of sacred relics a pewter can of gin, which he gave to the barber-surgeon to compensate him for his trouble and the long way he had come. The barber-surgeon tasted the gin. His face was transfigured, but this was immediately followed by an expression of deep concern.

"Many thanks," he said. "I'm at your service whenever you need me. Also in the event of burns, don't forget. But what am I to do to stop the crafty devil from stealing the gin?"

"Does the devil steal gin from you?" van Delle asked.

"Yes, as well as wine, must, beer, in short every kind of drink."

"Is the devil after you in other ways too?" van Delle asked.

"That's what I'm trying to say. Night and day," said the barber-surgeon.

"So the devil is after your soul?" van Delle asked.

"No, it's not that kind of devil," said the barber-surgeon. "Everyone has his own devil, and mine shares my marriage bed."

He took another swig from the pewter can, and Brouza took him to the gate in the wall and let him out on the main road.

At first light Brouza got up from the floor and rubbed the sleep from his eyes. Van Delle was awake. The pain in his leg, the strange surroundings and, above all, fear of the day that was now breaking had prevented him from sleeping. Brouza brought a copper wash basin, which was yet another relic, fetched water and washed his master's face, neck and hands. Then he brought him bread and cheese and, as usual, produced his motto for the day.

"Eat, sir," he said. "You'll find bread and cheese to your heart's content here. The bread light, the cheese heavy."

He put fresh compresses on the leg and then asked van Delle for permission to leave. He wanted to go back to the Castle and find out what the situation was there.

"There'll be a hellish row when they find out you've gone," he foresaw. "The Emperor's informants will get a great many cuts and bruises, and perhaps worse. He'll fly into a rage and throw at their heads whatever's within reach, candlesticks, plates, bowls, knives, boxes, figures of wood, stone or heavy metal, of which there are always plenty in the Emperor's room, so that he can throw them at people's heads, and perhaps he might even go for them with a sword. Once he threw at me a book with pictures of the passion of Christ. Afterwards he was full of remorse and shed bitter tears, not for my sake but because of the affront to the Saviour."

"And what will happen next?" van Delle, who was extremely worried, wanted to know. "The candlesticks and crockery are not likely to be the end of the matter."

"Certainly not," Brouza replied. "He'll send for the Chief Seneschal and the Chief Burgrave and give them a terrible dressing down, he'll rage and storm and say that it was they who helped you to flee, they were paid by Mathias for doing it. The Chief Seneschal will flush scarlet, but the Chief Burgrave will pacify the Emperor by promising to catch you and bring you back; and he'll have you sought for on every road and at every inn, but only for a week or two, because by that time the Emperor will have forgotten the whole thing, for in his head human feelings like anger, vexation, remorse, and also hope or trust, often change very quickly into their opposites."

"And they won't look for me here?" van Delle asked.

"No, here you're safe," Brouza assured him. "perhaps the very fact that you jumped from the ladder so badly that you couldn't go on shows God's love and concern for you. Now I'm going. I'll lock the door behind me. I'll be back this evening, don't let time drag too much while I'm away."

"I shall use it to contemplate the many vicissitudes of my life," the alchemist said. "Also I shall read this book, which will be a consolation to me in my troubles."

And he took the Seneca from his pocket.

But when Brouza had gone he found that he did not have the peace of mind necessary to follow up any thoughts whatsoever. The adventures and vicissitudes of his life from the course and outcome of which he hoped to gain confidence in his present predicament clashed confusedly in his mind and ended in nothing. He tried reading Seneca, but the words had no meaning for him, and he didn't know what he had read. He was tired, but couldn't sleep. Time refused to pass, and he tried to find a way to outwit it. He moved his foot, and pain overwhelmed him and became intolerable. Then it diminished, grew milder, lingered a little, and disappeared. A little time had passed. He repeated this game, but realised that the time gained had to be paid for with too much pain. His eyes settled on a snail on the wooden wall of the hut, and the creature seemed to him to stand for the hours of this day which crept along with such agonising slowness.

Towards midday he dropped off. It was a short and restless sleep, but he thought it had lasted for many hours, and when he woke he felt better. He now managed to read Seneca for a short time, but then he laid the book aside. He said to himself that the day was nearly over, it would soon be dusk, and it was bad to read in the failing light. In reality it was still early afternoon.

Nevertheless the rest of the day passed a little more quickly, for the Capuchin friars in their monastery close by started their bell ringing and choral singing. When Brouza came back at about nine o'clock in the evening he found him calmer than he expected. Van Delle tried to sit up, and immediately wanted to be told everything, but Brouza put his finger to his lips.

"Quiet, sir, quiet, there are two gardener's boys quite close outside, and they might hear us," he said.

Van Delle asked in a whisper what the situation was up in the Castle, whether there had been a great row, and whether they were already looking for him at the inns and on the roads.

Brouza put down his basket and wiped the sweat from his brow. Then he lit the lamp.

"There has been no row," he said. "They don't yet know you've gone."

"So the Emperor hasn't sent for me?" van Delle exclaimed.

Brouza opened the door a little and looked outside. The two gardener's boys' voices could be heard in the distance, but they were not to be seen.

"They've gone," he said. "No, the Emperor didn't ask about you."

"And he didn't send Palffy or Malaspina to see me?" van Delle wanted to know.

"No, none of the Emperor's gentlemen-in-waiting came to see you."

"I can't understand it," said van Delle, shaking his head. "Is today St Wenceslas's day, or is it not?"

Brouza made preparations for their supper. He moved the table close to van Delle and laid a white tablecloth.

"Perhaps just because it is St Wenceslas's day the Emperor was too busy to trouble about you," he suggested. "For St Wenceslas's day is always a very troublesome day for him. He has to walk in procession carrying a burning candle and show himself to the people, and he dislikes doing that. The archbishop and the Bishop of Olmütz were both received in audience by him, and they pleaded with him very eloquently not to deprive his devout Catholic subjects of the usual impressive spectacle at a time when Utraquism was raising its heretical head everywhere in the kingdom. His father, the late Emperor Maximilian II, now resting in the Lord, had never failed to walk in procession on St Wenceslas's day."

Brouza drew his hand across his eyes, and then produced a cold fish dish from his basket, as well as hard-boiled eggs, fruit, cheese and a jug of wine.

"Tomorrow," he said, as if he felt he must comfort and console van Delle, "His Majesty will certainly remember that you staked your head and lost."

Van Delle stayed in Brouza's hut for seventeen days, and for seventeen days nothing happened, the Emperor seemed to have forgotten him. At first he found it difficult to spend the day dreaming and in idleness, but then he found ways of helping to pass the time. He watched the ants in the hut. There were two kinds or populations of these, the red and the brown, and they resembled the human race in that they could not remain at peace, but made murderous attacks on one another instead. He looked at a spider's web and noticed how small flies got caught in it, while big wasps went straight through – another reflection and symbol of the age and of human affairs. He discovered that if he said his beads three times and recited the Creed twice it took him exactly eight minutes. He practised walking, first with the help of a stick and then without it, and at night he sometimes went outside the hut and contemplated the starry sky.

Brouza occasionally came to the hut in the day time, for caution was now less necessary, and he had long conversations with him. Van Delle talked to him about human nature, and the happiness of the rich and powerful, which was meagre in comparison with their insatiable desires; about the great forces that lay hidden in precious stones and metals, in the blood of certain animals, and in plants plucked when the moon was full. He told him about a sea-fish, known to the learned as Uranoscopus, which had only one eye, with which it gazed continually at heaven, as men, who were blessed with two eyes, did not. He showed Brouza two stars which tirelessly travelled east towards an unknown destination, one fleeing in great haste with the other in hot pursuit. This was a sign meaning the death of great princes, treachery by their servants, changes in the religion and government of many countries, in other words, great woes. An astrologer could foresee these events, but could not avert them. For the highest wisdom attainable was contained in the words: Lord, Thy will be done, on earth as in heaven.

In return Brouza told van Delle that the Emperor was furious with the Archbishop of Prague, the Bishop of Olmütz and St Wenceslas, because during the procession he had singed his beard with the candle. He had also approved the payment of two ducats to the court kitchen to gild the hooves of the wild boars that appeared on the imperial table. And the ghetto butchers, whose duties included supplying the meat for the wild animals kept in the deer park, had addressed a letter to the Chief Seneschal's office that began with a blessing and an appeal to God in the Hebrew tongue, and the Hebrew letters looked like pokers, walking sticks, stove pipes and flour shovels.

On the morning of the eighteenth day Brouza arrived at the hut at an unusually early hour.

"Sir," he said, as soon as he had shut the door behind him, "I hurried here so fast that I'm almost completely out of breath."

"And what news do you bring?" the alchemist asked.

"The best that you could possibly wish for," Brouza replied, and told him that the two arquebusiers who had been posted outside his workshop door had reported to their lieutenant that there had been no sign of him, van Delle, for a fortnight, and that on Sunday he had not gone to Mass as he usually did. The lieutenant had reported this to the commander of the bodyguard and added that the door was locked, and that when one knocked there was no answer. The commander of the bodyguard informed the Senior Seneschal, who ordered that the door should be forced.

"Which means that perhaps they're already on my tail," van Delle interrupted.

"No," Brouza said. "Wait a moment. When the Emperor was told that you had gone, he hardly looked up. He laid his hand on his forehead and then on his ear, meaning that he had a headache and didn't want to hear any more. Then he went on taking to pieces the works of a clock, which he had been busy doing the whole morning. Philipp Lang, who was present, said his Majesty should not be worried with the matter, he didn't need you any longer, another alchemist had been appointed who understood the art much better than all philosophers, alchemists, gipsies and practitioners of the black arts."

"Another alchemist?" exclaimed van Delle in a state of extreme agitation. "Who is he? Where does he come from? Where is he?"

"I don't know," Brouza replied. "Philipp Lang wouldn't say, he seems to be making a great mystery of it. But it must be true, because for some weeks the Emperor's pockets have been bulging with gold, and he spends it as if he were expecting a great deal more, and doesn't hide it in holes and corners as he used to. Only yesterday he paid fifteen ducats for a picture of Christ – he has a dozen already, but he can't get enough of them. What I say is that fools shouldn't buy and blind men shouldn't run. If I take him a big pebble tomorrow morning and tell him it's the stone Jacob was sitting on when he saw his ladder, I bet you he'll buy it."

Van Delle sat staring into space and said nothing. After some time he seemed to awaken as if from a dream. He asked Brouza to leave him, he wanted to be alone to take counsel with himself about what to do next. He grasped Brouza's hand, pressed it, and thanked him for having done so much for him and for having been willing to risk his life for him.

Brouza was embarrassed and bewildered. "Heaven forgive

me," he said, "but what need is there for such extravagant thanks? You know how devoted I am to you. I'd willingly be a galley slave for your sake."

When van Delle was alone he succumbed to the agonising realisation of how vain and useless his life had been. He had failed to find the mysterious formula, the essence, also known as the Red Lion, the Fifth Element and the dove of Trismegistos, required to transmute lead into gold, but someone else had found it. Disappointed again and again in spite of all his efforts, he had become an old man. What had life left to offer him? What aim? What hope?

In his mind he made obeisance to the unknown and mysterious alchemist who had been more fortunate than he. Once more he looked back upon his past life. It seemed to him to have been empty and vain. He slashed his wrists with his razor.

Brouza found him lying in his blood. He shrieked, and was about to hurry to get help, but changed his mind. He took one of the dead Emperor's shirts, tore it into strips and tied van Delle's wrists to prevent further loss of blood. Then he ran to fetch a doctor.

The doctor came, but all life had departed from van Delle.

When they took him away that evening to bury him in unconsecrated ground, Brouza followed the coffin, howling and crying out, behaving as if he had gone out of his mind and raging against himself, just as he had cried and howled and raged against himself when his master, the Emperor Maximilian, had been taken with great pomp to his tomb in St Vitus's.

THE BRANDY JUG

On a night lit by a pale moon in the week between the New Year and the Day of Atonement, which is known as the Week of Penitence, those who had died in the past year rose from their graves in the Jewish cemetery in Prague to praise the Lord. For they were granted a New Year festival just like the living, and they celebrated it in that ancient house of God, the Old New Synagogue, which seemed to have sunk into the earth up to half the height of its walls. And when they had sung the song of praise *ovinu malkenu,* "Our father and king", and walked three times round the Almenor, they called to the Torah. Those whose names they called were still in the realm of the living, but they would have to obey the call of those assembled there and join them before the year was out, for their death had been decided on above.

Late that night two musicians and wedding entertainers, Jäckele-the-fool and Koppel-the-bear, were walking in the streets of the ghetto. They were two tired old men, and were squabbling and scolding each other. They had been playing at a wedding party in the Old Town for a quarter gulden, Jäckele-the-fool on his fiddle and Koppel-the-bear on the Jew's harp, for Jewish musicians were in good repute with Christians and Jews alike, because they knew the latest dances. But after midnight a brawl had started among the guests, to some of whom the strong Prague beer followed by brandy had made an excessive appeal; and when the first tankard sailed through the air the two musicians had quietly slipped out with their instruments, for when Esau drinks, they reminded each other, it's Jacob that gets beaten up. But in the general confusion Koppel-the-bear had made off with a small jug of brandy, and it was about this that the two were squabbling. Not that Jäckele-the-fool would have begrudged himself or Koppel-the-bear a sip of brandy from the wedding table. But during the past year Koppel-the-bear had had a stroke and had been confined to bed for weeks, and he still dragged his left leg when he walked, and he was forbidden strong drink. He did not obey the ban, of course, but laughed at it, saying that lame dogs lived longest. But Jäckele-the-fool had grown almost morbid in his anxiety about his friend's health.

"You're a brazen thief, nothing's safe from your rapacious fingers," he told him. "You'd steal the Five Books of Moses, together with the eight commandments if no-one was looking . . . If at least you had . . . there was a kind of honey and poppy-seed cake there that would have been worthy of a king's table, and we have nothing at home for the sabbath but a plate of beans and a bit of fish. But brandy? What do we want with brandy? You're forbidden it, and I hate it."

"You hate it like a bear hates honey," Koppel-the-bear replied. "Also you know that it is written: Brandy with fish enlivens the dish, for God sent us the fish and still owed us the brandy. So I did a good and meritorious deed in taking from Esau's table what was meant for Jacob, for it is God's will that we should spend the sabbath cheerfully."

"But not with stolen brandy," said Jäckele-the-fool indignantly.

"Actually I didn't steal it," Koppel-the-bear pointed out. "I didn't know there was any brandy in the jug. I was concerned only with the jug. I wanted to prevent one of those violent men from hitting someone on the head with it. So by taking the jug I preserved the life and health of someone who was in grave danger. You can call it what you like, Jäckele-the-fool, but I call it a good deed. And I've got the brandy into the bargain."

"May it stick in your throat," Jäckele-the-fool said angrily and bitterly.

"God forbid," Koppel-the-bear exclaimed. "Though God wants me to revive, you don't want me to survive. Take care, Jäckele-the-fool, take care, you know that the first hours after midnight, when the cock stands on one leg and his comb is as

146

white as wolf's milk, are the hours of Samael, when bad wishes come true."

"Then my wish is that you take your brandy to the hangman, that you break your neck on the way, and that I never set eyes on you again."

"Very well, then, I'll go," Koppel-the-bear said tearfully, "and this is the last time you'll see me in this life."

He made as if to go, taking the brandy jug with him.

"Stop," Jäckele-the-fool called out. "Where are you going in the dark?"

"For you I can't do anything right," Koppel-the-bear complained as the two walked on side by side. "If I'm with you, you tell me to clear out, if I go, you stop me. If I sit down, you say I'm frittering away my time, and if I walk, I'm wasting shoe leather. My silence causes great offence. And when I talk I'm just as dense. Offered beer, you call for milk, or linen if I've brought you silk; onions if I've cooked you beans, or dumplings if there's only greens. If I'm well, you're feeling rotten, and if you're ill, I'm misbegotten. I light the fire, and what's the betting . . ."

"Hush," Jäckele-the-fool interrupted. "Don't you see something? Can't you hear something?"

". . . that you say: Stop, because I'm sweating," Koppel-the-bear ended his litany. Then he stopped and listened.

They crossed the Breitegasse and stood in front of the dark grey, dilapidated walls of the Old New Synagogue. A gentle singing and humming was audible, and there was a gleam of light through the narrow windows.

"It's strange that anyone should be there at this time of night," said Koppel-the-bear.

"They're singing the *ovinu malkenu* as if it were New Year today," Jäckele-the-fool whispered. "Come, let's go, I don't like it here."

"They've lit the candles and are singing," said Koppel-the-bear. "I'm going to see who they are. I'm going to find out . . ."

"What do you want to see and find out?" Jäckele-the-fool insisted. "Come along, I tell you, it's not good to be here."

Koppel-the-bear would not listen to him, but crossed the

road to the window from which the light came. Jäckele-the-fool followed him with quivering limbs. Great though his fear was, he did not want to abandon his friend and colleague of so many years to his fate. His fiddle was under his arm, wrapped in a black cloth.

"Something strange seems to be going on here," said Koppel-the-bear, who had gone to one of the windows and was looking down. "The candles are lit, and I can hear voices and all sorts of sounds, but there's not a soul to be seen. And someone's coughing just like Neftel Gutmann, the gingerbread baker, bless him, used to cough. You know, our neighbour the gingerbread baker, whom they took away last year."

"May he think well of us," said Jäckele-the-fool. There was cold sweat on his brow, and his whole body was trembling. "So Neftel Gutmann still bakes gingerbread in eternity? If so, who are his customers? Koppel-the-bear, I'm afraid. Come away from here, I tell you, it's eerie here – why won't you listen to me? They're celebrating their festival – what are we doing here? Come, let's go. It's cold now, and a drop of brandy from your jug before we go to bed will do us good whether it's stolen or not."

"I'm staying," Koppel-the-bear announced. "I want to see what happens next. If you're frightened, go."

"It's for your sake that I'm frightened," Jäckele-the-fool complained. "May you live for a hundred years, but you know what the doctor said and what the state of your health is, and I don't want to hear them calling you."

"Don't be afraid because of me," said Koppel-the-bear. "An old crock often lasts longer than a new mug. And what can happen to me other than being delivered out of all my troubles?"

"There you go again, doesn't it show that you always think only of yourself? You'd be delivered out of all your troubles, but you don't ask what will happen to me if I'm left alone without you. That's a fine example of brotherly love and devotion you show me."

"Hush," said Koppel-the-bear. "They've stopped singing, the *ovinu malkenu* is over."

"They're going to call to the Torah," Jäckele-the-fool said with bated breath.

And as he said this a voice arose from the invisible assembly below:

"I call Schmaje, the son of Simon. The butcher."

"Who keeps the butcher's stall in the Joachimsgasse," another voice added, as if to avoid possible confusion with someone else of the same name.

"Schmaje, son of Simon, you are called," the first voice repeated, and then there was silence.

"Schmaje, son of Simon, that's the butcher Nossek," said Koppel-the-bear. "I know him, and so do you. He squints a bit, but he has sold meat honestly all his life, he always gives full measure."

"Come away from here, I don't want to hear any more," said Jäckele-the-fool.

"And now he's tucked up in bed fast asleep, and he doesn't know his fate is sealed and that the angel of death has taken him in charge. And he'll get up early tomorrow morning and go to work as usual. We human beings are like chaff blown away by the angel of the Lord. Don't you think we ought to tell him what we have just heard and warn him to hold himself in readiness for his forthcoming transfer from time to eternity?"

"No," said Jäckele-the-fool, "it's no business of ours to bring him such tidings. Besides, he wouldn't believe us, he wouldn't believe his name had been called, he'd say we'd misheard it, or perhaps that we'd only been dreaming. For it's human nature even in the direst extremity to see a spark of hope and blow it into flames. Now come along, Koppel-the-bear, if they called your name, I couldn't stand it."

At that moment the unknown voice calling to the Torah spoke again:

"I call on Mendl, son of Ischiel," it said. "The goldsmith."

"He also buys and sells pearls, singly or by weight," the other voice added. "His house and shop are in the Schwarzengasse."

"Mendl, son of Ischiel, you are called," the first voice repeated.

"That's Mendl Raudnitz," said Koppel-the-bear when silence was restored. "There won't be much grief for him. His wife's dead, and he has been on bad terms with his children for years. He's a hard man, and when he takes his seat in the synagogue on holy days he quarrels with his neighbours. He has never done any good to anyone, even himself. Perhaps we ought to tell him he has been called, and that it's time he sought a reconciliation with his children."

"No," said Jäckele-the-fool. "You don't understand human nature, Koppel-the-bear. He'd say it wasn't true, and that we'd invented it out of malice in order to frighten him. He'd never believe it was true, and he'd find some lie and console himself with it. For he won't say goodbye gladly to this world and the gold and silver in his shop. When death meets him in the street and takes him to his destination, gold and silver he will leave, to his ultimate frustration."

Koppel-the-bear shook his head disapprovingly, for rhyming was his job in the partnership. Jäckele-the-fool's job was thinking up jokes to tell at wedding parties.

"Why in the street?" he objected. "The angel of God may just as well fetch him from his living room or shop."

"You're quite right," Jäckele-the-fool admitted. "When it's time for him to go, His gold and silver'll have to stay below."

"I don't much like the sound of 'gold and silver'll have to stay below'. What about: When God decides it's time for him to go, He'll leave his gold and silver here below? Doesn't that sound better?"

"Yes, that's not at all bad," said Jäckele-the-fool. "I've heard he's thinking of marrying again soon. But whether I shall be able to play at his wedding knowing – what did you call it? – it's time for him to go, and whether I shall be able to make a single good joke . . ."

"Whom is he thinking of marrying?" Koppel-the-bear wanted to know.

"I shall have to think whether I was told or not," Jäckele-the-fool said, "but if I was told I can't remember."

"You can't keep anything in your head," Koppel-the-bear grumbled. "You want to hear and find out everything that concerns you and doesn't concern you, you're perpetually hanging about the streets hoping to pick up something interesting, and if two people stop and talk, you make up the third. And then you forget everything you've heard and haven't heard, you don't remember a thing, and one day you won't remember your name or who you are."

"I call Jacob, son of Judah, known as Jäckele-the-fool," the voice said.

"Who has made a living by his fiddle all his life. Who has also often played in the synagogue on the holy sabbath to the praise and glory of God," said the other voice, as if there were in the ghetto or somewhere else in the country another Jäckele-the-fool who must not be confused with this one.

"Jacob, son of Judah, you are called," the first voice repeated.

For a minute there was a grim silence, and Jäckele-the-fool, deeply shaken, but yet composed, said:

"Praised be Thou, eternal and just Judge. Thy doing is without fault."

"Almighty God," Koppel-the-bear cried out, "Did I hear correctly? What has happened to you, Jäckele-the-fool? What do they want of you?"

"O God of infinite goodness, send me a lie," Jäckele-the-fool implored his maker, but could think of nothing that would for a moment deceive Koppel-the-bear. And so he went on, trying to introduce a note of indifference into his voice:

"What do you suppose has happened? I've heard confirmation that people enjoyed my playing in the synagogue on the sabbath. That's a great honour. Don't you grant it me?"

"Yes, I grant it you, and I grant you that you should be healthy and live long. But they called you. Didn't you hear?" Koppel-the-bear sobbed and lamented.

"Yes, I heard, I'm not deaf," Jackele-the-fool replied. "But I don't know – I don't feel as if I already belonged to the next world. I feel very much alive. Koppel-the-bear, I'm suspicious about all this. There's some mistake – or is there a hoax at the bottom of it? Didn't you feel you ought to be able to recognise the two voices?"

But the lie he had at last hit on did not catch on, and Koppel-the-bear went on weeping and lamenting. Jäckele-the-fool tried something else to console him.

"Listen to me, Koppel-the-bear," he began. "At today's wedding party didn't you play and sing the song: When money clinks in our pockets, there's nothing wrong with the world? Now, listen to this. We're not going to be short of money. I've been meaning to tell you for a long time, but I forgot until today. My savings amount to two and a half gulden, so now let us enjoy ourselves with it. Today you saw chickens, partridges, ducks and geese being served, we alone didn't eat any, to us it was unclean. But tomorrow we'll go to market and buy a capon or goose for the sabbath, because I want to enjoy a good meal for once."

"Don't talk to me about it, I refuse to listen, for there'll be no more enjoyment," Koppel-the-bear lamented. "For me, ashes will be my food, and tears will be mingled with my drink. When I think that they're going to take you away wrapped in cheap linen . . ."

Jäckele-the-fool behaved as if the only thing worrying Koppel-the-bear was the poor quality of his shroud.

"Don't make such a fuss about the linen, it may be good quality or bad," he said. "What do you expect? You know that for a poor person's funeral the burial fraternity pays no more than three kreuzer a yard. How could the linen be anything but grey and poor quality? You can't expect much for three kreuzer a yard. If only I were Mordechai Meisl. When his time comes he'll be carried to his grave in heavy double damask costing half a gulden a yard."

"I call Mordechai Meisl, son of Samuel. Who is also known as Marcus," the voice announced.

"Mordechai Meisl, you are called," the first voice repeated.

"Did you hear, Jäckele-the-fool?" said Koppel-the-bear. "Mordechai Meisl, the great merchant. He too has been called."

"Who is a poor man," the other voice went on. "Who hasn't half a gulden in the house. Who owns nothing, possesses nothing he can call his own."

"Yes, Mordechai Meisl too," Jäckele-the-fool said, beginning to laugh quietly to himself. "Mordechai Meisl, who is a poor man. Did you hear that? Who has nothing he can call his own? What do you think of that? Don't you smell a rat, Koppel-the-bear?"

"It's extraordinary, I don't understand. What does it all mean?" he asked in bewilderment. "That he . . . that you. . ."

"It means that there are two persons down there who have been hoaxing us," Jäckele-the-fool explained. "And it was a very foolish hoax. And now they're talking rubbish. Isn't it rubbish to say Mordechai Meisl, to whom money flows from everywhere, is a poor man? They're idiots to talk such rubbish. They took you in, Koppel-the-bear, but I thought from the first that I ought to be able to recognise those voices."

"And have you recognised them?" asked Koppel-the-bear, clutching at this small spark of hope.

"One of them is Libmann Hirsch, the gold embroiderer," said Jäckele-the-fool, "You surely remember that he was given the order to repair the embroidery that hangs in the Old New Synagogue. He did the job this evening, and to keep him company he took with him his cousin, Haschel Selig. The two of them always stick together, as you know."

"I think you may be right," Koppel-the-bear said thoughtfully and with a deep sigh of relief.

"They must have heard us coming," Jäckele-the-fool went on, feeling more and more confident that his explanation was correct and was the only possible one. "We were talking loudly enough, and they must have had the idea of making fools of us."

"They ought to be ashamed of themselves," said Koppel-the-bear. "Grown men behaving like that."

"Shall I call down and tell them they've been found out and ought to be ashamed of themselves, engaging in such boyish pranks?" said Jäckele-the-fool, who now had no doubt that it was the gold embroiderer accompanied by the button maker who were at work down below.

"Oh, leave them alone, don't bother with them," said Koppel-the-bear, who, as a result of his happiness at not being about to lose his friend and colleague, was in a forgiving mood. "It is written: Thou shalt not take notice of fools or answer them in their folly."

"So what I say is that we should stay here no longer, but go home and quietly and joyfully have some of our brandy," said Jäckele-the-fool. "A drop for you and a drop for me, and so we drink until we see, leaving both of us bereft . . ."

"When in the saucer nothing's left," Koppel-the-bear completed the couplet, when his colleague dried up.

"The saucer?" Jäckele-the-fool exclaimed. "What saucer? Since when does anyone drink brandy out of a saucer?"

"One could very well drink brandy out of a saucer," Koppel-the-bear said in self defence. "But as you wish, you can also do it this way: A drop for you and a drop for me. And so we drink until we see in an alcoholic fug not a drop's left . . . Well?"

". . . in the jug," Jäckele-the-fool ended the verse with a nod of appreciation.

"Yes, but where is it? I haven't got it any more," Koppel-the-bear lamented. "I must have dropped it in my fright when those men called your name."

Jäckele-the-fool went down on his hands and knees and groped about until he found it.

"Here it is," he said, scrambling to his feet. "Koppel-the-bear, my heart stood still for a moment. Praised be the Lord that He let us off with a fright. For a moment I thought it was broken."

THE EMPEROR'S RETAINERS

On the evening of 11 June 1621, nine years after the Emperor's death, Anton Brouza, former jester and later stove-attendant at Prague Castle, who now called himself his deceased Majesty's intimate friend, made his way as usual from his quarters on the Hradschin by winding steps, arched gateways, dark passages and steep alleyways to one of the taverns on the Kleinseite in which he found audiences for his jokes and generally had a meal at other people's expense, for he disliked spending his own money. This time he had decided to favour the inn At the Sign of the Silver Pike on Kampa island, where he had not been for several weeks and the landlord, who at the age of sixteen had been a kitchen boy in Prague Castle, treated him with special respect.

Six months had passed since the Battle of the White Mountain at which the fate of Bohemia was decided, and a great many things had happened in that time. The Bohemian Estates had lost their chartered rights and ancient privileges. The last King of Bohemia, known as the Winter King, was a refugee, and an imperial commissioner was living in Prague Castle. Jesuits, Dominicans and Augustinians disputed possession of the churches confiscated from the Protestants and the Bohemian Brethren. Protestant preachers had been expelled from the country. Those who had taken part in the rising of 1618, or were merely suspected of having sympathised with it or having aided the rebels, were in prison and, if they escaped with their lives, their property and possessions were forfeited to the exchequer. Thus old families were impoverished and disappeared from the history of Bohemia.

Other names were destined to survive in the popular

memory, including those of the twenty-seven members of the nobility, gentry and bourgeoisie who were executed for high treason on the Altstädter Ring in the early hours of that 11 June 1621. Among them were Count Schlick, a German, the leader of the Protestant nobility; Herr Wenzel Budowetz of Budow, the head of the Bohemian Brethren, who returned from political asylum in Brandenburg in order not to leave his country in the lurch at a time of crisis; Dr Jessenius, the famous physician and anatomist, who performed the first public dissection of a dead body in Bohemia; and Herr Christoff Harant of Pohlitz, the president of the Bohemian treasury, who in his youth travelled in the east and wrote a two-volume account in the Bohemian tongue of his adventures in Egypt, Palestine and Arabia.

The faces of those whom Brouza met on his way reflected fear, despondency and a sense of oppression, but he felt that this increased rather than diminished his prospect of scrounging a meal. He knew human nature, and was well aware that on a day like that no one liked being alone. Many wanted to hear what others, whom they regarded as better informed, felt about things, many wanted an audience for their own views, and everyone wanted some consolation, comfort and encouragement from others, and so they all went to the taverns.

Certainly times were bad. The war had been going on for three years already, and no one believed in an early peace. Trade and commerce were stagnant, markets were unattended, prices were increasing and money declined in value. You could not get for two gulden what in the Emperor Rudolf's time cost half a gulden. People wondered where it was all going to end. But by telling true or invented stories about Rudolf II, his court and his servants, Brouza sometimes found it easier than before to earn a meal or a little butter to put on his bread. For the present was so grim, gloomy and frightening that the citizens of Prague liked listening to stories about the past.

When Brouza walked into the bar at the Silver Pike, the only subject of conversation was the executions that had taken place that morning. Johann Kokrda, the court usher, who had spent the whole night on the Altstädter Ring to make sure of a good place in the crowd of spectators, was enjoying his hour of glory. He described everything he had heard and seen, one thing at a time, without allowing himself to be diverted by questions or interruptions. Work on the scaffold had gone on all night by torchlight and, after all the banging and hammering, it was ready in the morning, and it was very frightening. It was four yards high, twenty square yards in area, and everything, including the executioner's block, was draped in black. Stands were provided for officials and the clergy and nobility, and the square and the surrounding streets were packed with common people. Three hundred halberdiers and four hundred cavalrymen from Colonel Waldstein's or Wallenstein's regiments were responsible for maintaining order. Itinerant vendors offered sausages, cheese, beer and spirits to those whom they could reach in the throng. Then, to a roll of drums, the condemned men were brought to the scaffold one at a time, in their order of rank. The first, as was right and proper, was Count Schlick. He was wearing black velvet, carried a small book in his hand, and behaved in a cool and relaxed manner. When his head fell a woman in the crowd called out "You holy martyr", the cry was audible even in the stands, and Waldstein's cavalrymen tried to get to her to arrest her. A number of people were ridden down, one was trampled to death under the horses' hooves, but the woman escaped. Then, when order was restored, Herr von Budowetz mounted the scaffold unaccompanied by a priest, for the comfort and support of a Calvinist priest was denied him, and he refused to be accompanied by a Catholic priest. He waved a friendly farewell to the spectators in the square and tipped the executioner, and the people below called out: "Farewell, Wenzel, good luck to you in the next world all along the line." Everyone thought that the words "all along the line" must have pleased him, they were a favourite expression of his, for he was often to be heard saying things such as "Uphold the Bible all along the line", or "Resist the devil all along the line". Then it was the turn of Herr Dionys von Czernin of Chudeniz. When he mounted the steps of the scaffold his brother Hermann, who had a seat among the noble spectators, rose and left the stand, blowing his nose or perhaps wiping his eyes as he did so – from where he was standing he, Kokrda, had not been able to make sure which.

Brouza did not listen to all this, it did not matter to him, all he was interested in was his supper. He sniffed appraisingly at the various dishes being served, and his eyes fell on a plate of black pudding, herbs and dumplings being offered to one of the guests. The odour attracted him and he went over to the table, and behind the plate recognised a friend and drinking companion, the master saddler Votruba.

"So there you are, I hope you enjoy your meal," he said with the condescension with which he as a former court servant felt he was entitled to treat the rest of humanity. "Not everyone's as well off as you in these hard times, but only a scoundrel would begrudge it you, as Adam Sternberg, his deceased Majesty's Master of the Horse, always used to say."

Votruba, whose mouth was full, signed to him to be quiet and sit down and listen to Kokrda, who was just saying that one of the condemned men, Herr Zaruba of Zvar, could have saved his life by appealing for mercy, but he had refused and was beheaded with the others.

"Don't let it go down the wrong way," Brouza was meanwhile saying to Votruba. "Many a man has choked on black pudding with herbs and dumplings, I don't know whether it's a good way of dying or not. But, when you've swallowed what's stuck in your throat, tell me who's the first to notice the rain in this part of the world. That's a question I once put to His Majesty the deceased Emperor. The kind gentleman had to pay me two talers as he didn't know the answer. Rack your brains and perhaps you'll think of it. If not, I'll allow a special rebate. It'll cost you only a tankard of beer. Is it a deal?"

Votruba considered what advantage to himself he could derive from this situation. He found it in the elevating thought that the question that had been put to him had once been put to His Majesty the Emperor. Meanwhile Kokrda had finished his eye-witness's account. He shook a number of hands by way of farewell and promised to drop in again soon, and off he went to seek a fresh audience in another tavern.

"Well?" Brouza said to Votruba. "Is it a deal? I await your

decision and reply, as the deceased Emperor always said to his privy councillor Hegelmüller."

"Hegelmüller? Who's that talking about Hegelmüller?" said someone at the next table. "Good heavens above, it's Brouza. Let's have a look at you, man. How many years is it since I last saw your snub-nosed thief's face?"

"Sir," Brouza replied with dignity, "choose your words more carefully, I don't know you."

The man was surprised and amused.

"What?" he exclaimed. "You don't recognise Svatek? God knows how often you watched while I blooded His Majesty, crimped his hair and trimmed his beard. You don't know Svatek, you coal-dust swallower?"

"Svatek? The barber?" said Brouza with infinite contempt in his voice, for in his memory he had associated at Prague Castle only with the mighty, such as the Senior Chamberlain, the Chief Huntsman, and the privy councillors.

"A shaven-headed priest is the first to notice the rain," announced Votruba, who had been racking his brains, but was not rewarded with any applause for his answer to the riddle.

"You don't recognise Svatek, you wood-louse?" exclaimed the late Emperor's barber. "Svatek, who so often rubbed ointment into your back after our most gracious master had thought fit to give you a good thrashing."

"His Majesty the deceased Emperor himself and in person . . ." said Votruba in tones of the most abject servility.

"That's an infamous lie," Brouza declared in honest indignation. "His Majesty, my most gracious master, always treated me with respect, and often showed his liking for me and his appreciation of my services."

"Respect? Liking? Your what? Your services?" said the barber, laughing aloud. "Hold me up, somebody, or I'll fall down."

"I have evidence of the truth of what I'm saying," Brouza declared.

"Yes, on your back," said the barber.

Brouza decided it was time to put an end to this discussion which could do no good to his reputation among the citizens of the Kleinseite, and to turn his attention to the tankard of beer he hoped to obtain from the master saddler.

"Two are always together though they are sworn enemies," he said, turning to Votruba as though the barber were no longer present. "Who are they? Can you tell me that?"

"The stick and your back, it's obvious," the barber, who knew that the real answer to this riddle was the two words "yes" and "but", replied before Votruba had time to open his mouth.

"Clear off," Brouza told him angrily. "I have nothing to do with you, so join your own kind and leave me in peace."

"Now, now, Brouza, don't lose your temper," the barber said, trying to pacify him. "You'll have to put up with my company this evening. Didn't you come here to see old Červenka again?"

"I? Červenka? What Červenka?" Brouza asked.

"Our Červenka," the barber replied. "Didn't he let you know he was coming here tonight? He seems to be rather late. But, no, there he is."

Two men had come into the bar, and Brouza recognised them, though he had not seem then for nine years. One of them, a rather bent old gentleman who walked with a stick and had sparse white hair hanging over his brow, was Červenka, who had been the dead Emperor's second valet. The other, a rather shabbily dressed man with a hook nose, was Kasparek, who for many years had been the Emperor's lute player. Brouza rose to greet them. But first he tried to make sure of his tankard of beer.

"Just think about it," he said to Votruba, the master saddler. "Two are together but are sworn enemies. Who are they?"

"I assure you I haven't the slightest idea," said Votruba, whose mind was no longer on riddles. "I've never seen them here at the Silver Pike before. But ask the landlord, he's bowing and scraping to them and seems to know them."

"So here I am," said old Červenka, helping himself to the soup that the landlord had placed before him, "and it wasn't so easy for me to get here. My daughter, with whom I live, and her husband Franta didn't want me to come, they got it into their heads that something might happen to me on this trip. 'Stay where you are, old chap,' they said. 'Travelling about the world isn't anything for you any longer. Stop always thinking about the past. What happened, happened. Think about how much we need your help in the garden. Today you've got to pick the caterpillars from the cabbage plants, or are you trying to get out of it?' But I let them talk, and the caterpillars had a fine old time. Certainly, the whole tedious journey from Beneschau to Prague would have been for nothing if His Excellency Count Nostitz, to whom I humbly addressed my application, had not reserved a seat for me right at the top of the stand – in memory of the days when we passed each other daily up in the Castle, I with a 'I kiss your hand, Your Excellency', and he with a query about His Majesty's health or what sort of humour he was in, or, if he was in a hurry, with just a 'Good, morning, Červenka' – Well, to cut the story short, I had a seat right at the top of the stand, and so I really saw with my own eyes Dr Jessenius's head in the executioner's hands, just as my most gracious master the Emperor predicted in his last hours."

And he turned to the landlord, who had been standing by, listening curiously.

"Listen," he said. "After the soup I want an Olmütz cheese, a radish, a slice of bread and a half jug of warm beer."

"Did His Majesty the deceased Emperor," began the landlord, who lost his breath when he was excited, "did he really and truly read the future from the hand, as gipsies do at fairs?"

"I said a slice of bread, a radish, cheese and a half jug of warm beer, that's all, and be quick about it," the dead Emperor's valet replied abruptly.

The landlord was offended.

"Herr Červenka doesn't recognise me," he said. "I'm Wondra."

"Wondra? What Wondra are you?" Červenka asked.

"I'm the Wondra who ground the pepper down in the kitchen," the landlord explained, "and sometimes I was allowed to look after the roasting spit. I often used to see Herr Červenka" – he drew a deep breath – "when he came down to see whether His Majesty's soup was being properly prepared" –

he took another deep breath – "it was generally chicken broth."

"So that's who you are," Červenka said. "Nice to see you here. Do they let you grind pepper and turn the roast here too?"

The landlord stepped back and made a broad gesture to indicate the wide area of his responsibilities, which extended to the big bar, the small bar, the garden, the kitchen, the crockery and other stores and the wine cellar.

"I do everything here," he said proudly and excitedly. "I took over the place from my father last year."

"If you do everything here, bring me my order," said Červenka, who saw in him not the landlord and worthy citizen of the Kleinseite, but merely the kitchen boy of long ago.

"Hurry, hurry," Brouza said to the flummoxed landlord. "I know him, he doesn't like being kept waiting."

"I never noticed that His Majesty had the gift of prophecy," said the barber Svatek, who had been pondering the matter for some time. "To tell the truth, the poor gentleman often had difficulty in finding his way in the present. When did he tell you that about Dr Jessenius's head? Was it before or after the time when the three of us who are sitting here conducted the affairs of the kingdom?"

Several people at neighbouring tables who overheard these words exchanged glances or put their heads together and whispered. This annoyed the lute player Kasparek.

"Why can't you keep your mouth shut?" he said to the barber. "You know I don't like such talk. Particularly now that the heads of those who were once great and powerful sit so loosely on their shoulders."

"Quite right, quite right, that's what I've always said," remarked Brouza, putting his hand round his throat as if he were not sure his head was still there.

"It was when everything was over," said the former valet, lost in thought. "You, Kasparek, were in disgrace. It was when my most gracious master had lost his kingdom and his secret treasure and all his glory and power. It was during his last illness. He had completely lost his strength, for that man, Dr Jessenius, who was said to know the secrets of Paracelsus, had inflicted four days of severe fasting on him."

"Thus he was following the instructions of Galenus, who said that in cases of high fever one should not yield excessively to the patient's wishes for food and drink," the barber pointed out.

The former valet cut into thin slices the radish the landlord had brought him.

"He treated His Majesty with shocking severity," the barber went on. "I don't know anything about Galenus, I'm not versed in the art of medicine, but one thing I do know, that a little meat broth once a day and three spoonfuls of good Malaga wine in the morning, at midday and in the evening would have been sufficient to maintain His Majesty's strength."

"When I'm feverish, I eat nothing but boiled river fish, it suits me admirably," said the landlord, who had approached the table again.

The ex-valet looked at him with great displeasure.

"No one asked for your opinion," he said severely. "What gave you the idea of comparing your miserable fever with that of His Majesty? You fellows from the kitchen think you have to pour your gravy on every roast."

He turned to the barber.

"You, Svatek, were upstairs with me in His Majesty's sick room, you must remember," he said. "Don't you remember the day when Jessenius came into the room and shouted and insisted that all those useless herbs should be thrown out?"

"Yes, I remember it as if it were yesterday," said the barber. "As His Majesty could sleep neither by day nor by night, but kept tossing and turning and groaning, I fetched leaves and stems of nightshade and henbane from the apothecary's garden and, with the permission of His Excellency the Senior Seneschal, spread them on the floor, for their smell affects the head and induces sleep. Also I put a cloth soaked in cat's blood on His Majesty's brow, for that too encourages sleep, and patients must be helped in every possible way. And then, just when His Majesty started breathing more easily and no more moaning and gasping was to be heard, Dr Jessenius arrived . . ."

"Yes, that's exactly what happened," Červenka interrupted, "and he flung open both windows, and called out that air must be let in and those rubbishy weeds thrown out. When I tried to object, he told me to be quiet, and said he knew without my telling him what his Majesty complained of: thirst, heat, headache and pain in his limbs, trembling, anxiety, tiredness and weakness. And then he went over to the sick bed and called on His Majesty to get up, but His Majesty could no longer do so. Then he was so bold as to . . ."

He stopped and shook his head, as if he still could not grasp what had happened next. Then he went on:

"Jessenius was so bold as to take my most gracious master by the head and shoulder and lift him by force. And my most gracious master looked at him and sighed, and said 'God help you, you have laid hands on me. I wish you hadn't, but it has happened, and one day the executioner will lay hands on you, he'll hold your head high above his own, and you, redhead, will be among the spectators.' For my most gracious master still called me redhead, though my hair was already churchyard-coloured."

And he stroked his scanty white hair.

A number of guests had moved their chairs closer to the table in order to listen, and one of them made himself the spokesman for the rest. He rose in his seat, raised his hat, and said:

"If you will excuse me, sir, may I ask how Herr Jessenius took what His Majesty said?"

The ex-valet looked at him appraisingly and then granted him the honour of a reply.

"He laughed briefly, but it was obvious that he felt uneasy. He said that fever had unsettled His Majesty's life spirits, and that the nature of the fever was obscure and mysterious, it must be allowed to take its course, and every effort must be made to investigate its causes. Then he left, and today, in accordance with God's will, I saw him again on the Altstädter Ringplatz."

He crossed himself, drank some beer and put cheese and small pieces of radish on his slice of bread.

That was a good story and, by heaven and all the saints, one doesn't hear one like it every day, Brouza said to himself while tears rolled down his cheeks in memory of his dead masters. His only regret was that the customers of the Silver Pike had heard it without its having earned him a meal. He was hungry, but it

164

hadn't occurred to any of today's guests to offer him a morsel of anything, and there was no hope of getting anything from Červenka, who had been a skinflint and penny pincher all his life, and you could see from the cheese and the radish that he didn't order anything decent even for himself.

"Aren't you the master locksmith who has a workshop just behind the Loreto church?" the lute player Kasparek asked the man who had approached the table with an "excuse me please".

"Yes, I am. Georg Jarosch, locksmith to the imperial court, at your service, sir. I too followed the Emperor's coffin with the glass blowers, the wood carvers, the stone carvers, the medal makers, the wax modellers and all the others whose art was rewarded with honour and praise from His Majesty, but with very little money."

"So," the lute player said respectfully, "it was you who made the fine ornate grill that surrounds the statue of George of Podiebrad."

"We need another like him," someone at the next table called out. "We need a king of Bohemia like George of Podiebrad, then there'd be better times for us."

The old valet shook his head.

"No," he said. "Don't hope for better times. Have you forgotten that His Majesty, my most gracious master, cursed his disloyal city of Prague and called down the wrath of God on it? Today showed that God listened to him, Jesus and Mary, all that blood, may God have mercy on those miserable sinners. No, there will be no better times for us, and never again will the world see a king of Bohemia."

"That's what I've always said," announced Brouza, addressing the audience and vigorously nodding his head for greater emphasis.

The anxious voice of Votruba, the master saddler, came from a corner of the room. "For Christ's sake be quiet, both of you," he said.

"It's well known that the dead Emperor didn't like Bohemia, he wanted everything to be Italian or foreign," said someone at the next table.

"If it's true that he cursed Prague," said someone else, "he did so because his mind was clouded."

"No, he was in his right mind, no one knows that better than I, who bled him every day," said the barber. "To this very day I can see him standing by the window looking down at the city, pale, trembling, and with tears in his eyes. It was on the day when the Protestant Estates held him prisoner in the Castle. 'Prague gave me no aid,' he said to Herr Zdenko von Lobkowitz, the Chancellor of Bohemia, who came to him to bid him farewell. 'It abandoned me in my hour of need and did nothing, it didn't even have a horse saddled in my service.' And then my imperial master, overcome with anger and grief, flung his hat so violently to the ground that the big carbuncle stone that he wore on it instead of a feather disappeared and, in spite of all efforts, has never been found."

"Why are you looking at me?" Brouza exclaimed angrily. "If you're by any chance implying that I found and kept it, that's a wicked lie. Everyone knows that the responsibilities of the work I did for His Majesty the Holy Roman Emperor kept me so busy that I had no time for such trifles."

And, carried away as he was by the insult to which he had been subjected, he helped himself to a long swig from the tankard of his neighbour, the imperial court locksmith.

"If only our imperial master had been better advised," said the lute player Kasparek. "If only he had recognised the danger, seen the needs of the hour, and loosened his purse strings. With so much at stake, it's no use being stingy with one's resources. If only I had the chance, my most gracious master, who was so deeply affected by music, would have listened to me, as he had used to. But I was in disgrace, and because of that Diocletian, may God damn him, I was no longer allowed in the Emperor's presence."

"Your Diocletian is damned, you can be sure of that," the valet Červenka assured him. "He was an obdurate pagan, and he persecuted the Church."

"His Majesty was also a great connoisseur of ancient Roman coins," the barber was meanwhile informing the locksmith and a few others. "He had got together a fine collection of what he called his pagan heads, and scholars and antiquarians came from all over the world to see them. Even a copper piece in poor condition was not too insignificant for him, but Kasparek presented him with a big silver piece with a portrait of the Roman Emperor Diocletian on it . . ."

"It was a rare piece," Kasparek interrupted, "and His Majesty the Emperor would have taken great pleasure in it but for the fact that, to my extreme misfortune, Diocletian abdicated and renounced his throne. That put a fantastic idea into my imperial master's head, namely that my purpose in presenting him with that coin was to insinuate that he should do the same as Diocletian, and that therefore I must be in the pay of his brother Mathias."

"At every prince's court there is a goblin called suspicion," the imperial locksmith remarked when Kasparek, overwhelmed by his memories, fell silent.

"That's true, but I hoped for a better reward for my loyal service," Kasparek said bitterly. "The result," he went on, "was that when the rebellion broke out in the New Town I was in disgrace with His Majesty. You remember that the Protestant Estates met rebelliously and occupied the New Town town hall, and Count Schlick and Budowetz put themselves at their head and made Dr Jessenius their chief advocate, and Wenzel Kinsky went about telling everyone willing to listen that this king was no good, they must have another one, and there were negotiations with Mathias in the village of Liben. But His Majesty's cause was not yet lost, for at the time Prague was full of disbanded troops who swarmed through the streets, picked quarrels, brawled, and waited to be taken into the Emperor's service. If only my gracious master had not saved money, if only he had put his hand in his pocket and raised an army . . ."

"If, if, if," the valet Červenka interrupted. "There was no money there, even for everyday necessities. 'My alchemist, my money maker, has died,' His Majesty complained, 'and taken the secret of his art with him into his grave without leaving me even half an ounce of his gold.'"

"Who was his Majesty's alchemist whose death was so untimely?" asked the locksmith.

"You should have put that question to Philipp Lang before he left this world with a noose round his neck," Červenka replied. "He was His Majesty's confidant in the matter, I knew nothing."

"His Majesty employed all sorts of alchemists and adepts up at the Castle, but none of them produced anything of note," said the Emperor's lute player. "But, as for the last of his alchemists about whom there was so much talk, in my opinion he never existed. Who ever saw him? He was nothing but a figment of our gracious master's imagination, a creature of his dreams."

"No!" Brouza declared. "That alchemist was no figment, no creature of the imagination. I know who he was, yes, look at me, I, Brouza, know. And if I told you his name it would cause you great surprise and much shaking of heads."

"You know who he was?" the valet asked in a tone that revealed that he too was in the secret.

"Yes, I do, there's no question about it," said Brouza. "I often followed Philipp Lang, I know where he went and into whose house he always disappeared. And I told my master to his face what sort of alchemist he had to the detriment of many poor people, and that it was unChristian. At first my master the Emperor behaved as if he suddenly no longer understood the Bohemian tongue, but I persisted, and he began complaining and lamenting about how wretched his life was, and how heavy was the burden that lay on his shoulders, and there were so many mouths he had to feed, and it was impossible to defray the costs of his enormous household without this alchemist's assistance. And then he made me swear that so long as God left life in me I would not reveal his name or tell anyone about the matter, and that is what I have done to the present day."

"But surely that doesn't still apply after so many years?" the barber suggested. "Surely you can tell us, your old friends?"

Brouza shook his head.

"Leave this to me," the imperial locksmith declared. "I know how to deal with him." He turned to Brouza and said:

"And what would you say, brother, to a pancake with a herb salad to go with it?"

Brouza said nothing and shook his head.

168

"So you'd like me to order you something boiled or roasted? That's fiendishly expensive nowadays, the landlord's a thief, but never mind."

Brouza did not reply.

"Well, well, there must be something you fancy," said the locksmith. "What about roast pork with all the trimmings?"

At that Brouza looked up.

"Roast pork done in the way I like it?" he asked. "Not too fat and not too lean? And with some crackling?"

"Yes, with some crackling, as well as herbs and dumplings," the imperial locksmith assured him.

"You're in luck today, Herr Brouza," someone at the next table remarked.

Brouza sighed. He had had a short and violent battle with himself, and ended by resisting the temptation.

"No," he said. "I swore to my master the Emperor by almighty God and by Mary His mother and by the salvation of my soul for which I hope, and so in this life my mouth is shut. But perhaps, Herr Jarosch . . ."

He hesitated for a moment, as if briefly to reconsider what he was about to say. Then he went on:

"Perhaps God will ordain that we shall see each other again in heaven. If so, I shall make straight for you and tell you up there what I cannot tell you here below. May God grant us that grace. Amen."

"Amen," said the former valet, making the sign of the cross, and the others repeated: "Amen." But Brouza's former jester's spirit reawakened, he decided he had promised the locksmith too much and might have reason to regret it, and so he hastened to correct his mistake.

"But don't imagine you'll get it for nothing," he told the imperial locksmith. "No, it's obvious, a secret like that keeps its value for ever. It'll still cost you a dish of roast pork with herbs and dumplings up there."

He looked up to heaven and shut his eyes, and the thought of heavenly roast pork lay like a reflection of eternal bliss on his stubbly, snub-nosed, wrinkled face.

169

THE GUTTERING CANDLE

It was always late evening when Philipp Lang arrived at the house in the Dreibrunnenplatz where Mendel, Mordechai Meisl's trusted servant, awaited him and took him upstairs to his master.

During the daytime the house was full of people and their noisy activity. Merchants from many countries waited on Mordechai Meisl and offered him their wares: velvet, marten skins, hat ribbons, golden trimmings, spices from Asia, sugar, indigo and aloes from the islands of the New World. Grey-haired clerks sat at desks piled with papers, drafting letters or contracts or preparing bills. Young men from Vienna, Amsterdam, Hamburg or Danzig who had come to gain practical experience of commerce with Mordechai Meisl walked busily about with quill pens behind their ears or sat over documents of which they had to make copies. Bohemian noblemen who wanted to borrow money on the strength of a promissory note grew indignant if they were kept waiting, and complained to one another of the poor harvest and the unprofitability of cattle and sheep rearing nowadays, life would be different if only they could lend money like the Jews, to whom charging interest was the equivalent of the harrow and the plough. Messengers arrived breathlessly from the staging post with letters, a clerk called out for sealing wax and another for a freshly sharpened quill, and carriers who had been on the road for many days took their ease under the arcades down in the yard, stretching their legs, drinking beer, and watching the heavy bales and chests and barrels being unloaded from wag-gons and disappearing into the warehouses. And Meisl's little poodle dashed about happily among the carriers, horses and porters, yapping, sitting up and begging, and wagging its tail.

In the evening it was quiet. The clerks, apprentices and servants had gone, and only Mendel sometimes stayed and slept in the attic when Meisl needed him. He was staying that night, as later he would have to wait at table on Meisl and Philipp Lang.

During the day Meisl had checked accounts that had arrived from the Taxeira bank in Hamburg, dictated letters to his clerks, and received the aristocratic Herr Jan Slovsky of Slovic, the Emperor's treasury councillor, who had asked for more time for the repayment of a loan of eight hundred gold gulden. He had listened to reports by agents who had come from Milan, Augsburg, Marseilles and Nizhny Novgorod, and then returned to his living room earlier than usual.

After his evening soup Mendel brought him an infusion of marshmallow, cowslips and linseed, for, after a deceptive lull, the chest trouble from which he had suffered for years had opened a new offensive, the fever and painful coughing fits recurred at shorter and shorter intervals, and sometimes a coughing fit would be so violent that everything went black before his eyes.

He drank the hot infusion one sip at a time and, as he could not remain inactive, he tried reading Don Izak Abarbanel's book *The Eye of God*. But the meaning of the words eluded him, he could not grasp the famous man's ideas and, tired and disappointed, he laid the book aside and abandoned himself to the thoughts that came to him in his hours of loneliness and were always the same.

If only God had granted me a son, he said to himself, a son whom I could have left behind in the world when I died. I would have brought him up in wisdom and good doctrine, he would have been like a pomegranate in bloom, full of learning, and he would have had no difficulty in reading Abarbanel, he would have been an intepreter of dark sayings, wisdom and knowledge would have been the breath of his breath. But it was not to be, it was not God's will. I shall leave the world childless and my wealth will go to strangers. Is my misfortune a necessity in the plan of the divine wisdom so that it may be the foundation of another man's happiness? Who knows? Who can tell? God's wisdom is as deep as the sea.

He rose to his feet. His thoughts took their usual course. From thinking about his unborn son he went on to thinking about his wife. He took from a cupboard against the wall a small rosewood box that contained things she had been fond of. They were little things, not amounting to very much, and there were not many of them. Brightly coloured birds' feathers, a faded silk ribbon, a playing card that had once come into her possession, withered rose leaves that collapsed into dust when touched, a small broken silver knife, a stone shaped like a veined human hand, an amber ball, a glass ball, and something that had once been a brightly coloured butterfly's wing. Mordechai Meisl looked at all these things thoughtfully, he had not held the box in his hands for years. He sighed, locked it, and put it back in the cupboard. Its contents struck him as no less puzzling, baffling and hard to understand than the obscure and mysterious words in Don Izak Abarbanel's book.

God decided, and so it had to come about, he said to himself. He has taken her into eternal bliss. And I. . . There are many ideas and wishes in human hearts, but only His will prevails. It was like any other day, we sat at table, I spoke the blessing over the bread, and she served me during the meal, and then – that night – whose help did she call for when she lay dying? A stranger's name, that of a Christian. She had seen the Roman Emperor once and once only, when he rode through the Old Town into the ghetto, and the elders and the councillors awaited him, and the trumpets blew and the Great Rabbi held the Torah in his hands – her voice, that cry on her deathbed, Rudolf, help – was it he for whom she called? Or was it someone else of whom I know nothing? Alas, I shall never know.

A fit of coughing came over him, and he pressed his handkerchief to his mouth. The door opened, and Mendel's anxious face appeared. Mordechai Meisl signed to him that it was nothing, and that he did not need him.

His thoughts took a different direction. He was now a secret business associate of the Emperor, and his business affairs were also the Emperor's. The Emperor's treasury councillor, who had called on him that day, did not suspect that he paid the Emperor monthly interest, and that the Emperor had granted him, Mordechai Meisl, rights, privileges, freedoms and dignities that had not been granted to any Jew before him. "We, Rudolf II, by the grace of God elected Roman Emperor and King of Bohemia, at all times Increaser of the Empire, have decided to grant our loyal Jew Mordechaeus Meisl . . ." the charter establishing his rights and privileges began. No court could touch his person or property and no officer of the court had access to his house in his lifetime. Any case against him must be dealt with by the Emperor. The export of silver from the kingdom of Bohemia was transferred to him, and he alone was entitled to lend money against promissory notes to persons of noble or knightly rank, as well as to monasteries and other religious foundations. He could travel and trade freely throughout the Holy Roman Empire and, like any great lord or prelate, was exempt from the tax on coachmen and horses on his travels. And Philipp Lang had hinted more than once that the Emperor was contemplating the idea of elevating his loyal Jew Mordechai Meisl to Bohemian knightly rank.

He for his part had regularly given Philipp Lang, the Emperor's confidential messenger, quarterly accounts of income and expenditure and punctually handed over the Emperor's share of the profits. On his death half of his money and possessions would go to the Emperor. Was the Emperor waiting for his death? Would he prefer a capital sum to these quarterly payments? "A handful doesn't satisfy a lion," Philipp Lang had sometimes remarked with a shrug of his shoulders when he took the money. A handful? Four sealed bags of gold lay on the table, as well as three money orders for a total of forty thousand imperial talers, two of them payable at the Frankfurt fair and the third at the Leipzig New Year fair, which was also known as the "cold Mass". For another quarter was over, and tonight Phillip Lang was coming for the accounts and the Emperor's money.

To others, Meisl said to himself, making money often means great and often vain and painful efforts, and many staked their life on it and lost it. But to him it had always been merely a game. All his life money had chased him, had wooed and courted him and, when he had rejected it, it had come back. Sometimes he had tired of his good fortune, and sometimes it had actually frightened him. Money oppressed him, it wanted to be his and no one else's, and when it became his it did not remain in his chests and strong boxes, but bustled about the world for him as his faithful servant. Yes, money loved him and subjected itself to him. But what would it do, what would it put in hand, when he left it behind in the world unshackled and no longer guided by his hand?

A short but extremely violent fit of coughing came over him and shook him, it was so violent that he thought he was going to die, and when it was over the handkerchief in his hand was coloured red, and at the sight of the blood he was surprised that he was still alive. He felt he had long since reached the end of his life, but was not allowed to die. The Great Rabbi Loew, the light of the Diaspora and the jewel of Israel and the Only One of his age, had once sat in his room, reading the sacred books in which the God's mysteries are described, when the stump of the wax candle that lit the room started flickering and was just going out, and there were no other wax candles in the Great Rabbi's house. So the Great Rabbi had spoken a magic formula over the guttering candle, calling upon it by the ten Names not to go out, and it had obeyed, and had gone on burning steadily and without flickering all night, enabling the Great Rabbi to fathom God's mysteries, and not till it was bright daylight had the remnants of the candle gone out, leaving nothing behind. Was he, Mordechai Meisl, not such a guttering candle, that should have gone out long ago, but still went on burning? Why does God not let me go out? Why am I still alive? he wondered, still looking at the blood-soaked handkerchief in his hand. Why does God still need me in this world?

There was a knock at the door. Mordechai Meisl hid the handkerchief, and Mendel let Philipp Lang into the room, and Mordechai Meisl walked to within two paces from the door to welcome his guest as etiquette required.

Philipp Lang was a tall, lean man, standing a head taller than Meisl. His head and beard were tinged with grey. He dressed in the Spanish manner, and a portrait of Our Lady of Loreto hung on his chest.

As he entered he glanced at the four sealed bags and the money orders lying on the table; and, as he had so often done before on that day, he tried to work out how much would be needed to satisfy the Emperor on this occasion. The Greek marble statue that the Emperor had bought from an antique dealer in Rome had arrived and had to be paid for, and there were other debts that were less urgent. But the Emperor was also thinking of buying Dürer's *Adoration of the Magi* from the All Saints' Church at Wittenberg that the municipality of that town had offered him.

What he said gave no indication of what he had on his mind.

"I hope I have not come at an inconvenient moment," he said to Meisl. "There's a gale outside, and it's just coming on to rain. And how are you, my dear friend?"

He had taken Meisl's hand and was holding it in such a way that he could feel the pulse. It's very fast, he's certainly feverish, he's not at all well, he said to himself.

When Mordechai Meisl was asked how he was, he always gave the same meaningless answer. He told no one how he really felt.

"Very well, thank you," he replied. "What remains of my indisposition today will have disappeared tomorrow."

And he freed his hand from that of the Emperor's valet.

Philipp Lang looked at him and silently made his own prognosis. There was no doubt about it. In that emaciated body there was no strength left to fight the wasting disease and imminent death. Tomorrow he would be able to tell his master that he would not have to wait much longer, two or three weeks at most, for the secret treasure, the ducats and double ducats, the rose nobles and doubloons. And, according to Philipp Lang's plans and intentions, it was not just half of the Jew Meisl's wealth that was to go to the Emperor, but the whole of it, for lions and emperors did not share with anyone. To Meisl he said:

"Yes, we must be grateful that we live in the present age, when the doctors have made so many and such magnificent discoveries that they are able to use for our benefit."

"Yes, that is true," said Meisl, "but I don't need their aid. I feel better and better every day."

"That is excellent news, and I shall pass it on with great pleasure to my most gracious master, who gave me strict instructions to tell you that you must take great care of your health and be sure to look after yourself."

"I shall do that in loyal obedience to the royal command," Meisl replied. "May the Lord of the world prolong His Majesty's life and multiply his fame."

And, as both parties had now done enough to satisfy the requirements of politeness and etiquette, they started talking business.

Towards midnight when, after long negotiations, they had reached agreement on every point, Mendel served wine and a cold meal and hot almond cakes baked in oil that he had just fetched from the bakehouse. And Philipp Lang, while he ate and drank at his ease, talked about the imperial court and the strange things that often happened there. One of the Emperor's gentlemen-in-waiting, a certain Baron Palffy, kept a servant who had to swear in the most appalling way instead of his master when anything went wrong, because the baron himself was too God-fearing to do so. Everyone knew that Don Balthazar de Zuniga, the Spanish ambassador to the imperial court, was unfaithful every week to his beautiful young wife, but never with anyone named Mary which, he thought, would give offence to the Blessed Virgin Mary. Two learned gentlemen at court, Martin Ruhland, who was solving the problem of perpetual motion, and the Italian di Giorgio, who was making a great parabolic mirror, were at loggerheads because each thought the other was better paid than himself, and when they met they called each other more names than there are letters in the German and Italian alphabets combined. "Swindler! Idiot! Swine! Whoremonger!" from one would be answered by "Birbone! Furfante! Mascalzone! Furbo!" from the other, and all this in spite of the fact that the Emperor had owed both of them their salary for years. The young Count Khevenhueller, a second lieutenant in the Emperor's mounted bodyguard, had returned from the war with the Turks with a sabre wound right across his throat. The tendons had been severed, with the result that he had to wear a silver collar to support his head; and when he complained in the officers' mess that the times were so hard that, when one went into town to enjoy oneself, things were so expensive that one didn't have nearly enough money, a captain of arquebusiers sitting opposite him called out: "Pawn your collar, you fool, then you'll be able to go to your whores," and the result had been a fracas.

Philipp Lang stopped, because Meisl had another coughing fit, and Mendel slipped so quickly into the room with a bottle of medicine that he must have been listening at the door. He glided to his master like a shadow, took the handkerchief from his hand, and gave him another.

"It's nothing," said Mordechai Meisl when he had recovered his breath. "A slight cough. It comes from the dampness in the air. If it's a fine, warm day tomorrow, it will have gone, God willing."

And he nodded to Mendel, indicating that he could go.

"In the meantime," Phillip Lang said, "you should strew plenty of salt on the floor of all the rooms you use. Salt is a strong magnet that draws the water from the air."

The Hungarian and Portuguese wines to which he had done full justice during the meal began to go to his head. There are people who, when they have had rather more to drink than they are used to, get argumentative and try to pick quarrels with everyone, and there are others who hang their heads and get lachrymose and bemoan the state of the world. Philipp Lang belonged to neither of these categories. Wine merely made him talkative and boastful; and so he started talking about himself and his great gifts and boasting about the power he exercised. He said he had the last word with the Emperor about everything. He could fix anything, he could be very useful to his friends, and nothing could be done against his will. Many a highly placed gentleman of birth and breeding sought his friendship in vain, but those who showed themselves worthy of his approbation and liking were really to be envied; and he raised his glass and emptied it in a toast to his good friend Mordechai Meisl, his prosperity and lasting good fortune.

"So long as I retain my position and look after things in the kingdom," he said, "my most gracious master can spend as much time as he likes with music or seek diversion with the paintings in his art gallery."

Meisl pursued his own thoughts in silence. He had heard a great deal about the strange man up in the Castle who was the elected Holy Roman Emperor and King of Bohemia and allowed his valets and barbers to run the kingdom in his place. Only that morning, when Herr Slovsky of Slovic had called on him to discuss his debt, he had once more talked to him about his imperial master. "He doesn't like people," the treasury councillor had said. "He has a low opinion of them and despises and ridicules them. Surrounded as he is by a noisy mob of painters and musicians, soldiers of fortune and swindlers, scholars and artists of all sorts, quacks and fairground barkers, he lives a lonely life."

He, Mordechai Meisl, also led a lonely life in his house that during the daytime was full of noise and bustle.

"And why," he asked Philipp Lang, "has his Majesty the Emperor – may God increase his fame and multiply his days – why has he not a wife and children?"

"You're very outspoken," Philipp Lang said with a trace of disapproval. "But why should we not be frank with each other in view of our longstanding friendship? Why not tell you the truth? There has been no lack of marriage plans for my most gracious master. There have been negotiations with Madrid and Florence, secret couriers have ridden hither and thither, portraits painted by the hand of famous masters arrived and were viewed – but my most gracious master could not be persuaded to contemplate marriage, and all efforts to make him change his mind were in vain."

He fell silent for a while, and then went on in a whisper, as if apart from Meisl there were people in the room from whom such highly secret matters must be kept.

"My most gracious master confided to me that the reason why he did not want to marry was that he was hoping for the return of the woman he loved, who was always in his mind and whom he could not forget. He spoke about her in a confused and bewildering way, and I could not make rhyme or reason of what he said. She had been snatched from him, he said, but how that happened he could not say, and she had not come back. And, as my most gracious master spoke of her perpetual fear of God's anger, I think she must have been another man's wife." When Philipp Lang talked about the woman the Emperor loved, Mordechai Meisl's heart grew heavy, he did not know why, it beat and beat and would not slow down, and he was full of grief and anxiety.

He wondered why this strange unrest had suddenly come over him, he could not understand it, for there was no obvious explanation. He was surprised and puzzled, and then it struck him that what weighed so heavily on his heart was perhaps a great omission of which he was guilty; he had never set eyes on that strange and puzzling, exalted and glorious man, the Holy Roman Emperor, his business partner. It seemed to him that it was this omission that so oppressed him, and this idea made him feel better; and the more he thought about it, the stronger became his desire to see the Emperor up at the Castle.

He turned to Philipp Lang. Hesitantly and searching for the right words, he told him how great was his desire to express to His Majesty his due gratitude for the kindness, favours, honours and privileges that had been granted him.

Philipp Lang's first reaction to this request was that Meisl had committed an appalling if involuntary *faux pas*.

"Do I hear you correctly?" he exclaimed. "Are you being serious? You want to appear in person in the presence of His Majesty the Roman Emperor? Who on earth put such an unreasonable idea into your head?"

An alarming suspicion had arisen in his own head. He thought Meisl's mischievous purpose was to denounce him to the Emperor. But how could the Jew have possibly discovered that he, Philipp Lang, as just recompense for his loyal services, had on one occasion retained a quarter and on another a fifth of the Emperor's money? Had the Jew Meisl spies and informers everywhere? What an evil and treacherous race these Jews are, he said to himself, their intentions are always evil, they never behave decently and keep quiet as they should.

"His Majesty the Emperor," said Mordechai Meisl, "has heaped greater honours and privileges on me than have been granted to any other Jew. Hence my humble request . . ."

"*Non si può*," Philipp Lang interrupted angrily. He was born in the Trentino, and when he was angry or agitated he relapsed into Italian. "*Non si può*. It's impossible. It's out of the question. You don't know the court. You don't know what happens in matters of this kind with his Majesty. The King of England's ambassador has been waiting for two months to present his letters of credence, but has not been granted an audience, which is continually delayed and postponed. He writes letters of protest and complaint, threatens to leave Prague, but is not received. Colonel von Guenderode has a personal letter from the Elector of Brandenburg to hand to His Majesty, but is not received. His Majesty could not refuse to see Prince Borghese, the papal internuncio, who is a nephew of His Holiness the Pope, but he interrupted him and told him to cut short what he had to say and use as few words as possible, for he, the Emperor, was sufficiently troubled with affairs of state already. And you want to be received by His Majesty? What do you want from him? What idle chatter do you want to whisper into my most gracious master's ear? Have I ever given you any cause for complaint? Don't you know I'm a – what do you call it? – an *ohev Israel*, a friend of the Jews? And haven't I always been like a brother to you"

"I have nothing to complain about and nothing to suggest to His Majesty," Mordechai Meisl replied. "The only reason for my request is that with the indulgence and graciousness that is natural to His Majesty . . ."

"All right," said Philipp Lang. He saw that Meisl was determined to have his way, and at the same time realised that his request was not so dangerous after all and could be satisfied with very little trouble. "My friendship for you," he went on in an entirely different tone, "is too great for me to be able to refuse a request of yours, however difficult it may be to carry it out. You shall have your way. But I must ask you one thing, to have a little patience. Nothing will be lost if there's a delay of a day or two. I shall have to choose a convenient time and place to talk to His Majesty about the matter alone and undisturbed. For my most gracious master has to be handled carefully, nothing must be done over-hastily or at the wrong moment. Don't misunderstand me, all I ask for is two or three weeks."

Mordechai Meisl saw through him. Something in the sound of his voice, the expression on his face, told him what was behind these smooth words. Philipp Lang already included him among the dead, he allowed him no more than two or three weeks of life, and hoped to be saved trouble by postponing the matter.

"Thank you, I understand," said Mordechai Meisl.

Philipp Lang's carriage was waiting in the Niklasgasse, and Mendel escorted him there with a lantern, for it was easy to lose one's way in the narrow, crooked, ghetto streets.

When he returned to the house in the Dreibrunnenplatz he found his master still awake.

"As soon as it's light tomorrow morning go to the meat stalls," Mordechai Meisl told him, "and ask the butchers which of them is taking the Hungarian beef to the deer park this week."

No matter how much the Holy Roman Emperor kept himself hidden from the world, there were a number of people in the ghetto who could see him every day if they chose. These were the butchers and their assistants. For the Prague Jewish butchers were obliged to supply the Emperor daily with thirty-four pounds of good Hungarian beef for the two lions, the eagle and the other wild animals that he kept in the deer park, and so they and their butchers' carts were allowed freely through the gate. The Emperor never failed to be present at the animals' feeding time, he took care to ensure that each animal had its fair share, and he sometimes himself fed the two lions, which he had tamed and with whom he felt a magical affinity through the stars, and the eagle, which sat sadly and forlornly in its cage.

Mordechai Meisl, dressed as a butcher's assistant in a leather apron with straps over his shoulders and a small butcher's chopper in his belt, drove with the butcher Schmaje Nossek across the Moldau and up to the Hradschin, where they arrived about midday. They left the horse and cart in front of the porter's lodge inside the perimeter walls and went the rest of the way on foot, for the horse grew nervous if the smell of the wild animals reached it.

It was a frosty day with a clear sky and a biting wind that drove the withered leaves before it. They followed a drive that led between fruit and vegetable gardens and across some meadow land. They went through undergrowth and crossed a bare beech wood in which roe deer browsed and foxes had their burrows. They emerged from the wood to find themselves facing the wing of the Castle that adjoined the zoo.

The cages and the bear pit were in the shadow of ancient elms and beech trees. A tame bear that begged for its food in the court kitchen trotted along the path in complete freedom. The zoo keepers were housed in a single-storey brick building. There were three of them, but only one appeared; and, while he examined and weighed the meat and the lions roared and the monkeys chattered, the butcher Nossek pointed out to Meisl the gate from which the Emperor would appear. He described him as a small, nimble man with a curly beard. At this time of year he wore a short, gold-braided overcoat; Nossek thought the gold braid cost half a gulden a yard. He added that the Emperor was also easily recognisable by the way he walked, holding his right hand in front of him as if he were showing himself the way – it was a small hand with blue veins. Meisl would not have long to wait, for the animals were hungry and the roaring of the lions was audible all the way to the Emperor's windows.

When the meat had been weighed and found to be in good condition, the pay was handed out: four newly minted Bohemian groschen for the butcher and half a groschen for his assistant.

The other two keepers emerged from the lodge to go and meet the Emperor, of whom there was yet no sign. Schmaje Nossek pointed out a gardener's boy who was busy not far away on a bed of rose bushes but kept his eyes fixed on the

Castle gate. Nossek said he didn't look like a gardener's boy, and didn't know how to use his gardening scissors and knife properly. He said it wouldn't be surprising if the lad, whoever he might be, turned out to have been smuggled in with the gardeners' help for the purpose of meeting the Emperor.

As if on a word of command the two sentries at the gate struck the ground with their halberds, the gate opened, and the Emperor, in a short braided coat and holding his right hand a little way in front of him as Nossek had described, entered the deer park.

During the night the Holy Roman Emperor Rudolf II had been plagued by a dream in which he was pursued and threatened by his brother Mathias, the Archduke of Austria, in the form of a boar. When he awoke the melancholy that never completely left him was aggravated by the anxiety and despondency of the dream, which he could not shake off. Červenka, the second valet, who was on duty that morning, knew what to do to cheer him slightly. He arranged for the Emperor's Spanish and Italian horses to pass by under the windows of the royal bedroom. The sight of the fine, proud animals gladdened the Emperor who, still in his night clothes, flung open the window without minding the rough wind that blew into the room. He leaned out and called the animals by name. "Diego! Brusco! Adelante! Carvuccio! Conde!" Each animal raised its head and whinnied loudly when its name was called. But the Emperor's melancholy did not leave him.

While his breakfast was being brought up, the stove attendant Brouza appeared in the room with his shovel and tub to remove the ashes from the fireplace. The Emperor watched him for a while, and then asked:

"Brouza, whose side are you on? Mine, or my brother Mathias's?"

"Father-in-law," Brouza replied without interrupting his work, "I'm not on his side or yours. I'm on the side of my broom and shovel, because I can rely on them. You and Mathias are both tarred with the same brush, and to a poor man neither of you is any better than the other."

"Do you call yourself a poor man?" said the Emperor. "You have savings, you're rich. Will you lend me a hundred gulden? I'm short of cash."

Brouza looked up from his work, showing his snub-nosed face, which was covered in coal dust and ashes.

"Well, you *are* keen on money," he said to the Emperor. "Can you produce a surety? What security have you to offer?"

"You're to lend me a hundred gulden with no surety and no security, only on the strength of my name and my face," said the Emperor.

"No, young master," Brouza replied. "I'd rather lend a hundred gulden on the security of this tub of ashes than two on your face."

He slipped quickly out of the room, leaving his tub and shovel behind, for the Emperor had picked up the heavy silver bread basket, and Brouza said to himself that, having no hole in his head, he didn't need any plaster.

The Emperor spent an hour in a room used as a workshop by two seal cutters and a wax modeller. He watched them working, and they behaved as if they were unaware of his presence, as they knew he resented having his train of thought interrupted.

Then he went to the gallery in which works by Brueghel, Dürer, Cranach, and single paintings by Altdorfer and Holbein were hung. In the middle of the room was a marble statue that had come into his possession the day before, the work of a great sculptor of antiquity whose name has not come down to us. It was a statue of the boy Iloneus, one of the sons of Niobe, who in her pride challenged the gods and drew down their anger upon herself.

The boy, struck by Apollo's arrow, had sunk to the ground, but had not surrendered unresistingly to death. With his right hand he tried to extract the arrow from his breast and with the other to help himself to rise, so that he could flee to his mother's aid and protection. And so noble was his attitude, so handsome was his face, marked by death and yet turned towards life, that the Emperor's eyes filled with tears. His heart felt lighter. The fact that this marvellous work by a forgotten master had been recovered from debris and rubble and come into his possession consoled and reassured him and made him feel better.

Meanwhile midday had struck and he heard the roaring of the lions and the cry of the eagle calling him.

While he walked down the stairs and a flunkey handed him his hat and coat, he lost himself in a day-dream. If it had been God's will – so he imagined as he walked out into the garden, followed by two officers of the bodyguard – if he had been born, not in this age, but long ago in the century when that unknown master had carved the Iloneus, if – so he went on in his imagination – he instead of Augustus or Nero had ruled over the Roman Empire, which of the thinkers and scholars of his age would he have attracted to his court? He did not have a high opinion of the poets and dramatists, but he would have accepted Virgil as a scholar, and have had him and Pliny and Seneca about him constantly, and he felt a pang of disappointment when he recalled that in Augustus's time Plato and Aristotle, Euclid and Epicurus, whom he placed high above all others, had long been in their realm of shadows.

His thoughts reverted to the marble statue. If – so he went on dreaming – instead of being emperor in pagan Rome he had been the creator of that dying boy, would not his fame have been greater than that of the Caesars? Had not Titian's fame and glory exceeded that of the great Maximilian? And as he went on musing about the fame and glory of artists and Caesars – and imagined himself now a Caesar in ancient Rome and now a sculptor – as he walked on day-dreaming thus, a girl dressed as a gardener's boy intercepted him, went down on her knees and called out in a loud voice: "Rudolf, help!"

The Emperor, shocked out of his dream, started back a pace and made a defensive movement with his hand.

The girl on her knees in front of him was the daughter of one of his field commanders, a distinguished soldier, who had been captured by the Turks. As he was an old man and was kept in strict confinement by the Turks, she feared she might never see him again. She had managed to raise only part of the ransom money. Once before she had gone down on her knees and appealed to the Emperor, in the stables which the Emperor sometimes visited, and he had said yes, he would take up her case, but nothing had happened.

The Emperor did not recognise her. He took her to be one of the kitchen boys, who, as Červenka had told him, had twice gone to sleep instead of turning the roast and was now to be whipped by order of the Senior Seneschal, who was responsible for the discipline of the court servants.

"This is the second time you have done this," the Emperor said to the kneeling girl. "Never do it again. I'll tell Lichtenstein" – that was the Senior Seneschal – "to excuse you this time. You have done harm. Go away, and never do it again."

He walked on quickly. The general's daughter rose to her feet and was utterly bewildered as she watched him walking away. He had spoken kindly to her, he had said he would talk about her case to someone who evidently had a great deal of influence, but she could not understand what harm she had done by appealing to him for a second time. Or had she damaged one of the rose bushes with her secateurs? She was still wondering about this when one of the two officers of the Emperor's bodygyard went up to her, raised his hat and, with the politeness due to a person of rank, asked her to follow him.

I'll send Červenka to see Lichtenstein, the Emperor said to himself. He'll talk to him and tell him my wishes in this matter. I don't want to see him, he would only ask for money. They all want money from me, Lichtenstein, Nostiz, Sternberg, Harrach, the kitchen people and the people from the silver store, as well as the preacher in the chapel and his musicians and singers, they all want money and more money and still more money, they all want a share in the secret treasure. But I'm not letting anyone touch that, I need it desperately to defend myself against Mathias's brotherly love . . ."

He had reached the lions' cage. He took a piece of Hungarian beef from the keeper's hands and walked into the cage. The lioness, who had been waiting for him, rose and laid her paws gently on his chest. She took the meat from his hand while the lion had his huge head on the Emperor's shoulder to greet him.

The Emperor spoke to his lions. It was the time of day when

he felt happiest and most carefree. He did not and could not suspect that this was the hour when he lost his secret treasure for ever.

Rudolf, help. Mordechai Meisel, standing outside the keepers' lodge, with his handkerchief over his mouth because he had another fit of coughing, heard the words that his young wife Esther had called out when she felt the angel of death coming for her. Rudolf help. In her last moments her thoughts had been of this man who now walked past him.

Hitherto the Holy Roman Emperor in his Castle had been merely a phantom, a power of which one was aware, a distant glamour. But now he saw him – a man walking with hurried steps, with bent shoulders and bowed head, his shoes crunching the gravel. This was the man who had taken the woman he loved.

He was possessed by the idea that Esther, his wife, whom he could not forget, had become the darling of another man, the darling of the Emperor, the man walking away over there, the darling of the Emperor's heart of whom Philipp Lang had spoken when his tongue was loosened by wine. And words that she had spoken or whispered while she, the Emperor's darling, slept by his side returned to his memory. Now he could understand them and he felt he should have always recognised the truth.

There was grief in his heart, and greater even than his grief was his hate and the burning desire to avenge himself on the man who had taken his wife.

When he returned to his house on the Dreibrunnenplatz he had already made his plan.

On his death half of all his wealth was to go to the Emperor. So he was determined to leave nothing whatever behind when he died.

Not much time was left. Getting rich had been easy for him, almost a game. But getting poor – was that something he could manage? Gold clung to him, and now he must get rid of it. He must throw it away, spend it, squander it, fling it to the winds to the last half gulden. He had blood relations, a sister, a brother, and three nephews and nieces. Nothing of his money and property must fall into their hands, for the Emperor's judges and advisers could easily get it back by means of imprisonment and torture. Only the most meagre possessions such as the poorest had would go to them: the bed in which he slept, his coat, his parchment prayer book.

And where was the money to go?

It would buy a poorhouse for the ghetto. A pest house. An orphanage. A new town hall. A house in which to read and study. A big and a small synagogue. Not enough, money would still be over. Ducats in chests, valuables in vaults, money in the hands of others – all of it must go. The narrow, crooked ghetto streets would be paved and lit. The Emperor and his advisers could grab the ghetto paving stones.

If only he were left enough time to get rid of it all. His only remaining wish was to become a poor man who had nothing, nothing whatever he could call his own. Guttering candle, you must go on burning till that happens. And then. . .

Then go to sleep, Mordechai Meisl. Sleep and forget your troubles, sleep and forget your grief. Guttering candle, go out.

THE ANGEL ASAEL

During the nights of the new moon a maggid, a teaching angel, descended from the heavenly spheres and entered the room of the Great Rabbi, who was called the Crown and the Diadem and the Firebrand and the Only One of his time. He was sent to reveal to the Great Rabbi the hidden things of the world above that no living being can fathom. And there are many such things.

The angel did not come in human guise. Nothing about him was fashioned in a way to which the human eye is accustomed. Yet he was very beautiful.

"The great forces and powers that maintain the course of the world are contained in the signs that you use to form words," he instructed the Great Rabbi. "And know that everything on earth that is formed into words leaves traces in the world above. Aleph, the first of the signs, contains truth in itself. Beth, the second sign, contains greatness. It is followed by Elevation. The fourth sign contains within itself the nobility of God's world, and the fifth the power of sacrifice. The sixth is Compassion. Then comes Purity, then Light. Study and Knowledge. Justice. The Order of things. Perpetual movement. But the last in the series of signs is the noblest. It is taph, with which the sabbath ends. Contained within it is the balance of the world, the guardians of which are the five angels of supreme holiness: Michael, the lord of stone and metal; Gabriel, who is set over man and the animals; Raphael, whom the waters obey; Feliel, who is responsible for grass and all plants; and Uriel, who rules over fire. They watch over the balance of the world which you, a mere grain of sand, a son of dust, once frivolously disturbed."

"I know, Asael," the Great Rabbi said to the teaching angel, and his thoughts flew back to the day on which the Roman Emperor had ridden into the ghetto on his white horse. He, the Great Rabbi, had awaited him with the Torah in his hands and had spoken the priestly blessing over him. And, as it happened, a confidant of the Emperor's, the Wuk of Rosenberk, a member of the highest Bohemian aristocracy, had chosen that time and place to make an attempt on the Emperor's life, for he begrudged him the Bohemian crown. One of his servants hid on the roof of a Jewish house with a heavy stone taken from a wall which, when the trumpets sounded and jubilation broke out all round, he dropped in such a way that it would fall on the Emperor's head. And, without waiting to see the outcome of the attempt, he hurried down to escape to the streets of the Old Town and to let it be thought that the Jews had made a treacherous and dastardly attempt to assassinate the Emperor.

But the Great Rabbi saw the stone dropping and used the power that was lent him to transform it into two swallows that flew away over the Emperor's head and climbed and vanished into the sky.

The angel anticipated the Great Rabbi's thought, and said:

"When you made the swallows out of lifeless stone you interfered with the plan of creation and disturbed the balance of the world. Those living in the world outweighed the dead. You diminished Michael's realm and increased Gabriel's. Thus discord arose among the five angels of supreme holiness, for the angels Raphael, Uriel and Feliel took sides and intervened in the dispute. And, if the dispute had lasted a little longer, the rivers and streams on earth would have flowed backwards, the forests would have moved from their places, and the mountains would have collapsed in ruins. The world would have perished, like Sodom when it was touched by God's finger."

He called God by the ninth of His names, which is Shadai.

"But the dispute came to an end," the angel went on, "for the patriarchs Abraham, Isaac and Jacob arose and met and joined each other in a combined prayer. And that triple prayer has such primal force that it can undo what has happened and cause what has not happened to happen. So the balance of the world was restored, and harmony returned to the choir of angels."

"I know, Asael. I bear the yoke of my double guilt," said the Great Rabbi, thinking of the day on which he fell into guilt a second time for the Emperor's sake.

During his ride in the ghetto the Emperor noticed in the throng that gathered on both sides of the streets a face that captivated him and would not let him go, and he knew that it would remain in his heart for ever. It was, he thought, a child's face, that of a Jewish girl. She was standing against a gate post, her big eyes looked at him, her mouth was half open, her brown locks hung over her forehead. And when his eyes looked away from hers and he rode on, leaving her behind, a great sadness overcame him and he knew he had fallen in love.

He turned and ordered the servant riding behind him in the procession to stay behind and follow the girl wherever she went, for he was determined to discover who she was and where she could be found again.

The servant did as he was bidden. He stayed behind, saw to his horse and, when the crowd began to disperse, followed her through the ghetto streets. She walked as if she were in a hurry to get home, she looked neither to the right nor to the left and did not turn. As it was beginning to get dark, he stayed close behind her. But unfortunately in one of the streets leading to the Dreibrunnenplatz a number of street dealers who were making their way through the ghetto with their lamps and candles got in his way and offered him their wares and, by the time he managed to shake them off, the girl had gone and he looked for her in vain. So all he could tell the Emperor was that he had lost her from sight in the ghetto.

At first the Emperor thought it would not be so difficult to track the girl down, if not today then tomorrow, and so at his bidding the servant went to the ghetto every day. He wandered about the streets and spied around, but found no trace of the girl.

And as time passed, the Emperor's hope faded, and he thought he had lost her for ever. But he could not forget her face, or her eyes, which had sought his. He grew melancholy, and found rest and consolation neither by night nor by day. And, being at his wits' end, he sent for the Great Rabbi.

He told him about the Jewish girl whom he had seen in the ghetto. He complained that he did not know how it had happened, but he could not forget her night or day. He painted her face in words, and the Great Rabbi realised that he had seen the young Esther, the wife of Mordechai Meisl, who was beautiful beyond all measure.

He advised the Emperor to think of her no longer, for there was no hope for him in this matter. She was a Jewess, and would never give herself to a man other than her husband. But the Emperor took no notice of what he said.

"You will bring her to me at the Castle," he ordered the Great Rabbi, "and she will be my beloved. And don't keep me waiting long, because I couldn't stand it. She has been keeping me waiting too long already. And I don't want anyone else, I want her only."

"That cannot be," said the Great Rabbi. "She will not transgress against God's law. She is a Jewess, and will not become the beloved of any other man."

When the Emperor saw that the Great Rabbi again refused to help him, a great thunderstorm of rage came over him and he swore an oath.

"If you disobey my command, and I get no loving response from her who is ever in my mind, I shall expel all the Jews from my kingdoms and territories as a disloyal people, that is my decision and my will, so help me God."

Then the Great Rabbi went and planted a rose bush and a rosemary under the stone bridge on the bank of the Moldau where they were hidden from men's eyes, and over both he spoke words of magic. And a red rose opened on the rose bush, and the rosemary flower nestled up to it. And every night the Emperor's heart entered into the red rose and the Jewess's heart entered the rosemary flower.

And night after night the Emperor dreamt he held the beautiful Jewess in his arms and every night Esther, the wife of Mordechai Meisl, dreamt she lay in the Emperor's arms.

The angel's voice, in which there was disapproval and reproach, recalled the Great Rabbi from his meditation.

"You broke the rosemary bloom," the angel said, "but the red rose you did not break."

The Great Rabbi raised his head.

"It is not for me," he said, "to weigh the hearts of kings, it is not for me to examine them for guilt. It is not I that puts power into their hands. Would David have become a murderer and adulterer if He, the Holy One, had allowed him to remain a shepherd?"

"You children of men," the angel said, "are poor and full of troubles in your life. Why do you burden it with love, that disturbs your reason and makes your heart wretched?"

The Great Rabbi looked up with a smile at the angel, who knew the secret paths and ways of the world above, but to whom the ways of the human heart had grown strange.

"At the beginning of time," he said, "did not the children of God go together in love with the children of men? Did they not wait for them at the springs and wells and kiss them in the shadow of the oaks and olive trees? And was not Naamah, the sister of Tubal-cain, lovely, have you ever seen her like?"

The angel Asael dropped his head, and his thoughts flew back through the ages to the very beginning of time.

"Yes, Naamah, the sister of Tubal-cain, who forged clasps and gold chains, was lovely," he said softly. "She was lovely and she was delightful. She was as lovely as a garden in spring when day is breaking. Yes, the daughter of Lamech and Zillah was lovely."

And as he remembered the beloved of his distant youth, two tear-drops ran down the angel's cheeks. They were human tears.

EPILOGUE

At the turn of the century, when I was fifteen and a pupil at high school – a bad pupil, who continually needed extra help – I saw the Prague ghetto for the last time. For a long time, of course, it had not been called that, but was renamed the Josefstadt, but it remains in my memory as I saw it then: tumbledown houses huddled together, sagging with age and in the last stages of dilapidation and decay, with extensions and shorings up that blocked the narrow streets, those winding, crooked streets in the maze of which I could easily get lost if I did not take care. Dark passages, gloomy courtyards, holes in the wall and cave-like vaults in which hawkers offered their wares. Wells and cisterns, the water of which was contaminated by the Prague disease, typhus, and at every hole and corner a den in which the Prague underworld foregathered.

Yes, I knew the old ghetto. Three times a week I made my way through it to the Zigeunergasse, that led from the Breite-gasse, the "broad street", or main street, of the old ghetto, to the neighbourhood of the Moldau bank. My tutor, Jakob Meisl, a medical student, lived there under the roof timbers of the house "At the Sign of the Lime-kiln".

I can still see it in my mind's eye, in half a century it has not faded from my memory. I still see the wardrobe that would not shut, revealing to the visitor two suits, a raincoat and a pair of knee-high boots. I can still see the books and papers on the table, the chairs and the bed as well as on the coal scuttle and the floor, singly and in piles, and I can see on the window ledge the three flower-pots with two fuchsias and a begonia which my tutor said he had only on loan, they belonged to the landlady. A boot jack, shaped like a stag beetle with huge antlers, protruded from under the bed. And I still see the damp-stained, smoke-blackened and ink-bespattered walls, the medical student Meisl's crossed rapiers, and his five tobacco pipes with their porcelain bowls that displayed in lively colours the heads of Schiller, Voltaire, Napoleon, Field Marshall Radetzky and the Hussite leader Jan Zischka of Trocnow.

My last visit to the ghetto has stayed in my memory more distinctly than the earlier ones. It was a few days before the long summer holidays, and I made my way with my school books, which I carried in a strap, through the former ghetto, the demolition of which had just begun. To my surprise, I found that big holes had been hacked by pick-axes in the Joachimsgasse and the Goldenengasse, and through the holes I could see into streets and alleyways that were previously unknown to me. And I had to clamber over huge mounds of debris and rubble, broken bricks, roof shingles, bent lead pipes, rotting beams and timbers, battered domestic utensils and other rubbish. I reached the medical student's room late, tired, covered with lime and dust.

That is not the only reason why my last visit to the ghetto remains so vividly in my memory. For that afternoon my tutor showed me Mordechai Meisl's will, which he had inherited. Both events, the demolition of the ghetto and the emergence from the past of the legendary will, seemed to me to be interlinked and together to mark the end of the story my tutor had told me in the course of many winter afternoons, the story of Meisl's wealth.

I had always been familiar with the term Meisl's wealth. It implied possessions of every kind, gold, jewellery, houses, real estate, vaults filled with all sorts of goods in bales, chests and barrels. Meisl's wealth meant, not just riches, but riches in super-abundance. And when my father said he could not afford some expense that one expected of his generosity, he would say: "Yes, if I had Meisl's wealth."

My tutor produced Mordechai Meisl's will from a worn leather briefcase in which he obviously kept documents and old family letters. It was written on an old yellowed folio sheet that had disintegrated into five or six pieces, for in the course of time it had only too often been unfolded, read, and folded up again. My tutor carefully took the separate pieces and arranged them into a whole on the table top.

The will was written in the Bohemian tongue. It began with an appeal to God, who was addressed as the Eternal and the Everlasting and the Creator of the world. Then, in a few lines in which the writing had faded and was hard to decipher, Mordechai Meisl described himself as a poor man who had no money or valuables he could call his own and had nothing left but a few things of daily or holy day use which he was disposing of in this, his last will and testament. He added that he had no debts and that no one could justify or rightly make any claim against him.

Then he went on:

"The bed in which I sleep as well as my wardrobe are to go to my sister Frummet so that she may think of me. May she be blessed, may God increase her happiness and preserve her from suffering. My everyday coat and my holy day coat, as well as my seat in the Old Synagogue are to go to my brother Josef. May God grant him and his children long life. My daily prayer book and my parchment prayer book are to go to Simon, the son of my sister Frummet, and the five books of Moses, also of parchment, as well as my tin platter for unleavened bread are to go to Baruch, the son of my brother Josef. The four books of Don Izak Abarbanel that are called *The Legacy of the Fathers*, *The Collected Prophets*, *The Eye of God*, and *The Days of the World* are to go to my brother Josef's son Elias, the scholar, who advances from stage to stage. To all of them I wish their heart's desire, also health and peace from the Lord of the world and that He may grant them children and grandchildren who will live in wisdom and according to the teaching."

Under these provisions accompanied by words of blessing were the signatures of the two witnesses. The medical student Meisl had found out that one of them was the secretary of the Prague Jewish community, and the other was the "caller to the synagogue", whose job was to ensure that the members of the community turned up for divine service punctually and in full force.

"On the day after Mordechai Meisl was buried," my tutor said, "law court and Bohemian treasury officials descended on his house to lay hands on all his money and valuables and all the goods in his warehouses. But there was nothing there, and their surprise must have been great. Philipp Lang was arrested and charged with being implicated in the disappearance of Meisl's wealth. Mordechai Meisl's relatives were arrested too, but were soon released, as they could prove that no part of the vanished wealth had gone to them. The exchequer then sued the Prague Jewish community for the restitution of Meisl's property, and the case dragged on for 180 years and was dismissed only in the reign of the Emperor Josef II. The papers are in the royal and imperial archives in Vienna, and if you go through them line by line you will find not a single reference to the real legal title on which the Crown based its claim."

My tutor carefully laid together the pieces into which the will had disintegrated and put them back in his leather briefcase.

"That Elias who was advancing from stage to stage is said to have been my direct ancestor," he went on, "but the four books by Don Izak Abarbanel have not come down to me. They must have gone astray in the course of three centuries, they've disappeared, heaven knows which of my ancestors took them to the pawnshop. For all of them were poor, not one of them made a success of anything. Perhaps they brooded too much about Meisl's wealth and why none of it had come down to them. Perhaps they were always looking back to their lost inheritance instead of looking to the future, to life. They remained humble people, and what am I? An idle student. But perhaps now, when Meisl's wealth . . ."

He did not put into words the idea that passed through his mind, but paced silently up and down the room for a while. Then he raised his voice in a lament for the death of the houses of the ghetto that were being demolished, for his heart lay in everything that was old and destined to disappear.

"They've torn down the house 'At the Sign of the Cuckoo's Egg'. They've torn down the old bakehouse to which my mother took her sabbath cakes every week. Once she took me with her, and I saw the copper-lined tables on which the bread was kneaded, and the long shovels used to take it out of the oven. They've torn down the house 'At the Sign of the Tin Crown', and the Great Rabbi Loew's house in the Breitegasse. It was last used as a warehouse by a box maker, and when the boxes were taken away, recesses were found in all the walls. They were not used for any mystical purposes, but the Great Rabbi kept his cabalistic books in them."

He stood still and went on with his enumeration of the houses that no longer existed.

"The house 'At the Sign of the Mousehole', the house 'At the Sign of the Left Glove', 'Death house', 'the Gingerbread Nut' house, the little house in this street with the strange name of 'No Time'. Until recently the last so-called heyduck tailor had his workshop in it. He made liveries for servants of the nobility and gentry.

He went to the window and looked out over the gables, the yards, the building sites, and the ruins where houses had been.

"The pest house was over there," he said, "and that's the poorhouse. What you see over there is Meisl's wealth."

He pointed to two buildings of which only the bare walls still stood while the pickaxes went on with their work. And we watched while Meisl's wealth collapsed into debris and rubble and rose up again as a thick cloud of reddish grey dust. While it hung there it was still Meisl's wealth, and we watched as a gust of wind blew it away and it disappeared.